Kenn

CW00392881

DEDICATION

I dedicate this to all those who have made things work for me over the past 45 years. I further dedicate this to my mother and father who encouraged me to be the best that i could be, in everything that i did in life.

I also dedicate it to my wife's and all my sons (no! I only had one at a time, wife's that is) it is tough being a musician's partner or dependent finally, to you who have bought my books, music, and guitars.

I THANK YOU

CONTENTS

1
GOOD HOMES NEEDED

The rain seemed to be perpetual today, as it pounded on the tin roof of the kennels. Jenny had spent her entire life trying to save all waifs and strays. The trouble was there seemed now, to be so many more of these poor animals, with less and harder to find homes, for these poor and often maltreated animals.

Originally when Jenny had opened her small rescue centre, it was meant to be a temporary home. It was intended as a local rescue centre, for dogs and also for the odd cat. Most of the animals, had come to her via other rescue organisations, like the RSPCA. Although many were just dumped on her doorstep, late at night. It was not unusual to find some poor bedraggled dog, tied to the gatepost leading down the pathway to her home.

Jenny gave it her best shot, but she never seemed to have enough time to care for all of the animals that found their way to her.

Then her husband of twenty something years, said he had enough of these 'Mutts' messing up the grounds to their home. He had at that point, given her an ultimatum, although he knew what the outcome would be. It was a simple one 'Either the dogs go, or he would.'

Jenny had refused to throw all the dogs out on the street again. They had bought the house with money that had been left to her, when her mother passed away, so the house was in her name. Jenny missed her husband, not just for the company, but for the fact, that she did love him.

He had built a set of twelve kennels at the bottom of their vegetable patch. Billy was the perfect handyman to have about. However, Jenny could not in a clear conscience, see any animal in distress, and not do something about it. It was this alone that drove them apart. It was not any lack of love or romance. Still, it was what it was.

There had been enough money left over after the purchase of the smallholding and farmhouse for them to build the kennels. Now though her husband Billy, had since moved in with his brother, who lived just down the road from her house.

Billy's brother Jack, had settled here when he had retired from the police force. Jack had gained a lot of notoriety, after he had solved the Yellow Jacket murders in Swindon and London. The police had promoted him to Detective Chief Inspector, and they had given him his own taskforce when Swindon had been plagued by a serial killer who had modelled himself on Edward Theodore Gein, probably the most emulated serial killer in American history.

That had all happened after the death of his wife a few a couple of years before. Some five years after the death of his first wife. Jack had finally taken a new wife, Janet she was one of the nurses who had looked after his wife in her final year and in the end providing her with palliative care.

Jack's wife Janet, was delighted that since Jack had left the police force, she now had her husband home at nights. They had sold his bungalow in Swindon and moved to Frithville in Lincolnshire.

Jack had bought an old four bedroomed house with just over two acres of land, that Janet was now using, at least in part to become, self-sufficient with vegetables. The excess they sold to local shops that wanted their 'Organic Products'.

Billy worked part time with Jacks wife and part time on his own plot. He still maintained a sociable friendship with Jenny. He did not hate her, for the kindness that she showed to the dogs and cats. It was just he needed her to be full time in their own relationship. The strain of running the rescue centre entirely at their own cost meant that it was always an eighteen hour day when he lived there, which left no time for each other, no time for love, not the way things used to be.

Jenny would get a telephone call in the small hours of the morning. Then she would get up and go and collect one animal or another. They had tried on many occasions to work it out, but Jenny would end up spending more time and money on other peoples, unwanted pets, than she did on their marriage. Billy wished her well.

Jenny placed adverts in all the local of the newspapers, endeavouring to obtain quality homes for her waifs and strays. This cost money, that originally she had to start with. She struggled to find it now and that was another reason that Billy had left.

Most of the other rescue centres charged 'Voluntary Donations' which were sums ranging from £250 to as much as £500, depending on the breed of the dog and the cost of running their rescue centres.

There were kennel-maids to be paid, then the cost of running a van to collect and deliver cats and dogs around the county. The expenditure of feeding these animals had soared over the last year. At was now at the point where Jenny, knew she would have to wind things up. The realisation that saving animals cost real money.

Then like a miracle and totally out out of the blue, a man had come to her one day and offered to pick up the tab for the running cost of the kennels. Jenny could hardly believe her luck. This man owned a sizeable farm, less than a half mile from her own home.

He had responded to one of her adverts requesting help in running the rescue centre. Her advert had read 'Wanted someone to help out with the day to day running of a small but quality private rescue kennel. Work would be on a voluntary basis only'

So when her new help arrived, in a very new very flash pearl white Range Rover, she had been more than a little surprised. His name was John Perkins and he had offered immediately, to take two of her rescue dogs, which he said he would keep on his farm with lots of space for them to run and play.

As with all her placements Jenny had not taken it on face value but she had visited the farm and after speaking to the farmer and his wife, Jenny had looked around the area where the dogs would live and play. Jenny was so happy that she never bothered of ask for a voluntary donation of £50.

The next day Mr Perkins had arrived with a large cheque, which he said, was to help with the day to day running costs of the kennels. John said that he was a bit of a philanthropist who had made most of his money in the city. Now he was just happy that in part at least, some of that money would be going, to good use.

Janet had told Billy about her new benefactor and said that perhaps she would be able to spend less time in the kennels, as she would be able to pay for a couple of kennel staff, due entirely to the new benefactor.

Now not only would she be able to rescue more animals, but she would be able to do so while spending less time doing the hard work, which it involved.

After checking with her new benefactor, she asked Billy to extend the Kennel block effectively double the space. Mr Perkins had suggested that Jenny might like to have an indoor cattery, behind the kennel block. Once again he offered to pay for, not only the building but the running costs.

He had helped with the design by using a friend of his who was an architect, then after the plans were drawn up, he had helped some more by getting the planning permission, through the local council. John Perkins, told Jenny that if her husband wanted the fully paid job, of building and maintenance, then the position was his. Billy of course accepted. John had paid Billy proper wages, to build the extra kennels and cattery.

Jenny now not only had the space, but her kennels had a quality of the accommodation, which was way beyond, the rest of the rescue centres in the county. All this though, created another problem.

They had more space, than they had animals to put in them. It was then, that John Perkins asked her, if she was willing to take rescued animals from central and eastern Europe.

He had shown her pictures on Facebook, of the maltreated dogs and cats. There were rescue centres in these countries, but when compared to those in the UK, they were pitiful. Jenny had asked him how they could help as there would be all sorts of things to sort out, like dog and cat passports. Added to this, there would be the horrendous cost, of bringing the poor beasts over to the UK. John said that he was willing and able to take care of all these niggling little things, so as he was in a position to, he would help make the dogs and cats lives better than the life they currently lived.

John Perkins and his wife had been a Godsend. Jenny was now becoming closer to Billy again, because she had staff to clean the kennels along with feeding and general care of the dogs and cats. All Jenny had to do was to act as the manager and complete the paperwork, along with vetting the prospective new owners.

John had great contacts and within weeks of the new kennel block opening. John had managed to find homes for all the dogs that Jenny had rescued from Lincoln and the surrounding areas. Now there was only one old and scruffy looking Labrador and a female tabby cat with her litter of kittens that were too young to be taken from their mother.

John had come up with another idea, why did they not employ a Vet on a retainer basis? It sounded like a great sentiment, but where could they find a

Vet, that would do work, that would be affordable to their kennel. After all they did not have the same finances, that the larger rescue companies had with their charity status. Once again John said to leave it with him, and he would sort something out. Jenny wanted to ask him, why he was spending so much money on what was effectively her project? One day she finally plucked up the courage and ask.

"My dear Jenny, did I not tell you? I have a large farm that I inherited about a year ago from my uncle. He also left me a sizeable bank balance. My wife and I have always been animal lovers and spent some time working in Romania. So we have seen the way that some of the Romanian Gypsies treat their so-called pets. We always vowed that when and if we could, then we would try to eradicate pet cruelty, wherever we saw it. When we found out about your rescue centre, my wife said that we should help you in your work. Do not worry we are not in it for the kudos, nor do we wish to own your Kennels and Cattery. We are just fortunate enough to be in a position to help you financially in your work and our passion." He said as they sat having one of their now almost daily brainstorming sessions.

"What about the Vet, surely no Vet will work for free and I can't see any of our local Vets working for less than their standard fees. The only Vet that works in this county that way, is the RSPCA Vet, and he is on a parable wage with other UK Vets." She had replied.

"As I said Jenny, leave it with me. I might know of a man who will come and work for us. He and his wife are keen to come to the UK. He is a Vet and his wife she is a Veterinary nurse. I will let you know in a few days' time. Meanwhile do you require anything else for the kennels?"

"Wow that would be amazing. I really don't know how to thank you John." She responded.

"No need for thanks. It is you who's doing great works Jenny and it is my pleasure to be able to offer a little help." John had said and then he finished his coffee and left.

Jenny waved him off and went down to the new cattery where Billy was busy finishing off the electrics. It was amazing everything they required, John had paid for. Central heating for the Kennels as well as the Cattery. Effectively it was a luxury hotel for cats and dogs.

"Hi Billy, John thinks he can get us a Vet, that will work for free. Though I am sure that is going to be pretty difficult, even for him to achieve."

Billy put the screwdriver down in his toolbox and looked up at Jenny. He thought before answering her.

"Don't you think it's all a little strange, that John keeps throwing money at your kennels? All this without asking anything in return. He must have spent £30,000 so far on all the little additions that he has made. Not to mention the wages for the two part time kennel maids will work out at £15,000 a year. I wish I had that sort of money that I could just throw around." He said.

"I think he is just like me Billy an animal lover. He hates to see any animal in distress. Have you seen the pictures he took in Romania and Russia of the way some people treat their animals? They would be jailed if they did those things in this country."

"I don't know Jenny, it just seems too good to be true." Billy replied to her.

"Have you never heard the saying 'don't look a gift horse in the mouth' They are still my kennels and my rescue centre. He has no controlling stake in any of it. It is all voluntary donations. He told me the other day that he was able to write off large chunks of his tax by giving to charitable institutions."

"Jenny you are a voluntary rescue centre, which the RSPCA and the Dogs Trust, have Vetted and both use you. But you are not a registered charity unless anything in that line has changed over the last six months?"

"Billy I understand you worrying about why he is spending a lot of money and no I am not a charitable trust yet. I think he and his wife just love animals and are fortunate enough to be able to help people like us. So that we can make a difference." She said.

"You are probably right Jenny. I do still worry about you know. Technically I am still your husband, so it is still my job to watch out for you."

"That is nice of you to say so Billy. Do you fancy having dinner with me tonight? No strings attached".

"That would be nice, thank you. I will be up at the house in about an hour after I finish this little job off." He said and went back to his work.

Jenny walked up to the house and started to prepare a simple meal of fish and mashed potatoes with a creamy cheese sauce to pour over the top. It was one of Billy's favourites.

During the evening meal, Jenny deliberately kept away from the subject of her rescue centre and tried as much as she could to talk about how Billy was getting on helping at his brothers.

Billy was the one who had been blessed with all the hands-on skill set like joinery, electrical and plumbing skills. He had completely re-plumbed and rewired their home when they bought it. Then he had decorated it to a high standard. He had also set up a good vegetable garden, before he pandered to Jenny's longing to save animals. She knew of course that he would be a great asset to Janet when it came to their smallholding.

After dinner they sat down in the lounge in front of the traditional fireplace that Billy had renovated. The pair of them sat on cushions and drank wine while watching the flickering flames of the logs that burned in the hearth. It had been a wonderful night, almost like when they were first married, and they would sit with a bottle of wine and curl up in front of the fire and talk into the early hours of the morning. That was then and this was now. Jenny wanted what they had but was unsure just how to get it back.

At 1:00am Billy said he had to go as he was going to have to make an early start over at Jack and Janet's in the morning, especially if he was going to have any chance of finishing the plastering in Jenny's new cattery later that day. He got up and kissed her on the cheek, then thanked her for the great dinner and a very pleasant evening, then he was gone. Jenny waited until the sound of his VW Beetle had faded into silence, then she too, got up and went into the kitchen and washed up the pots and pans before turning out the lights and heading up to bed alone, well alone except for her Cavalier King Charles Spaniel and her Persian cat who followed her upstairs.

The cat would sleep on the floor, but the miniature cavalier would always sleep on the bed. It had done this even when Billy was in bed with her. Sometimes Jenny would wake up to find the cavalier with its head stuffed between Billy and her, with its head on their pillows.

Jenny woke refreshed and ready for the new day, she went to the bathroom and completed her ablutions. Then she went downstairs and made breakfast for herself and the two pets that shared the house with her. After breakfast she let the dog and cat out. They never ran away even though they could, if they so wished.

There were no fences around her property as they backed onto fields on three sides with a long driveway that separated two fields. To the rear of the house was her land where she had a small field filled with vegetables and beyond that, the area was the kennels and cattery then a small, wooded area that belonged to one of her farmer neighbours. He had given her permission to walk the dogs in the woods area.

Jenny used to do it herself but when the kennels were full, the kennel maids would carry out this task.

As soon as the coffee was brewed she poured herself a large mug of the steaming black liquid. Jenny liked it strong and black and after just a few sips her mind would be racing on the tasks of the day. She looked at the clock on the kitchen wall.

8:15 the two kennel maids would be here in about 10 minutes. Both the girls were 16 years old and had just left school that summer. They were good hard workers and never complained about any task.

The first of which would be to go to the kennels with a wheelbarrow and clean away any solid waste before scrubbing down the concrete floors with disinfectant. Then they would feed any dogs that were in the rescue centre, before repeating the whole process in the cattery. The wheelbarrow would then be tipped into a large container not unlike a septic tank. This tank was emptied every three months by a specialist company, who would then dispose of the slurry.

The two girls would come up to the house for a coffee and chat, before taking the dogs for a walk around the woods. Now there was not a lot of work for them to do, but John has said, that Jenny should keep them on, and he would cover their wages.

Billy was now splitting his time equally between Jack and Jenny. So, all the little and sometimes big jobs that would have cost a fortune to call a qualified tradesman in, were now being completed by Billy. The big difference now compared to before, is that he was being paid for the work, that he did to the kennels and to the cattery.

Jenny walked down the slabbed pathway to the kennels and cattery in her right hand she had her mug of coffee and in her left she carried the cordless phone, there was still good reception at the to the kennel block.

She looked at the new tiling to the bottom half of the 8 feet high walls that separated the individual kennels. The top half of the walls were whitewashed. All but one of the 12 kennels were empty and there were no cats in the cattery. John had told her not to worry as they would soon be extremely busy. The new stainless-steel doors to each enclosure looked fantastic, again this was something John had ordered and paid for. The cattery was much the same except that there was now space for 32 cats. Both the dogs and cats, had indoor and outdoor enclosures. Jenny was rightfully proud of the way her rescue centre looked now, especially when compared to her amateur efforts before John had come into their lives.

Jenny tried not to compare Billy and John, but it was difficult not too. Billy had never really been interested in her idea of running a rescue centre for cats and dogs, yet it seemed to be the only thing on John's mind. John had wanted everything to be the best.

He was due down later today to check in on how the work was coming along. The truth was that Billy had already completed all the work and was now just titivating things and tidying up behind himself.

Billy had even built a large storeroom where they could keep foodstuffs including frozen meat along with nice shiny new stainless steel feeding dishes. The final item to be installed was to be a new custom sewage tank complete with a macerator motor and pump, allowing the waste from the kennels to be diverted back into the main sewer system. This would negate the requirement for the tank to be emptied every few months. All the metal fittings in the kennels were made from high grade stainless steel and all concretes surfaces were either tiled or rendered smooth and painted.

John had invited them over to his home for dinner tonight, where they would discuss the first batch of animals to come in from a shelter in Romania.

2
ROMANIA

Jenny and Billy, arrived at the rather more lavish home of John and his good lady wife. Before tonight Jenny had only seen John's wife from a distance. Billy pressed the polished brass doorbell and it could be heard ringing in the house.

A woman in a traditional housemaids uniform opened the door. Jenny started to introduce Billy and herself but the woman said nothing, she just indicated they should enter the house. Then she stood there before taking their coats and walking off.

"Ahhh Good evening. How are you both? Please come in" John said without really giving them a chance to answer the question about their health.

John led the way down the wide hallway and to the double doors of what was obviously the dining room. He moved aside to allow them to enter.

"I don't think you have been formally introduced to my wife. Darling these are the kind people who have have the rescue kennels. They have very kindly allowed us, to help them in their quest to protect man's best friend. Jenny, Billy, please meet my long suffering and beautiful wife Natasha.

Natasha stepped forward and kissed Jenny first on one cheek and then the other before doing the same to Billy.

"It is a great pleasure to formally meet with you Jenny. My husband talks so much about your love of dogs as well as for cats." Natasha said.

Billy tried to place her accent but all he could glean from it, was that she was from Eastern Europe. Billy need not have bothered as John continued with his introductions.

"My wife is from Zapsillya in the Ukraine. just in case you were wondering about her accent. Like myself she is a lover of cats and dogs, we are both saddened to say, that in her homeland a lot of these wonderful animals are not treated with the love and respect that they so justly deserve. I am afraid that it is a bit of a hangover from the old days of the Soviet Union." John had said.

Billy noted the incredible beauty of Natasha. It was an honest appraisal and not a personal attraction. She had the poise to go with her outward beauty. It would not have surprised Billy if her husband had introduced her as a distant member of the of the former Russian royal family. Her hair was blonde although probably not natural going by her well groomed eyebrows, her high and well defined cheekbones could have allowed her to be a model walking on any of Europe's fashion runways. Billy took his eyes from the face of Natasha and shook John's hand.

Billy was not alone in noticing the elegance and beauty of Johns wife. Jenny was a tad jealous of the natural beauty that Natasha had. Jenny had dressed up for tonight and by normal UK standards she would have tuned heads, but not when standing next to this Ukrainian beauty. The simple sleeveless dress that Natasha wore, fitted perfectly to every curve of her body. Everything about her seemed to be perfection right down to the uncomplicated cream coloured high-heeled shoes that Natasha wore.

After they were seated at the fine dining table that would have easily seated a dozen diners. A man came through and served them wine before dinner. John introduced him as Alexi, and that Alexi was his wife's guardian, when John himself was not around.

The rest of the time he worked as a driver and butler. Alexi's wife was the housekeeper and cook.

On hearing that Alexi's wife was the cook, both Jenny and Billy had expected the meal to be some Eastern European style of food. They were wrong, to have made such sweeping assumptions.

Their fine meal started with a French onion soup, which was followed by Beef Wellington that was served with seasonal vegetables. all of this was finished of with a Chocolate bomb laced with brandy. It had been a delightful meal by any standards.

After dinner they went through to the equally opulent lounge, which was exactly the way that Jenny had imagined it would be. Tastefully yet luxuriously decorated and filled with a mixture of East and West of Europe. When they were seated and when Alex had refilled their glasses. John said

"I have a friend of mine from the Ukraine, well to be honest, it is a relative of Natasha's. He, like us is ashamed, of the way that some, and not just their countrymen, but people around the globe tend to treat so many poor defenceless animals. My friend qualified as a Veterinary Surgeon, just over a year ago and basically has been working for food and board, at one of the rescue centres in Romania. He has said he will come and work for us. I will pay his wages and we can find him a small house nearby or he can stay with Natasha and me, here on our farm."

Jenny was truly in awe at this sudden announcement.

"But wont he require a surgery to operate from?"

"I am sure he will Jenny and I shall build that here in the farm. Not only will it benefit the Rescue centre but it will be good for us, as Natasha wants to get some horses and we were thinking about building a small stud farm. Billy you look troubled?"

Billy rolled the half full crystal glass between his palms, as he thought how best to answer the question. Then he put the glass down.

"I don't want you to take this the wrong way John and I know that you have the same love of animals that Jenny does" He said before John interrupted him.

"You look so serious Billy, I cant help feeling that there is a 'but' coming up?"

"You are right John. Why pick Jenny to help when there are so many other bigger and more organised rescue centres. I mean, we all want to get something out of life. What is it that you will get from spending all this money. The work that you have paid for at Jenny's small holding, has already doubled the value of her property. You are taking a huge financial risk. As a rule of thumb, rescue kennels are paid for either by a registered charity or by the money generated by those that adopt the animals. Will the rescue centre not become a bit of a millstone for you? The cost of transportation alone will run into tens of thousands I am sure. Are you a secret millionaire?"

Jenny was mortified that Billy had been so blunt in asking these questions from their hosts. Were it not for a similar line of thought running through her own head, she would have stormed out leaving Billy to find his own way home.

"Billy we should not ask such personal questions of our friends." Jenny said while placing her hand on Billy's arm.

"I am sorry. Jenny is of course right, it is none of my business where or how you have made your money. Please accept my apologies John." Billy said. Even though, he really did want to know.

John sipped his drink and looked at Natasha. Billy watched and he was sure there was just a tiniest of nods from Natasha to John.

"Of course you should ask these questions, were the situations reversed I would be asking you the same. When I first met Natasha she was living in Russia, even though she is from the Ukraine. She had been married to a man in the Oil business. However he divorced her in favour of a younger model. At the time I was in investments, Natasha came to me with her divorce settlement and ask me, to help her make the money from her alimony, work for her, rather than her for the money. Bitcoin was just starting to surface and it was something new, but it seemed to be catching on. In 2010 for $0.08 you could buy one bitcoin, we invested £10,000 well that is to say I invested for Natasha. So last year it was worth £35,000,000. We cashed it in and bought a home in Ukraine and this farm here, which I inherited. So I modernised it and cleaned it up a bit. Did you know my father?" John asked

"No John the people before you kept themselves pretty much to themselves." Jenny said.

John continued.

"Well financially, this left us with quite a bit left over. So in answer to the other questions you have. We are independently wealthy, and we just like to spread a little cheer to those, that are kind people. Jenny you are a kind and caring person. You opened your small kennels to animals that needed rescuing and you did so at your own cost, with no outside financial help. I would think, the strain that it caused the pair of you, is probably the main reason that you split apart. Perhaps without that stress, then even that can be mended. I apologise if this is too forward of me. So now you know that if the total setup that we can do for you is £100,000, then is it not that much of a drain on our resources. At some point the Kennels will become self sufficient, or at least it will break even. Now let us drink a toast to its success and you will have to think of a name for your revamped rescue centre something with an international flair." John said.

They drank their toast and then a few more John called a taxi for Jenny and Billy, saying he would have their car returned to them tomorrow morning. Billy should have been going to his brothers home but Jenny told him to come 'home' for a coffee first. Initially Billy had declined but as Jenny persisted he eventually accepted.

When they arrived home they went into the Kitchen and Jenny put the water on to boil for the

Cafetière, which he had spooned some arabica coffee grounds into.

"What do you think" She asked

"About?"

"About John and Natasha, silly."

"He has more money than sense if you ask me. But I guess it's his money and he can do with it as he pleases."

"That's not what I meant Billy. I mean what do you think of them on a personal level."

"Seriously, I think he is punching way above his weight. His wife has to be twenty years his junior. Also did you notice that it was her money that he invested and not his own. Hell I wish I had put a few quid into BitCoin when I had the chance."

"You had a chance to do that?" She asked him

"Yes, a mate of mine was a computer geek and he said it would be a good investment, but as he had no money of his own to speak of, he never invested so I decided not to as well. Hindsight is a wonderful thing Jenny. So what do I think about John and Natasha? I think that he is a very lucky man. Obviously going on what he has said, the wealth is hers and he is fortunate that their views on rescuing animals in distress is similarly aligned." Billy said.

"Do you think she is the driving force behind him or what?" Jenny asked while pouring the coffee.

"I think it does not really matter Jenny. What matters, is that you can run your rescue centre, completely free from financial worries. I think if you asked him to pay you a wage for your services, then he would do it." Billy said as he carried their coffees through to the lounge. Jenny went in first and switched on the lights before dimming them down a bit.

Jenny put on some background music before she sat down on the corner sofa next to Billy.

"I just don't understand, how we got so lucky? Mums money will run out soon and I will have to find an income to live on. Honestly I nearly broached the subject with them at dinner but I held off for fear of spoiling the night." She said as she curled her legs underneath her bottom.

"Well if I were you. I would strike while the iron is hot so to speak. Call him in the morning and ask him to pop over. I can be there for moral support for you." Billy said putting his cup down on the small coffee table next to where he was sat.

"Would you Billy? Would you really do that for me. I mean, I know you never liked the idea of me running a kennel."

"I never said I disliked you running a kennel, what I objected to was you doing it all for nothing or even worse, running it as a financial and social lose. When we were first married we would spend lots of time together. We would curl up on this sofa and listen to music, while we shared a bottle of wine. Then you seemed to forget about us, and spent all your time, money and effort on the stray dogs and cats. I know I can speak to you freely these days, as things are no longer strained between us. If you had run it like the other rescue centres, so that it did not run at a loss, and that you managed rather than did everything yourself, then I don't think we would have split."

Jenny was stunned by his honesty but also happy that he had opened up to her finally about exactly what it was about the kennel that had driven a wedge between them.

"You know what Billy. You are right. I will call John in the morning and see if he can perhaps fund a wage for me until the kennel is up and running properly." She said. Feeling that a big weight might suddenly be lifted from her shoulders.

They finished their coffee, then opened a bottle of wine and listened to Jeff Wayne's album 'War Of The Worlds' just like they used to. Billy stayed that night and true to his word, he was there in the morning for moral support. After calling John and asking him to come over as she wanted to finalise a few ideas with him. She put a fresh pot of coffee on and with butterflies in her belly, she awaited his arrival.

3
NEW ARRIVALS

John arrived not long after that, Jenny watched him as he got out of his shiny new Range Rover and tried to avoid the many muddy puddles, caused by the previous nights downpour. Billy went to the kitchen door and opened it allowing John to enter.

"Morning John, coffee?" Jenny asked holding up the percolator, which was still gurgling having only just having been removed from the Rayburn stove.

John wiped his feet on the door mat before replying.

"That would be nice Jenny. Morning Billy"

Jenny put the coffee on a trivet, in the middle of the scrubbed pine kitchen table and then got a jug of milk from the fridge. She laid three stoneware mugs on the table. before sitting and waiting for the two men to do likewise. She poured the black coffee into the mugs and gently shoved one over the table to John. Billy took his black but he liked it sweet and three spoonfuls of sugar from a small bowl on the table. Jenny waited until John had added sugar and milk to his before starting the conversation.

"I know you have done so much for us already John and I really do hate to ask you to do more for the kennels, but until we are fully operational I cant afford to pay all the normal bills of my own life. I put all my mums money into this venture. Me and Billy were just getting by when we only had a few dogs to look after and find homes for, and yes I do know we have no dogs here at the moment, but I have no other income." Jenny said.

She was starting to become flustered and a bit embarrassed at the very thought of asking him to pay her as well as all the other running costs. Jenny knew her cheeks must be glowing bright red. So she thought, just grow a set and ask. Although she need not have bothered, as John put his hand up to stop her. Shit! She thought now he is going to pull the plug on the entire venture. She felt a profound sense of shame for even asking him. Jenny could feel the tips of her ears burning and knew full well that her face would have gone scarlet red by now, that feeling of shame that creates a sickness, rather than butterflies.

"I don't know why you did not mention it to me before Jenny, I was too mortified to come out and plain offer you a wage, in case you thought me too forward and trying to buy your services. So please let me rectify that right now. We pay the kennel maids what £250 per week each? Right?" He asked her.

Jenny stuttered out a simple "Yes John"

"Well you have to be worth at least the value of two kennel maids, so lets make this easy. £500 per week for you and if Billy would like to stay on as handy man and driver here, for about the same? Is that enough?" John asked

Jenny was just about to say that was way too much and so much more than any manager of a rescue centre in the UK was getting. Billy though, cut her off.

"So long as you are sure John? Then it is perfect. I will be able to maintain everything to a high standard and I am sure it is a great weight off Jenny's mind."

"Jenny you have only ever shown yourself to be a wonderful human being and a true lover of animals. It is an expensive business looking after other peoples, cast off pets and animals that are in need care. I do though have another job for you Billy and it has to do with the Kennels. Although this time it will be over at my farm. There are a series of outbuildings next to our house which I would like you to turn into a Vets Surgery. The buildings are sound, they just need some internal TLC and a new concrete floor. All the equipment for the surgery will be arriving in two weeks time. Do you think you could complete the work by then?"

"Wow that's a lot of work John and I might need to call in some extra help to get it done in time."

"You get the hired help and I will pay them, also there will be a bit of a bonus for you when the job is done." John responded and then said he had some work to do but would make the arrangements with his own accountant, to sort the wages for Jenny and Billy.

They waited until his car had left, before sitting back down at the kitchen table. It was a while before either of them could speak, but it was Jenny who broke the silence.

"I feel like I have just won the lottery Billy, now we both have jobs. What are you going to say to

Jack and Janet? You wont have time to continue to help him with his smallholding?"

"I will let him know and help him find some green fingered person to assist him, that or else he will have to crack the whip on Janet." Billy said with a smile.

Now they had no worries about money, they were far more relaxed. It flooded over into their personal relationship too. Jenny found herself and Billy growing close, it was like things used to be when the first met all those years back.

It was great, they no longer squabbled over the little things, in fact they no longer fought about anything. Billy had been over and sorted out some help for his brother Jack, so now that was another problem taken from his shoulders.

Jack had been down and looked at the all new kennels and cattery, he was impressed. The last time he had seen anything on the scale of what Jenny and Billy had built up, was a professional setup at Battersea Dogs Home, albeit that Jenny's was a smaller operation.

Jack was sorry to lose his younger brothers help on the smallholding he had, but wished him luck in his new venture with Jenny. Secretly he was glad that Billy might be out from the home that he shared with his wife Janet, at least now they would get their privacy back.

Jack though could never understand why someone would throw tens of thousands or pounds of their own money, setting up and paying for a kennel, that someone else would own. Still Jenny's benefactor must have his reasons, perhaps it was some way of making sure the taxman did not take as big a cut of the man's money.

A week or so later John came to the kennels and he had some good news to tell Jenny

"We have six dogs coming in from a Romanian refuge and they should be with us in three or four days. They will first go to Dover and then from there, they will come here. Billy you will have to collect them from the immigration kennels and bring them up here. They need to stay in the kennels here for two weeks before they are allowed to be re-homed. Before that they will of course have to be checked out by our Vet. They will all be inoculated and chipped or re-chipped where required. You will notice that all the dogs arriving have already had some surgery for injuries. This is one of the reasons I have helped you set up your rescue centre. Most of these poor animals would normally have been destroyed, rather than to receive expensive Veterinary treatment. Any further surgery that may be required will of course be done by our in-house Vet. He will work only for me and your kennels. As soon as I get the details of the dogs coming in I will message you Billy, so that you can collect them. I have also managed to convince another good friend of mine to produce a professional website for your kennels. I have asked good local photographer, to come down and take some pictures, and as soon as the dogs are ready. This means that you will have professional photos of them put up on the site. Due to the fact that you will be getting up to ten dogs at a time from eastern Europe. This means that you will of course require a suitable and reliable van. I have taken the liberty of buying you a brand new Ford Transit van which I shall have wrapped in the graphics of your Kennels, it will be registered to you Jenny and it has also been insured for either of you to drive. That's it we are now ready to go." John said then he finished his coffee and left. Jenny and Billy were both left slack jawed and stunned at his generosity.

Jenny called the Kennel maids up to the house and explained everything to them, so they would be ready to do the job they had been employed to do.

The next few days were spent in adding final touches to everything Billy had built a large summerhouse to the side of the kennels which would now function as the main office. Billy had connected up all the mains utilities to it along with high speed broadband.

The old mud and gravel driveway had been replaced with a new Concrete driveway and proper car park area to the other side of the Office. All the buildings had been painted white, this also included the outside of their own home. It gave the place, a clean and professional look.

Signs were made and posted 200 yards both side of the entrance to the kennels, so that anyone driving along from either direction would be able to find the place with ease. They had named the place after Jenny's mother, 'The Marjorie Rescue Centre for Cats & Dogs'. John had arranged for all sorts of fund raising merchandising. The sort that could be sold to prospective owners as well as to the general public at large.

Finally the say came and the call they had all been waiting for from Dover. Billy waited the two days and then drove down to the animal holding area at Dover Docks. There were only to be five dogs rather than the six that John had originally told them about.

His Vet in Romania had ensured that all the dogs were correctly microchipped as well as ensuring that they had all been vaccinated against rabies at least three weeks before their travel. Each dog had also been vaccinated against tapeworm, as well as having received any flea and tick treatment as necessary.

Every dog was in a separate crate with a description labelled to the front. All of the dogs were described as 'mixed breed' and they were aged between 12 months and 4 years.

Billy passed over the paperwork that John had provided and the crated dogs were wheeled out to the front and then put in the rear of Billy's air conditioned Ford Transit van, which was now emblazoned with the logo of their kennels. Billy made sure that each crated dog had water in their anti spill feeding bowls before they set off for home.

The first part of the journey the dogs were barking so loud that Billy could hardly hear himself think but after thirty or forty minutes they settled down and he turned the radio on and listened to some nondescript radio show to pass the time away.

It was almost 8pm when Billy arrived back at the kennels. As the kennel maids had gone home hours ago, Jenny and Billy took the cages to separate kennels and let the dogs out, into their individual runs. Billy noticed that all the dog has received some form of surgery as all but one, wore one of those cone devices, that they put on dogs to stop them nagging at any stitches or wound that they may have. The fifth dog has received surgery the back of its neck so did not require a medical collar. None of the dogs showed any form of aggression and they all ate heartedly from their feeding bowls.

Jenny took the documents from each transit cage and placed them in their respective holders outside each kennel. She would complete all the necessary paperwork in the morning along with checking on any health issue, that there would be to follow up on. When they had secured the kennels and turned out the lights Jenny walked arm in arm with Billy back up to the house.

"This is it Billy, we are doing this for real now. I am so excited I am fit to burst" She said

Billy said nothing but gave her a gentle squeeze and then kissed her full and passionately on the lips. They had a drink and then they both went up to their marital bed.

3
Regular Routines

Both Billy and Jenny were up early, keen to start working in the kennels. They had their breakfast by 07:30 and awaited the arrivals of the two kennel maids, whilst they only had five dogs, there would still be plenty of work for the two girls. First things first they had to get everybody settled into a regular routine.

Jenny filled the coffee pot and laid out a tray with cups, sugar, milk and a plate of biscuits just as the girls arrived together. They were both dropped off by the parents of Abby who was the slightly younger of the two girls.

"Morning Mrs Hamilton" Abby said and the other girl who was called Bella, followed suit.

"I have some sweatshirts for both of you" Jenny said and handed over two clear packages containing the sweatshirts printed with the rescue centre logo. to each girl. They in turn thank her and opened them excitedly before putting them on. Now everyone including Billy wore these professional looking tops.

After pouring out coffee for everyone Jenny invited them to sit down at the kitchen table. When everyone was settled she took a fat brown envelope and removed the documents from within. There were five sets of A4 paper stapled together and each had a see through plastic envelop that contained copies of the dogs essential documents like their inoculations and chip numbers. The attached paperwork described each dog in great detail, along with, where and why, surgery had been done on the animal. There were drawings of each section of the dog from left, right, top and underneath in order to show areas of any injury.

One of the pieces of equipment that John had bought for the rescue centre was a chip reading wand. The same as the ones that would be used in a Vets surgery. Jenny passed this over to Abby and showed her how to use it.

The girls would have to keep detailed records of the type and quantity of food, that would be given to the dogs. As well as records of any medications administered. So it was essential that the records matched exactly with the correct animal.

Next she passed the daily feeding chart to Bella. Jenny herself, would see to the medications, at least for now. At this point there was not much for Billy to do as everything was perfect.

The same applied to the Veterinary block of building he had helped to set up at Johns. The Vet would be arriving later today and he had a small apartment at the side of John's sprawling home.

The Dogs would be taken over one at a time when the Vet was ready, for now though Billy decided that he would help the two girls with cleaning out the kennels and making sure that everything ran smoothly especially when it came to the waste tank system.   After they girls had finished their coffee they left with Billy. Billy grabbed a sack of dog food from the purpose built storeroom and loaded it into a two-wheeled barrow and they all walked down to the kennel block.

Jenny opened the medication folder and looked at the first page. It was printed in colour and there was a photo of the dog at the top of the page. Under the picture was the dogs name and immediately below that was a chip number. Next to that there was a location box, in which was written 'Between the Shoulders' Then there was another box that said Tattoo. This space was left blank. The description panel said that it was a Grey and species box just stated Dog. Below that was another box for the breed. This simply said Mixed Breed. Next to this was yet another box, this one was for the sex and inside this box it stated Male Neutered. Then there was a box that said Date of Birth which said approximately 18 months with the same date as the Microchip Box had stated. The final box on this section was for the Coat of the animal. This box simply said Grey. The next section said at the top of its page Vaccination Against Rabies. The date this had been done was just over a month ago and there was a Veterinarians stamp, along with his or her signature. There was another page for Parva Virus and Kennel cough all pretty much the same as the page for Rabies complete with date stamps and signatures. Then there was a page for De-worming shots. Then there was a section for de-flea and de-tick. Finally there were pages for clinical examination.

This dog had been treated for cuts caused by becoming tangled in barbed wire. Its wounds had been treated and stitched by the same Vet who had administered the Anti-rabies inoculation shots. There was a note for the wounds to be treated and redressed at the next kennel location. This was of course Jenny's rescue centre.

After reading this dogs documents Jenny read the other four and they were all pretty much the same except for how they had come by their wounds some were to removed growths others were caused by accidents. The result though was pretty much the same all of these dogs required a lot of tender loving care.

Collecting up the folders Jenny walked down to see the dogs in the daylight and to check on their condition as well as to see how they behaved with people. Jenny had looked after dogs for many years and had experience of dogs, who were inherently bad natured, also of dogs who have become unstable due to their environments.

There were many reasons why dogs ended up in rescue centres and not all were due to the dogs fault. Often a big change in circumstances of their owners were the reason why dogs were given up. A move to a place where pets were not allowed or perhaps a pregnancy.

There could be a millions reasons, although quite often the truth was much more disheartening than that. Sometimes their owners just had no time, in their ever busier lives for the dog or cat.

There were sometimes more emotional reason such as, the animal would come into the care system because their owner had died. Dog and cats pine and mourn for their owners in the same way as we would if they were to die and leave us alone. Much more rare were the ones that were born feral.

Abuse of animals seemed to be on the rise around the world. Dog fighting and coursing, in Europe was quite prevalent. There were still a small percentage, who had been deliberately harmed by sick individuals.

Over the Years Jenny had seen all the reasons for rescue. Each animal though, was a sad story. Jenny had kept very detailed logs on ever single animal that had ever passed through her doors. These newer additions would get the same level of care and love. Jenny knew from reading the files on the first five dogs, that they would be in her care for at least four weeks, before they could be advertised for re-homing.

Jenny walked down to the all new kennel block, where the girls were weighing out the dog food as per each dog. The amounts having been set by the Vet who had examined them prior to the dogs making the journey to the UK. The quantities of water were also being monitored through automatic water troughs.

They worked on a simple ballcock system dropping one litre or water each time the level dropped. This was linked to a simple counter which would be reset each morning. Consequently Jenny would be able to tell the Vet, the daily intake of food and water for each animal.

The importance of this for dogs with any form of digestive or kidney problem, could not be understated and Jenny had stressed this to the kennel maids. They in turn would keep a log and hang the clipboard outside each kennel with the dogs name on.

The next job for the kennel maids would be to clean the kennels and the concrete dog runs, scrubbing them out with disinfectant. After that job was done, the dogs would be taken for some light exercise depending on their injuries. Again this was closely monitored and anything the girls noticed about the way a dogs walked or is it had antisocial tendencies would be recorded in that dogs folder.

It was almost lunchtime before all these chores had been completed. Billy was cleaning out the back of the van and wiping it down with a cleaning agent, just in case any of the dogs had brought anything unsavoury with it, or if there had been any leakage of blood from their wounds and of course, any soiling the dogs had done in the back of the van. Even though they were crated when they arrived. Jenny said you could not be too careful.

Jenny called Billy in for some lunch and the two kennel maids joined them as well. They were quite excited about their first real day on the job. Jenny was beaming with pride. Billy kicked off his boots as he joined then in the house.

He had just sat down at the table when a car pulled up outside, it was followed shortly by a knock on the door, which was then opened and Janet popped her head in.

"Any chance of a cuppa Jenny?" Janet asked

Jenny, rose to meet her sister-in-law who was followed into the kitchen, by Billy's brother Jack. Jenny kissed Janet on the cheek and then gave Jack a big hug.

"Come on in you two and yes of course, there is plenty of tea in the pot." Jenny replied, even though Billy and her drank coffee. After refilling the kettle she put it on the stove and put three teaspoons of tea leaves into the earthenware teapot.

The two kennel maids politely excused themselves and even though Jenny said for them not to go. They said they had some chores still to complete. down in the Kennel block. Jenny knew this was bullshit but appreciated that they knew this was to be a family gathering.

Jack pulled a chair out from the table and sat down. Since he left the police force he had been bored out of his mind. They had bought a smallholding just along the road from his brother Billy and his wife Jenny.

Jack and his new wife of two years, grew organic fruit and vegetables. jacks first wife had died almost five years ago. Initially they had run their organic smallholding without a profit, but things had started to turn around. This was in part due to a new craze, for everything organic and partly due to a new luxury housing village about three miles from them.

Janet had made flyers and gone around and dropped one in every house. Within weeks of that flyer drop, they were selling everything they produced.

Whilst growing organic was less expensive it was much more labour intensive. Good honest labour keeping the weeds and pests off the produce by hand, meant they kept the quality and the quantity of their products high.

Janet had even suggested that they should see if they could buy the two acre field next door to their smallholding before some builder bought it. Jack had contacted the man that owned it and whilst they had a deal verbally, he would have to wait for the owner to return from working abroad, before they could finalise things.

"So Jenny how are the all new rescue kennels" Janet asked as Jenny poured the steaming tea into two mugs that she had placed on the table along with a small milk jug and a sugar bowl, she could never remember if Jack took sugar.

"After you have had your tea, you should come down and see them, we just took in five dogs from Romania."

"Oh wow you never know, Jack and I might adopt one" Janet said

Billy could see Jack roll his eyes, he knew that Jenny had seen it as well but Janet had not.

"You never know" Jack said flatly and then continued

"Do you folks want to order any potatoes? They should be ready next week, the only reason I ask is I have pre-orders that I am not even sure I can fill. Family always comes first with me though. By the way that lad you sent down to help me, is really a hard grafter. More importantly he knows the difference between a weed and a plant.

Oh if you want a day or two shooting rabbits, I could do with a bit of a help there as there are lots of baby bunnies trying to eat me out of business." Jack said

"Oh Jack how can you be so cruel?" Jenny said. Jenny loved animals but could never get her head around the fact that there was a constant battle between food growers and pests.

"Its not cruel Jenny. If I don't have products to sell we don't make a proper living. I have rabbit fences up but they still burrow under or some other critter like a badger chews a hole in the fence and then the rabbits just come in and have a gourmet supper. I have managed to control the snails and slugs and now. I have a good few hedgehogs who keep them at bay. So I am being 100% organic there, which is natures way of controlling any pests, put in a predator that sees them as dinner. Trouble with rabbits is that hedgehogs don't eat them. Besides Jenny you could use the meat for your dogs, just boil up the carcasses and mix the rabbit meat with the dog biscuits 100% natural food for the dogs."

"The hell with that Jack you know I like rabbit pie. You know you will do better with a night shoot using high beam torches" Billy said to his brother

"I am sure that is illegal Billy." Jack replied

"Probably true Jack but we are way out in the country and shooting on your own land. We used to do it as teens or have you forgotten?" Billy replied

"No I still remember but we are talking almost fifty years ago and the guns laws have changed dramatically since then Billy" Jack replied

"OK Jack you hold the torch and I will shoot. That way you will not be breaking the law." Billy responded

"What and let you have all the fun, no way" Jack chuckled.

Janet finished her tea and then she and Jenny took off for the Kennels. The girls were gone for almost an hour and when they came back up to the house Jack said that they should be going as he had deliveries to make and he prided himself on getting orders to his customers in a ten minute window. Saying goodbye Billy and Jenny returned to the Kennels

4
The New Vet

The following morning John called them to say that the New Vet would be calling around and checking on the dogs. So they arranged that he should come at 10:30am after the dogs had their morning walk.

Spot on time, Johns's Range Rover, pulled into the parking area of the Kennels. John and a tall bald headed man exited the car. The tall man wore a brown storeman's coat on and carried an aluminium flight case

"Hi Jenny this is Mario he is our in house Vet. Please be patient with him as he only speaks a small amount of English. Mario like my wife is from the Ukraine. But he is a highly qualified Veterinarian who specialised in dogs but is also perfect with other domesticated animals. He has given up a work in a large practice in Kyiv, in order to work as my personal Vet. Today if it is OK with you, he would like to view the dogs in the kennels." John said

"Of course you may Mario, and it is good to meet you. If you would like to come with us I will show you to the dogs. Will you be able to act as an interpreter for us today John?" Jenny asked

"It would be my pleasure Jenny to help in any way possible." He replied and they walked down the slabbed pathway and into the kennel block.

Billy chose to stay up at the house not wishing to crowd Jenny. So he busied himself checking on the website, which for now had blank pages ready for the dogs details which at the moment other than the dogs names there was not much else there. The website appeared visually to be Russian. Not that it really mattered, Billy knew that folks who gave homes to rescue dogs, invariably gave the animals new names. When Jenny came back up to the house with John and the Vet, they all seemed quite happy with every thing.

Back in the kitchen and Jenny made coffee for everyone. John and the Vet were talking in Ukrainian, at least that what both Billy and Jenny presumed as neither of them spoke anything other than English other than enough Spanish, to order a couple of beers.

When John and Mario had finished their conversation, John put his cup back down on the table and turning to Jenny

"Mario has said, that whilst the care here is excellent and he can see that all the animals in your care are incredibly well looked after. He would like to be able to complete a thorough examination on every animal that comes to you as a rescue from eastern Europe. He tells me that not all the Vets are as conscientious as he is. So just to be on the safe side He would examine any that have had surgery to ensure there is nothing, that will come back to give their new owners any cause for worry." John said

"Ohhh Well obviously we would never have a problem with any Vet checking over the dogs. If you have employed Mario as a Vet for your personal animals then that to me proves that you have confidence in his ability. So when would he like us to bring the dogs to your home?"

John and Mario had a brief conversation and then john turned back to Jenny again.

"Mario says why not start as we mean to go on, could you bring dog number 1 down to his surgery at my home tomorrow morning?"

"I don't see a problem with that. Do you Billy?" Jenny said

"No problem at all John I will bring dog number 1 in a crate around 10:00am if that is good for you?"

"Perfect Billy. While you are there Natasha has asked if you would be able to install a fountain at the front of the house?" John replied

"I am sure I can sort something out." Billy said

"Right folks, I have to get Mario settled in his new home and make sure he has everything he needs for his surgery. So if you will excuse us, we will get off." John said and then after saying something to Mario they both stood up and left.

"What do you think of the new Vet then?" Billy asked

"He seems nice enough although if he is going to be a Vet in the UK, I would have thought that he would require the ability to speak English?" Jenny asked

"Yes that is a bit strange, but perhaps he has a wife or assistant who can act as a translator for him. Right I had better get going I have a water feature to create for Natasha. I will take Number 1 with me and that way we can kill two birds with one stone." Billy said while draining the remnants of his coffee before rinsing the cup and leaving it to dry on the draining board.

"OK Billy will see you later" Jenny said as billy walked out from the kitchen, to do his job.

Jenny went about the business of the administration that any business requires. Time passed by as it does when someone is deep in work. She was still doing her bookkeeping when Billy arrived back for his evening dinner.

"I am sorry Billy I lost track of time."

"Not a problem lets order a take-out." Billy replied.

Hoping that this was not the slippery road back into the life where they had no time for each other and wishing that it was just an exception to the rule.

They ordered Chinese and while they waited for it to arrive they each talked about their days work.

"The reason I forgot the time was that I was doing the books today Billy, is that I was working out the size of the investment that John has done into our Kennels. It will take us about 4 or 5 years before he will even break even, on what he has spent so far. I am not complaining, and I know that because of his money, no other kennel in the UK can compete with us." Jenny said

"Remember what John said, when he was investing into your rescue centre. He said that both he and his wife are doing it, because they really love animals" Billy replied

"I know that Billy and that we are so lucky because of that. Just saying its a strange thing to do. Like why not open his own place. Our house and kennels are now worth much much more than they were originally When mum was thinking about selling the house and plot of land she had it valued at £180,000. Now with all the work that has been completed by you but paid for by John it is probably worth close to £400,000 and as a working business it will probably add another £200,000. so you can see that our home has at least trebled in value."

"Then let's not dwell upon it and just thank our good fortune" Billy said even though, in truth he had his own reservations about John's massive input into their life.

"There is one thing I would like to change Billy" Jenny said

"Ohh What's that then?"

"I was thinking that you should move back in here properly, as into our bed as well." Jenny said and was afraid that she might have moved too fast.

Her fears were put to rest as Billy reached for her hand and said.

"There is nothing in this world that I would like more, Not to mention I think Jack would like it also." Billy said and held Jenny in a way that he had not done for a very long time.

Leaving the dinner plates on the table they walked up the stairs and to the marital bed. Morning came all too soon and they made love once again before sharing a shower and going downstairs. Jenny had only just made the coffee when the two young kennel-maids arrived. Jenny thought because she felt different this morning, so full of the joys of spring that she might look that way.

"Hello girls how are you both today?" she asked

Then Billy came down the stairs and into the kitchen, where Jenny had a cup of coffee waiting for him. He walked over and gave Jenny a peck on the cheek and whispered

"I Love you and you look positively radiant this morning."

The two you girls and smiled in a very knowing manner.

"Right when everyone is finished smiling. Billy and I are back together. So now you know. We have one dog at the Vets and it should be coming back today. So get to your chores girls, those kennels will not clean themselves. And you Mr Billy Hamilton you need to go down to Johns get to work on that job for the Natasha." She said giving Billy a hug and a long lingering kiss.

"Get a room you two." said one of the girls and they walked off giggling to do their work.

Billy drove down to the Perkins farm and had Natasha describe in detail, what it was that she wanted in way of a water feature. When he got there John joined Natasha.

"Morning Billy, I have just had a quick chat with Mario and he said that dog number 1 can go back to the kennels and you can bring dogs 2 and 3 back after you have done that. Natasha honey, you know that Billy has to do his work for the kennels first and then he can sort your fountain. If that is OK with you Billy?"

"Sure you are the boss. I will go and collect dog number 1 from Mario. Is he in his office?"

"Yes the dog is all good to go. I think Mario checked the wound and redressed it." John said and then went back into their farmhouse.

Billy got back in the van and drove around to the back of Johns house. to part of the stable-block that he had renovated into Johns private Vet's surgery.

Mario a was waiting for him with dog number 1 on a leash. Billy stopped the van and opened the side door before opening the large dog crate that was in the back. Realising that dog number 1, had been in surgery Billy picked the dog up carefully and guided it into the cage before eclosing it up and shutting the van door. He was surprised when Mario spoke to him in English as John had given Billy the impression, that Mario spoke no English at all.

"Two more yes?"

"What, of yes OK, I will go and fetch the next two dogs. And I will be right back." Billy said

The Vet just stared at him, obviously not entirely understanding the syntax of a full sentence. Instead he just smiled and went back to his office come surgery. Billy drove the relatively short distance to Jenny's, kennels. He put dog 1 into its compound and collected dogs 2 and 3, before returning to the Perkins farm.

This time John was not there and Natasha brought him a picture of a large ornamental fountain that was surrounded by a circular fish pond. Natasha also brought a drawing, which she had obviously done herself. It showed the driveway to the farmhouse as it was now and then a drawing of what she wanted. Which was a driveway that came down to the fountain and all the way around it.

It would require quite a lot of work and some heavy plant would have to be used to break up the existing concrete farmyard and complete resurfacing of not just the yard, but the road down into it. Billy told her that this would be extremely expensive, whilst he could do most small jobs himself. He also pointed out that he did not own the equipment that would be required to do the work. Again she said that was OK.

Natasha told billy that he could project manage, rather than break his own back. To which he agreed, then he took dogs 2 and 3 around to Mario and left them there, before returning to Jenny at the Marjorie Rescue Centre for Cats and Dogs.

Jenny had made sandwiches for their lunch. Billy told her about Natasha's big plans for John's driveway.

"So what type of farm has a fountain in the farm-yard?" Billy said

"A very posh one I should think. Perhaps they are planning to hold grand evening balls, at their home. Possibly they are going to have a high end stud farm. All I know is that it is regular well paid work for you, and you don't even have to break a sweat doing it." Jenny replied while placing a mug of coffee in front of him.

"Yes you are probably right Jenny, it's not really my business. So how is dog number one?"

"Well according to the paperwork that came back with him the old wound had to be opened and re-cleaned inside as there was still a small part of a the cyst that was left behind from its original surgery in Ukraine. So in a week we should be able to do his photo shoot and get some pictures up on the new website which by the way looks amazing. We even have a dot com now."

"Well Jenny I have to say it looks like everything is going perfectly. Having a Vet on hand not only is good for the animals it reduces the delays on getting an animal re-homed. What are your plans for this afternoon?"

"I guess I have to find a specialist company for their driveway as well as a company to supply and fit her version of some palatial home fountain. But its her money, so I guess my afternoon is going to be spent trawling the internet for suppliers and companies for this specialist sort of work. My bet is that she will want it made yesterday."

"OK Billy but remember to take breaks from the computer." Jenny said giving her husband a hug and a kiss.

Billy was still in the office searching for contactors and suppliers. He had about a dozen sheets of designs printed out along with the approximate costings. On a budget it could be done for as little as £20,000 but Billy thought that it would not be up to the standard that Natasha would like given the interior design of her home. The top end budget came in at the region of £100,000. As such Billy tried to find as much in the middle range and just a couple in the top and bottom prices. While he was doing this the telephone rang.

"Good afternoon Marjorie Rescue Centre" He said automatically into the telephone.

"OK Dogs are good. You come now for dog please"

"I am sorry who is this?"

"Is Mario Vet, yes you come?"

"Oh sorry Yes Mario I will come and collect the dogs. I will be there in ten minutes." Billy said and put the telephone back in its holder.

On arrival at the Vet's office, Billy found Mario as he had this morning. He was standing outside of his office holding the two dogs on their leashes. Both dogs had new dressings on their previous surgeries. Billy parked up and opened the side door of the van, then thought better of it and went to the back where there were two cages. After helping the two dogs in he closed the cages and vans double doors. Billy was just getting into the drivers door when the Vet stopped him.

"Please you bring four and five" In his heavily accented voice. It was clear enough though for Billy to understand.

So he drove two and three back to the kennels and then collected 4 and 5 and taking them to the Vet. He handed the wad of paperwork concerning the driveway and fountain over to Natasha for her to see the designs and also some photos of other peoples ornate driveway water features.

5
Sick Kitties

After the first five dogs had been seen by the Vet, all of the animals were photographed for the website. And then also advertised on various social media sites. Almost immediately, there were several interested parties and Jenny had already decided at the start of the rescue kennel project, even prior to John and Natasha's involvement. That they would first inspect any of the homes, that her animals would go to. This was to be a hard and fast rule that was set ins stone. This was to enure not only the safety of the animal, but also to make sure that any prospective new owner, would understand that caring for any animal was a serious task. Even more so for an animal which in the past, may have been abused.

While the first group of rescued dogs came from Ukraine, John had said that there were some cats coming from South Africa. He said that a lot of people in the cities, like to own speciality breeds because of them being a status symbol. Then when they learn that they have to look after them they just throw them out on the street and many die on the roads in and around the main towns and cities.

John said that between him and another philanthropist, they had set up a shelter in Johannesburg.

They also had several cats due in two days. They would arrive at Gatwick and first go through health checks before being released later the same day. So Jack would have to drive down to London and collect them.

So now with all five dogs promised to their prospective new owners, which they would get after the Vet had removed any external stitches and given them their final health checks. All the prospective owners had paid a £50 non-refundable deposit and they would be responsible for all the updates of the inoculation after they left the care of the rescue centre.

All of the kittens had also found new homes after the Vet had neutered them. John said there was a van filled with dogs coming in from Romania towards the end of the week.

So the following day all the dogs were collected by their new owners. The first batch of happy dogs. The voluntary donations ranged between £5 and an amazing £500 from one happy owner. The kennel had invested in feed and other merchandising to sell. Everything from dog collars to sweat shirts bearing the name and logo of the Marjorie Rescue Centre.

The following day. Jenny and Billy came down to breakfast early. In order that Billy could drive down to London to collect the Cats.

Unfortunately John and Natasha had taken a trip to Bahrain to talk to some cat rescuers there. Before he left he failed to tell them just how many cats were to be collected. All Billy knew was that they would all be coming in their own transit crates and that he was to collect them from the animal reception centre at Gatwick. As such Billy cleaned out the back of the van and wiped everything down so it was clinically clean.

Like the Dogs from Ukraine, these cats which were arriving from South Africa, had all received surgery for one problem or another, even if it was just for them to be Neutered. As such, they would all be going over to the Vet at the Perkins farm, in small batches.

Billy kissed Jenny goodbye. The two kennel maids said they would spend the day double checking the Cattery enclosures. Jenny made sure that she had all the blank paperwork for the cats.

Working on John's system of just giving the dogs a number, it was decided they should use the same system for the cats. All the animals were registered with their chip and a name, but owner invariably changed the name of the dog or cat, especially when they came from outside of the UK and had been named in a different language.

Billy arrived at Gatwick and was parked in the short stay multi story park right next to the airport. After going to information centre. they pointed him in the direction of the Animal Reception Centre. Here he handed over his driving license as a photo I.D and one of the business cards that they had made up for the rescue centre. Before leaving the UK, John said they would be expecting Billy at the Airport and all he would require would be proof of identity.

The man from the animal centre said that Billy needed the paperwork for all the cats, as in a copy of either the export or the import documents. These documents Billy did not have.

Billy made a call to Jenny, in the hope that she could get hold of John and get him to fax the documents through or the cats could not be released into their care. Jenny said that she would telephone John and send an email as well. If she did not get a reply in an hour she would call Billy back and then take things from there. Jenny suggested that Billy should go get a coffee and wait for her to call him.

About thirty minutes later Billy's mobile phone rang it was a number that he did not recognise. So he pulled it out and answered it.

"Hello"

"Billy?"

"Yes who is this?"

"Hi man. This is is Babdile Johnson" the man said with a heavy South African accent. Before continuing.

"I work with the Johannesburg Cat Rescue Centre. I understand that you are missing some paperwork for our cats?"

"Yes that's right I called at the Animal Reception Centre and they said I was supposed to Have this paperwork before they would release the cats to me."

"OK I should be able to help you out, can you tell me first, the name of the person who organised this transit?"

"John Perkins for the Marjorie Cats and Dogs Rescue Centre."

"And which airport did you say they were sent to?"

"Gatwick UK"

"One more thing sir your name please?"

"Sure its Billy Hamilton."

"OK Just hold on a moment and we will see if I can sort this."

All the time Billy was walking back to the animal reception centre as he knew what the final question would be. He was not wrong.

"Can you give me the Fax number for the animal import centre?"

Billy asked the man at the desk and then repeated it to the man from South Africa.

"We are just faxing the documents through to them now. You should have my number, so if there are any problems, just call and I am sure we will fix things. OK"

Billy thanked the man and hung up the phone. He waited for about another twenty minutes and then the man from the animal centre appeared with a large wad of paperwork.

"OK Sir everything checks out, I am going to issue you with a temporary pass for you so you can take your vehicle to the rear of these offices and there you can collect the animals. They have all been given food and water and had a quick check over. Nice to see that someone is so willing to look after injured and sick animals." He said as he passed over the paperwork which he had now put inside a card folder.

Billy took the paperwork and headed back to his van and then followed the instructions to the rear entrance to the Animal Reception Centre. At the gate he showed his temporary pass to the gate guard and then drove to the rear reception area and parked up.

Another man was behind that counter and he asked for the paperwork. Billy handed over the complete folder. Ten minutes later a series of trolleys were wheeled out with multiple crates on each.

In total 15 crates, which was considerably more than he had imagined there would be. Each crate had a name and a flight number on it, along with their final destination printed on a tag attached to the top of each crate. Billy knew that he could easily fit them into the van but he would have to first fit the middle shelf that was in the van. This allowed the van to carry two levels of animals. The man handed back the folder of papers and asked Billy if he needed any help in loading the cats into the van. Billy thanked him but said no it was OK, he would get on better on his own."

All the cats loaded Billy switched on the air conditioning in the van and drove back to the security gate he had entered. The security guard asked for the temporary pass back and then opened the gates to let Billy through.

Billy arrived back home at midday and drove the van right down to the cattery block. He left the unloading of the van, to the two kennel maids while he walked back up to the house to talk with Jenny.

"I'm back" he shouted out as he walked in

"Everything go OK?" Jenny asked as she walked into the kitchen.

"Yes and no really, I guess you could say." Billy said and then he explained the situation and the fact that they had double the number of cats than they had expected. Billy waited for the explosion that did not come. It seemed that jenny was happy to have so many animals. Well if Jenny was happy then he was also happy.

The girls came up from the cattery and said that they had put them all into the individual blocks. That left space for just one cat. Once everyone had lunch Jenny joined the girls down at the cattery. To sort the paperwork for each enclosure.

Billy went over to the Perkins place to check on how the contractors were doing on the new road layout and to make sure that they had brought a water and electric supply from the house under the road and to the centre of where the water feature would be placed after the road was finished.

Back at the rescue centre Jenny was going over all the cats first checking their breeds off against their cages. Some of the breeds were indeed very sought after most were just labelled cat even though Jenny could clearly see either a 100% pure bred cat or what she would label as almost certainly one breed or another. Of the fifteen cats that arrived only three she could describe as a 'Moggies'. Personally taking a photograph of each cat she went up to the house to print off two copies of each One for her personal files and one to be attached to the documents of the corresponding cat enclosure.

Checking on the internet against the pictures that she had taken There were a pair of Norwegian Forest cats, easily recognisable these large cats with their long fur coats. They prefer human company or the company of other animals. The Females weighed in at around 10 pounds and male male cat was almost half of that again at 16.5 pounds. Jenny was surprised to find this as a cat coming from South Africa as they tend to prefer the colder climates with their long multi layers of fur.

She also identified three Savannah cats all three of them were boys. There were a couple of Long Hair Rag-doll Birmans. A Long Haired Himalayan male cat as well. The breed that there were most of, were the beautiful pure white Persians. These were expensive cats by any standards with some of them fetching as much as £3,000.

It never ceased to amaze her how people could invest so much money and time into a pet and then just chuck it out when things got tough or they were just bored with it. Still she would have no problem in finding new homes for this shipment. Like the dogs all had received surgery of one form or another and most just a short time before being exported to the UK and to a new life.

She had asked John just before he went on his trip to Bahrain, would it not be easier for the Vet to come to the kennels to see to the animals. John had said that because of the language barrier it would be better for the animals to go to him, also Mario had his clinic set up on the farm. That seemed reasonable enough so Jenny left it at that.

Now it was time to go back down to the Cattery and have a close look at all the cats and let them out of their crates into their enclosures. When she got there she found the two kennel maids each with a cat in their arms, both being loved but it was wrong to do this before they had been inspected. Who knows what damage may have been caused to them in transit.

"Come on girls you know the rules, put them back in their cages so that we can go about checking them in properly."

"Aww they are so cute can we keep these two" one of the maids said

"We can talk about that later but you know the rules we keep them all separate for the first week just in case any of them are sick or have any parasites on or in them." Jenny replied

The girls did as they were told. Then with their assistance each cat was checked in and a drawing of each wound area was added to their file the cat passport were put in each file pouch are they were scanned and the number checked off against the chip database. All the cats seemed to have only been chipped after they came into the care of the Johannesburg Cat Rescue Centre.

Jenny found that really strange especially on such valuable animals. How could most of these animals not have been pre-owned, rather than just being feral street-cats? Well, they would be well looked after while they were in the care of her centre.

Billy returned just as Jenny was finishing logging the cats in. So he helped out with the feeding and the litter boxes in their enclosures. Then they all walked back up to the house.

Jenny called to the Vet and managed to let him know there were 15 new cats.

"So you bring five cats tomorrow please" was all he said.

"Have you heard from John?" Billy asked Jenny

"Yes he said he would be coming home tomorrow and that he had set up a rescue centre there. He will be home for a week then they are jetting off to Pakistan to see if they can set up there. John also said that Natasha will be staying at the farm while he is away."

"Wow that is some jet setter lifestyle they lead so back in the real world how are the cats?"

"Well they are all chipped and all the cats have been recently neutered. All the males have some injury or other. Most seem to have had cysts removed as best I can tell from the shipping documents, which by the way if you had read them then you would have noticed they are in Afrikaans. So we will need those translating before we can put them up for adoption."

"I guess like all things these days, it will cost a packet."

"Perhaps when John gets here tomorrow he could ask the Johannesburg rescue centre could re-send them in English as am sure that it is a bi-lingual country."

"I am afraid I would not know, but I will take your word for it." Billy said, as he opened the back door to their house and was greeted by their Miniature King Charles. Billy did as he always did and fused over the dog.

6
More Sick Cats

John arrived at the kennels with the Vet at eight the following morning.

"Hello Jenny. I am sorry I was unavailable for the arrival of the batch from South Africa, but I am here now. So what sort of condition are they and how many?"

"That's no problem, you lead a very busy life. Besides you are here now. Well all the cats have had some form of surgery. And there are a total of fifteen cats."

"Wow I only expected five or six, well you can handle that number, can't you?" John said

"Yes we have the space and the ability to look after them so long as your Vet does not mind the extra work that this is bringing him. I know that you are planning to have some horses and cows coming for your farm. Will Mario still be able to cope with the animals from our rescue centre?"

"Why of course he will, as for the horses they are from this country at least to begin with, so they will have had a full medical before I buy them at auction. We changed our minds on the cattle, so it will just be horses and Natasha will oversee them. Oh Billy, the road looks perfect and I am told the fountain will arrive later today and will be assembled and fitted tomorrow. So everything is working according to plan. Is it OK, if Mario selects the cats that he needs to check on first?"

"Oh well I am sure looking after horses is easier than running a dairy herd, as they would require milking twice a day. As for the cats Mario is welcome to chose whichever ones he wishes to check first. Billy will take them over to him in the van." Jenny said.

"Good good As soon as we have space I have some cats that will be coming over from Bahrain. We are also setting up a dog sanctuary in Pakistan. I believe that they are actually bring dogs cross border from Afghanistan. Unfortunately as you no doubt will know from the new on TV, there are a lot of poor animals who have been left without care when the British and American troops pulled out. There were a couple of service men who had previously set up a dog rescue in Bagram base. When it closed, they were only able to get about one third of the dogs out. So we will have to see if the Pakistan authorities will be helpful in getting this poor animals out. Many of which have had terrible injuries as result of the continuing conflicts out there. Not to mention the psychological trauma the war causes."

"Oh the poor things" Jenny said. And then continued

"When do you expect the Bahrain centre to send us their animals?"

"Ohhh don't worry about that at the moment, as it will only happen when you have the space. I would say that there is a good chance that the dogs from Pakistan will arrive first, even though we are just setting up things. It is is a financially driven government out there, so I will grease a few palms and use some of my wealthy friends to put pressure on the small government officials."

"Ohh we we had better get the kennels ready. Are we talking weeks or days before they arrive?" Jenny asked

"My best guess would be the former. There is no point in having long term plans in an unstable country." John said

The Vet said something in his native tongue and John nodded twice before turning to Billy

"Mario has a busy day ahead of him could you take the van down to the cattery and load the cats that he choses, into the van then drive them over to the farm please."

"Sure no problem" Said Billy. He wondered why things were started to shift into a higher gear. Worse he wondered how this pressure would affect Jenny and his newfound relationship with her.

Billy got in the van with Mario and they drove down to the cattery. The Vet just chose cats one to five, so there was no real reason for him to have been here. But he did a quick look along the enclosures, he seemed to be making mental notes as he went, then returned to the van.

Billy drove the cats and Vet back up to the house. The Vet got out and had a long conversation with John who shook his head and seemed to be angry about something. As they walked away from Jenny's home. Billy noticed that John and the Vet's conversation became more animated and even though the level of their voices had reduced there was definitely more anger from John in their talk. John walked around one side of the Range Rover and the Vet got in the passenger side, as they left John spun his tyres on Jenny's driveway before fishtailing it onto the main road.

Billy followed at a more sedate pace so as not to frighten the crated cats. He arrived at the Perkin's farm and the Vet was standing outside his surgery. Just like the time before the Vet carried the cats in and said

"Thank you. I call soon, for more cat"

John and his Range Rover were nowhere to be seen. Billy returned to the rescue centre.

"What did you make of all that?" Billy asked Jenny.

"Buggered if I know perhaps the Vet screwed up on some stud horse or something."Jenny replied

"No I don't think it was that. I think it had something to do with the cats that just came in."

"Like what?"

"Now that is the question, but whatever it was, it was serious, he left tyre marks on the driveway and the road. Oh well, probably not our business. What's for dinner?"

"Well I thought you could drive the girls home and pick up a Chinese takeaway from Boston. I have been so busy sorting out the cats I completely forgot about doing dinner,"

"OK Not a problem" Billy said and drove off with the girls and then into Boston for the takeaway.

The following morning the Vet called and asked for five more cats to be brought. Billy did and collected the five he had left there the day before and returned them to the cattery. The girls put the cats back in their enclosures. Jenny would check on them later. This morning she was over having a chat with her sister in law. Before they both went and did their weekly shop. She had several homes to check today, this was in order to ensure that they had brought their homes and gardens up to pet safe standard.

Janet also had some supplies for the Rescue Centre to pick up from Pets4Us. They supplied her with bulk food for the dogs and cats, now though she was going to see the manager as she would require a lot more litter than she had been previously. Hopefully he would be able to give her a reasonable discount or she would have to buy from elsewhere. She guessed that with the exception of the RSPCA, that her centre was one of the biggest locally. Now looking at the volume of animals that had just started to come in, they would have to expand. That would give her buying power.

Later that day when Jenny returned with Janet from their shopping trip and they were having a cup of tea, one of the Kennel maids came racing into the kitchen, in a terrible state. She had blood all over her hands and arms.

"Please Jenny, can you come quick one of the cats is in a bad way."

Jenny automatically got up slipped her boots on and excused herself from Janet, before running down to the Cattery. When she arrived one of the Savannah cats was staggering around its enclosure with blood literally dripping from a wound on its stomach. Jenny went and looked the wound. The blood was coming out from between the stitched area on its belly.

Jenny raced to the phone and dialled the Vet and the phone was answered

"Yes?"

"Mario one of the cats is sick can you come here?"

"Yes?"

"Do you understand me Mario we have an emergency."

"You come yes?"

"Can you come?"

"Yes you come please."

Jenny put the phone down

"Ahhh Fuck It Beth. Can you get a large crate and a blanket?"

The girl came back with a large crate complete with a soft blanket in the base. With the help of Beth they managed to get the squirley cat into the crate. Billy was out so they would have to use Jenny's beat up jeep. After putting the crate in the back, Jenny left Beth in charge and she drove the injured cat to the Perkin's farm Vet.

When she arrived outside the Vet's surgery she carefully lifted the crate out and carried it to the surgery door, expecting it to be open as he had just spoken to him on the telephone. So she was shocked to find it locked.

"Mario" She shouted and Hammered on the door.

"Mario where the hell are you?"

One of the windows opened, and Mario popped his head out.

"You wait please. I come to you yes?"

"Whatever" Jenny replied although she was pissed of, this was an emergency.

The cat was loosing blood at an alarming rate. This was one of the cats that Mario had treated just yesterday. Mario should have come to the Rescue centre, That was the original agreement. Also unless Mario was going to learn English, then she would talk to John about using a different Vet.

The door to the surgery opened and Jenny went to step in but Mario blocked the doorway.

"Please" He said with his hand outstretched for the crate

Jenny handed over the crate, which Mario took and then said

"I call Yes?"

"OK" Jenny said as Mario closed the door

This just would not do, he never even asked what was wrong with the animal. He would not have known where she was bleeding from, until he opened the crate and looked at the cat. Something was wrong about the Vet.

She knew that it was a proper surgery as Billy had done all the alterations and installed the specialist equipment, before Mario arrived.

Previously she had used a local Vet, Alasdair. He had always been her Vet before and he would quite happily come out in an emergency. Sometimes he even sent medicines by taxi if for some reason that Jenny could not make it to the surgery. And more importantly, was that you could talk to him about your sick animal, in the full knowledge that he understood the problem and he was always sympathetic.

She waited at the surgery door for a few more minutes and then got back in the jeep and did pretty much the same sort of thing that John had done on their drive the night before. She left burnt rubber on his brand new driveway.

That night after talking with Billy it was agreed that they would have to talk with John over the Vet situation.

The following morning immediately after breakfast Billy called John's mobile number and explained what the situation was with the Vet and that it was leading to an unworkable relationship between the Rescue Centre and John. John explained that he was already at the airport, getting ready to fly back out to Pakistan. John promised to take action as soon as he got back home, which would be the day after tomorrow.

That done Billy went back over to the Perkins farm, specifically to check on the cats welfare after which he would oversee the construction of the large and elegant stone water feature that was being installed in the centre of the ring shaper driveway.

Billy knocked on the surgery door and waited for Mario to open it. Eventually the door was partially opened.

"Yes?"

"Good morning Mario. How is the sick cat?"

"The cat?"

"The cat that Jenny brought over yesterday in the late afternoon."

Mario just shrugged his shoulders. So Billy asked again. All to no avail. The Vet closed the door.

In a rage Billy went to the main house to talk with Natasha. He pressed the doorbell and the maid answered after saying it was important to talk to Mrs Perkins, he was invited into the main lounge, where he waited on Natasha.

Five minutes later Natasha entered the room and greeted him

"Mrs Perkins please I need your help in talking to Mario I don't think he understands some very important things. We had one of the cats that was bleeding very badly after the Vet had previously seen the cat, and that last evening Jenny had taken the cat back to Mario as an emergency. Then this morning the Vet did not seem to know what I was talking about.

"Ohh my this is not so good." Natasha said as the maid appeared carrying a tray with a coffee pot and two cups.

The maid left and Natasha poured out two cups of coffee before speaking again.

"We will have a coffee and then go and see Mario. You can also update me on the progress of the fountain."

"I am sorry to put this on you Natasha, but you did say at the start of your association with us that you would act as a translator." Billy said and sipped his coffee.

"Of course Billy. I am sure it is just a case of Mario not understanding English." she said

"Yes you are probably right." Billy replied.

Niceties over and the coffee finished Natasha and Billy walked over to the Vets. Billy knocked on the door and once again Mario half opened the door.

"Yes?"

Natasha started to speak in Ukrainian to Mario. It seemed to start off friendly enough, but soon both were shouting at each other. It became blatantly obvious that Natasha was the boss, both in social standing and as an employer.

Then it came out, the truth.

"I am sorry." Mario said to Billy

"OK no problem so now can you tell me how is the cat."

Once again Mario said

"I am sorry yes?"

"I'm not sure I understand? Natasha?"

"Billy what Mario is trying to say to you, is that he is sorry. Last night after your wife brought the cat over. The animal died during surgery." Natasha replied.

"Ohh. Right well I will let Jenny know when I get back home." With that Natasha and Billy walked away from the surgery. They walked to where the fountain was being constructed and talked for about half an hour. Billy got back in the van and drove home to the rescue centre.

When he told Jenny that the cat was dead, she was devastated. Whilst she had been rescuing animals for some years now she had never before lost a previously healthy animal, be it dog or cat, during a Vets surgical operation.

"I think we should go back to using Alasdair as our Vet" Jenny said to Billy, after the girls had gone back home that night.

"I tend to agree with you, but John says he will fix things when he gets back here the day after tomorrow. Lets reach a half way agreement. We stop sending any of the cats to Mario. All the other cats appear to be quite healthy and are in no need of emergency treatment."

"He will have to get rid of Mario as the Vet for us, because I am not letting him touch another one of our animals, ever again." Jenny said as she was crying.

7
Dogs Galore

The next day was Sunday and the kennel maids day off. Billy helped Jenny with the cats and the hand over of the dogs, that were all going to their new homes today. As such it was a busy day for the both of them.

Jenny told the new dog owners that she would be doing some sporadic checks on the animals, over the next few months, just to makes sure everybody including the dogs were happy.

At 4pm Billy's mobile phone rung. It was John. Obviously, Natasha had been in touch and informed him of the situation.

"Billy I am so sorry that Mario has not worked out the way we had hoped. So, I have a new Vet coming with me tomorrow. His English is perfect and he has until last night been working for the Bahrain cat rescue centre. I have convinced him to come and work for us. His wife is also a Veterinary nurse. Natasha was so angry with Mario that she sacked him after calling me last night."

"OK that will probably sort the issue with Jenny as she was thinking about going back to our old Vet. I have asked her to hold of until she could speak with you."

"Thank you for that Billy. Now on to another matter. I know when we last spoke we talked about dogs coming to you from Bahrain,"

"Yes?"

"I think I said it might be weeks but it could be days."

"Yes?"

"OK well as I am coming back today, well tomorrow in the UK. I thought I would bring some animals with me and I would like you to go to the animal reception centre and collect them. It will be much quicker for me to get away from the airport if you sort out the dogs. I will meet you back at your rescue centre. If that is OK?"

"Sure no problem. Will all the documentation be their for me? Or are you going to fax them to us here?" Billy asked

"They will be waiting at the Animal Reception Centre at Gatwick. As I already Emailed them over" John replied and almost hung up.

"Before you go What time do you need me there for?" Billy asked

"Flight lands at 7:30am so around two or three hours after that I would guess. Once again please say sorry to your wonderful wife, for my failing with Mario. Is there is anything else?"

"Yes John, how many dogs?"

"There are eight adult dogs." He replied and ended the call.

Billy relayed all that information over to Jenny

"Well at least he took our concerns seriously" Billy said

"OK, But the jury is out over the new Vet, I am going to check his credentials out before he treats any of our animals." She replied.

Jenny was starting to have some serious misgivings about John. But time would tell so she let it rest for tonight.

The following morning billy set off at 6am in the van. He drove to the short stay and then went and collected his temporary pass before retrieving the van and heading over to the security gate for the animal reception.

Billy did not have long to wait and the crated dogs were brought out to the handover along with a large folder of paperwork, which included the dogs travel passports. The eight dog crates loaded into the van. Bill then set off for home.

He arrived back just before two in the afternoon. Driving directly down to the kennels he left the van there, for the girls to unload the dogs and put to them in their individual kennels, reminding them, that they would have put the paperwork into the pouches next to their doors. Billy walked back up to the house to find Johns Range Rover was parked outside.

When he entered the kitchen John was sat at the table with Jenny and an Arabic looking man and woman. Billy correctly assumed that this was the new Vet and his wife.

"Hello Billy, did everything go smoothly this morning?"

"Yes no problems at all in getting the dogs handed over."

"Good, good, good. I would like to introduce to you Dr Kareem Hussain, who is our new Vet, along with his wife Fatima. Kareem was actually considering coming to the UK, even before I approached him. Obviously given the short notice. I could only gain them temporary work visas and I had to pull a lot of strings to make that happen so fast. Fatima is also a fully accredited Veterinary Nurse. I have all their certificates here and tomorrow I will have them professionally translated for you. Needless to say, Mario will be gone from the surgery by the time I get home. I came here straight from the airport first to apologise to Jenny and to introduce my new Vet to you both." John said

"OK so I am happy if you are. Billy? We can all start with a new clean sheet." Jenny said

"If you are happy my love then I am happy." He replied

"That's settled then. Why don't we all have dinner over at mine tomorrow. I will send my maid to pick you both up, that way you can have a drink with out fear of drink driving. How does that sound to both of you?" John said

Jenny said it sounded good, then John and the Veterinary couple left in the Range Rover.

"The first thing I am going to do is check out the new Vet and make sure he is as good as John claims he is. Just as soon as I have checked the dogs in." Jenny said

After checking the dogs in, Jenny drove the girls home and then set about doing online search for the any information of the new Vet Dr Kareem Hussain. It would appear that everything that John had said about the Vet was correct. The rescue centre in Bahrain had not updated their website and it still listed Dr Hussain as the senior Vet and his wife as a Veterinary Nurse and Practice Manager.

After Dinner Billy and Jenny went down and prepared the Kennels for their new arrivals. The photographer came and took the photographs for the website. Whilst not really a commercial business, the Rescue Centre was running at close to break even. Of course that would not be the case, if she had to repay John his investment and of course the cost of importation of the animals which worked out at an average of £350 each.

The next day the new Vet came with John's Range Rover and collected the cats in batches for them to have their wounds checked.

Then later that day he brought back the cats. Billy drove over with all the dogs and Kareem said he would give them a call, as soon as they were ready to come back to the kennels.

Jenny checked all the dressings on the cats and they were all perfect and the cats whilst a little slow due to being medicated in order for the Vet to check and redress their wounds.

Tonight the plan was to go out for a meal with Jack and Janet. It would be good to have a proper catch-up. Perhaps Jack could do a little digging into John and Natasha Perkins. Jenny wondered if she was just being petty or just lashing out over the death of a cat which the previous Vet had been treating. Had she just started a witch-hunt, where no witches exist.

"You look amazing tonight babe" Billy said as he zipped up the back of her dress and kissed her on the nape of the neck.

"Why thank you Billy, you are looking pretty damn dapper yourself. Its been along while since we had a proper night out. I know we went to the Perkin's posh place but here in the real world. I am looking forward to a nice sit-down meal with Janet and your brother.

The plan was that Jack would come over in his nice 3 series BMW. Jack had two cars the other being a vintage MGA, but in truth whilst it did have two rear seats, they were only big enough for small children. Jack loved to drive it around the narrow Lincolnshire country roads. But Jenny preferred the comfort and classiness of the BMW. Five minutes later Jack appeared. Jenny and Billy got in the back and sat holding hands like teenagers.

"Where are we eating tonight?" Billy asked Jack.

"I thought that we would try that new Middle Eastern place that has opened up in town. How's that sound?" Jack said

"Sounds great by me and I know that Jenny loves Arabic spices." Billy replied.

Jack parked up around the corner from the restaurant.

"Fancy a pint first Billy?" Jack asked

"Sounds like a plan Jack. Girls?"

They both said yes and the two girls walked arm in arm behind their husbands. They were talking and giggling like a pair of schoolkids. Billy was so happy to see that his wife, for the first time in a long long time, was totally happy and relaxed.

In the pub Jack got the order in and the girls grabbed a table. When they were all settled down the talk soon swung to the rescue centre. Billy told Jack about the new Vet and Nurse, who could actually speak English. None of them were in any way raciest but they all also agreed that there were some positions where a full command of the English language, was not only a preference but it was totally essential.

It was when they were having their drinks when Billy thought he recognised a voice from somewhere behind him.

"Yes I have, so give me money please" The voice said in broken heavily accented English.

Then it became a bit of an argument. The voice he recognised said

"You bastard! you fucking cheat me. You owe me now pay up or I tell police." The voice said

Then things became quiet and the noise from the beer garden stopped. As the two men who were having an argument walked away.

"Wow that sounded like an unhappy bloke" Jack said

"It surely did, and I think I recognised the voice. I think it was the Vet that John sacked yesterday. But the other person in that little tate-á-tate, was not John, so I guess the he must have managed to upset someone else already. Anyway I can't see Jenny or I coming to his rescue anytime soon." Billy said

"What did that fellow do to you?"

"Truthfully Jack, he managed to somehow or other cause a massive bleed in one of the cats that he checked a wound on. The cat died and he did not seem to give a shit. He had no empathy for animals they were just a commodity to quantify his job. He was arrogant, to the point of pure bloody rudeness."

"I did not want to fall out with John but I told him I would go back to using Alasdair. John said he would fix it and the very next day he had sacked Mario and employed a very nice polite Arab Doctor Kareem Hussain and his wife Fatima, even better she is a Veterinary nurse. They both speak perfect queens English."

"Well at least it sounds like you have the problem of the Vet sorted." Jack said and continued.

"Right drink up the table is booked for about now."

It was only a two minute walk to the restaurant and the night air was wonderful. Being mid week the town was quiet, especially when compared to the Friday and Saturday nights in Boston.

Boston Town which for a variety of reasons had become the murder capital of England. Per head of capita that is. Sometimes the weekend crowd of heavy drinkers things would get a little out of hand. There was a time where Saturday night drunks would fight with their fists or the incredibly drunk, would fight with handbags at five paces. Now though it seemed they fought with knives. There appeared to be no reason as to why the majority of murders in Boston in the past ten years, had been committed by transient workers from Eastern Europe. So decent folks tended to avoid the town centre on weekends. It was not a lawless state or anything like that is was just neither Jack or Billy and their wives enjoyed confrontational inebriated individuals looking for a reason to fight, where none actually existed.

At the restaurant they were shown to the table by a pleasant young man, who asked if they would like to order drinks while they perused the menu.

They did and the drinks were brought swiftly. There were two other tables with customers at and a table in the back corner of the room that had two Arabic looking men, who were busy playing some card game. From the way they were dressed Jack had surmised they were probably part of the family that owned the eatery.

Jack and Billy both ordered the griddled Lamb Shawarma, Jenny had Falafel with the deep fried Halloumi, Janet went for the Cauliflower Steak, with Hummus. As the waited for their orders to arrive, Jenny talked more about how well the rescue centre was now doing and how so far, all the animals that had come in since John had started to help them had now found new forever homes. With the singular exception of the Savannah cat that had died. The Dogs pictures would be on the net and soon people would come to view the dogs, and she would start to Vet them.

Billy knew where this conversation was heading. Jenny was going to ask Janet to help her Vet the new homes with her. Fortunately the food arrived before the question was asked.

They started to tuck into the meal and it was absolutely delicious. Then there were some raised voices from the kitchen, not being able to speak

Arabic, meant that Jack and his extended family had no clue as to what was going on. The pair of men in the corner of the room gave up their game of cards and walked down and into the kitchen. And then everything went quiet. The young man who had taken their order came out and offered all the tables a complimentary drink, as their apology for the disturbance.

Of course each table accepted this free drink, and they all continued to eat their fine meals. Then it kicked off again only this time there were several voices involved in the argument. It was much more heated than previously. It became very obvious to all those in the restaurant, that there was a physical fight going on in the kitchen. Then once again it went quiet. The owner came out and apologised to all this in the dining room for the disturbance, although he did not say what it was all about.

After finishing their meal they got the bill, Jack paid for everything and would not let Billy pay his share. When they were walking back to where the car was parked, Billy saw the ex-Vet in a confrontation with another man. While he watched, the other man pulled a knife and stabbed Mario in the neck and then the attacker ran off as Mario slumped to the ground with blood spurting from a severed artery, while Mario tried to stem its flow.

"Ohh my God" Jenny cried.

She had never really liked Mario, but would never wish anything like this to happen to him.

"Call 999 and wait here said Jack as he ran to the injured man to offer his assistance. Billy called the ambulance and police. Then went to assist Jack, but by the time Billy got there, it was pretty obvious that Mario was beyond any medical help. The gaping wound had extended from behind his left ear to his Adams apple.

The police arrived first and Jack spoke with them, describing what had occurred and what they had seen and heard leading up to the incident. Jack returned with Billy and told them all that they would have to go down to the police station and give their statements now, while it was fresh in their minds. As the police station was only a short walk, Jack decided to leave the car parked where it was.

Almost an hour and a half later, they were back in the car and heading for home.

"What about that then, do you think that perhaps any of that was our fault by getting him sacked?" Jenny asked to no one in particular.

"Of course not Jenny, whatever it was they were arguing over, it had nothing to do with us, nor the Rescue Centre. Lets face what do cats and dogs have to do with Middle Eastern restaurants. Or pubs for that matter. Whatever it was that caused that guy to pull a knife on him probably had more to do with money or perhaps they owed him some money and he pressured them for it but definitely not our fault." Billy said

Very quickly Jack and Janet also agreed with Billy. When they got home Jack told Billy and Jenny to have a stiff drink and he poured them both a good measure of Havana 7 Cuban Rum, while pouring smaller ones for Janet and himself. After he had made sure that his sister in law and brother were OK. They said goodnight and drove the short distance home.

"Do you think we should call John and let him know?" Jenny asked

"Lets leave it until morning." Billy said and wrapped his arms around his wife in a supportive hug.

8

More Cats

Billy called John in the morning to give him the news on the death of Mario. Apart from the obvious shock, John seemed more interested in who had done it and what Billy and Jenny had heard in the arguments that had preceded the murderous attack. Billy told John the apart from the first argument that they had overheard in the pub, the other arguments were in a language which they did not understand. However that said Billy said that he though it might be one of the Middle Eastern languages. John ask Billy not to talk to anyone else about it as it might adversely affect his business. Billy said goodbye and went about his business.

All the dogs had now been seen by the new Vet and all had their previous dressings, which had been done prior to them being exported to the UK. Jenny looked at the Vet's work and it was of a much higher standard than Mario's work. The dressing were well attached, also where he had to clean and re-suture, his needle work was neat and tidy.

Over the next few weeks dogs and cats came in from pretty much all corners of the globe. There were cats now coming in from Burma, Dogs from

Columbia, Cats and Dogs from Russia, Cats from Bahrain, Dogs from South Africa, Dogs from Pakistan, and Dogs from South America.

The situation now was that within a day of a kennel or a cattery space becoming vacant, then there would be a new animal to take it over.

Things had been moving on without any hitches. It made Jenny feel good about things. The fact that she could find homes for these poor injured animals, which had now been treated and were ready for new families.

Billy and Jenny were in the kitchen taking a well needed break from working with their current stock of animals, when John and Natasha arrived in their Range Rover. They knocked and entered.

"Hello Natasha" Jenny said and then she greeted John.

"Tea? Coffee?" Jenny asked

"Coffee Please both black and no sugar thank you" John said and then he sat down at the table.

"I see everything is working out fine with the new Vet, and you are easily able to find loving homes for these poor animals."

"To be quite honest John, due to most of the animals being either rare breeds or much sought after breeds. I have a waiting list of clients just looking for just the right animal, to complete their family."

"Yes well about that, it is what I have really come to ask you?" John said taking a sip of his coffee.

"Oh?" Said Billy

"We were wondering if you would like another injection of facilities to your wonderful Rescue Centre." Natasha said.

"Not quite sure what you are really saying Natasha?"

"Well we know that there are thousands of poor animals in some countries that don't really place any value on domesticated animals. We, as in Natasha and myself are in the position, to be able to rectify that situation, if only by a small degree." John said and took another sip of his coffee, before continuing.

"How would you feel about doubling up on the size of your rescue centre, we would of course cover the extra cost in that setup including the funds to employ more staff and transport. So what do you think?"

"Wow that would surely require bigger kennels and Cattery, which would cut down on the available land that we have for exorcising the dogs." Jenny said

"Yes well we thought about that and the land behind your grounds came on the market yesterday, so I bought it. Now I am willing to sign over the title deeds to that land which is a parcel of 10 acre's. So you would still be able to have double the size of the Kennels as well as a bigger plot of land for your vegetable garden and a much bigger exercise area."

"What is the catch?"

"No catch just more animals that you can help us save."

"And this includes the building costs?"

"Billy, all Natasha and I want to do. Is to try and save as many animals as we can. I think I told you before, we made our money from what was a very small investment, in bitcoin, when it all started and we pulled out when it reached its peak. So you see we were lucky. We both love cats and dogs as such we are sharing our good luck and love with them. You and Jenny are good people with big hearts. So you deserve all the help that we can offer you. Don't answer just now, think about it overnight and you can give me your answer in the morning." John said and then they made their excuses left a shocked, Jenny and Billy.

"What do you think Billy?"

"It would mean double the work for both of us. John said he would pay for more kennel maids and more transport so I guess that would mean another driver as well. He he said he would cover all the new costs. Plus he would give you that ten acre plot of land next to ours." Billy said

"Lets sleep on it Billy and see what the morning brings, as my worry is that you would have to do all the building work and it is a lot of work for one man. Right lets get dinner on the go."

9

The Big Build

The following morning over the breakfast table, Jenny decided that it was far to good an opportunity for the rescue centre to miss out on. Although she did actually have some stipulations and one of those was that, the building work would not have to be completed by Billy as he was far to busy not just collecting the animals but general day to day upkeep of the Rescue centre as it was.

They had only just finished breakfast when John, polled up at the front of the house in his Range Rover.

"Coffee?" Jenny asked as he came in.

"That would be nice." He replied

Jenny poured a coffee for him and refreshed Billy's at the same time. Then she sat down between the two men.

"Lets get straight to the point. Have you two managed to come to a decision about the extension of the rescue centre?"

"We have" Jenny said before continuing

"It might seem a little cheeky to ask you this but I want my Billy to have a long life and not be worked to death." She said

"Well of course." John said

"So….. Can you have some professional builders do the new build work as Billy is already busy maintaining what we already have, as well as transporting animals to us and to the new families when they are ready to be re-homed."

"I don't see a problem with that, and its not cheeky at all. Also one of the other things I wanted to talk to you about was for you to have a Vets surgery, on the premises. This would stop the need to transport sick animals back and forth in cages, which only causes more stress to the poor things. My plan being if it is OK by you is to have the Vet come here on a daily basis, to carry out any work and also to check the animals as soon as they come in. This will save Billy a lot of time and allow him to get on with the day to day maintenance. As Natasha said last night we have bought the large plot of land that back on to your property and it is yours for the Rescue centre all you have to do is to sign for the land and its yours. Should you decide in the future that you no longer wish to rescue animals that land and the kennels would still remain yours. You still own the rescue centre and it is yours to run as you please. Natasha's and my only interest is to save as many animals as we can." John said

"How soon can you get builders in to work and we would obviously need planing permission and will that not take a lot of time" Billy said

"You would be surprised just how quickly things can happen, when a large donation is made. I am sure that by tomorrow the whole thing can be rubber stamped. I can have the groundwork started by tomorrow while we wait for the wheels of planing permission to work. I will have my lawyer contact the land registry and get the land in your name. So what do you say? Do we have a deal?" John asked

Jenny looked at her husband and then down towards the kennels before looking back at Billy with almost pleading eyes. Billy nodded and Jenny turned to John with an outstretched hand and they shook on it.

"I will have a groundwork team in here by this afternoon. You tell them where you want the new cattery and kennel blocks and they will clear the ground and have it ready for tomorrow. And we can get the foundation laid and then get the builders in a few days after that. I bet we could get the whole thing completed in under two weeks. Right I better get off and start organising things. See you soon. Ohhhh I hear some rummers going around that the thing with Mario, was all about drugs he was selling Ketamine to some local drug dealers to fund his online gambling addiction." John said

"That would sort of tie in with what we saw and heard I guess." Jenny replied

John left and an hour later an architect rolled up at the house

"Hello I am James Anderson, from Anderson and Hawes architects. John Perkins, said to come over and draw some plans up for you." He said

"Ohh Right please come in" Jenny said

"Thank you Mrs Hamilton." he said and walked into the kitchen.

"So what sort of thing are you looking for?"

"Well you better talk to Billy, just one moment, I will get him up, he is down at the kennels." Jenny said and picked up the phone and spoke quickly and quietly, before putting the phone back on the cradle.

"He will be here in a moment, would you care for a tea or a coffee." She asked and he politely declined.

Billy arrived and then the two men walked down to the existing Kennels and Cattery. Just one hour after the Architect left a groundwork crew arrived with a bulldozer and JCB digger. Just two hours after that the ground to the back of the kennels and cattery had been levelled and trenches dug for the foundations and also for the electrical, water supply and sewage. The foreman of that team came up and said they had done all they could today. They would have to wait for the concrete to be poured tomorrow morning. With that the six man groundwork team left for the day.

Billy arrived back up at the house at 5pm with the two kennel maids, who he drove to their homes and returned just as Jenny was taking a pie that she had cooked, out of the oven.

"Mmm that smells delicious."

"Its been a while since we had Steak and Kidney pie, I hope your hungry, I made lots." Jenny said

Over dinner they sat and Jenny talked excitedly about all the modernisations that were happening to the Rescue Centre. How this would make them the single biggest rescue centre in Lincolnshire.

Billy was secretly worried that things were moving way too fast for Jenny's dream. Was it Jenny's dream any more? Or was this John and Natasha's dream. Were they deep and passionate animal lovers but without the need to be hands on, true that part of things was messy and at times seriously hard work. Were they playing at being the Lord and Lady of the manor? Why invest so much money into Jenny's home and rescue centre. They had now put in almost £250,000 into making The Marjorie Cat and Dog Rescue Centre, one of the best in the country. It was clean and modern with lots of space, and now an in-house Veterinary surgery. This vision was way beyond what Billy or Jenny had ever dreamed of. It might be worth asking his brother to take a look into the background of Mr and Mrs Perkins

The next morning as promised the cement trucks turned up along with the groundwork crew from the previous day. By the end of the morning the foundations and roughed out floors were laid. The groundwork crew were not finished yet. They then went and removed the bottom fence to the property before bringing in a ground leveller and made sense out of the large plot of ground that now belonged to Jenny.

Multiple truck loads of hardcore were laid in a road like manner, that went around the outside edge of the property. They were followed by as many truck loads of course sand. Now the bottom field looked like it had an outside path or roadway. The men finished for the night they left, saying they would return again in the morning.

They did indeed return first thing the following morning. This time with two lorries laden with rolls of AstroTurf, which they rolled out on top of the sand road. Borders were dug on the outside edge and planted with several hundred small bushes.

The foreman came back up to the house and said that their work was complete and if Jenny needed any further groundwork doing, all she had to do was to call the number on the card he gave her. With that they all left, leaving the rescue centre in peace and quite with the exception of the barking dogs. Billy told Jenny he was just popping down the road to see his brother Jack.

"Hello Billy what brings you down to our little abode." Janet said as she answered the door.

"I was looking for Jack, is he about?"

"Yes he is."

"In the garage?"

"Where else would he be. I swear he loves that old car, more than he does me." She said laughingly

Janet, was referring to Jack's love for his old MGA classic British sports car. Billy had already rebuilt this car from the chassis up once before.

Originally it had been their fathers car. Billy remembered it always breaking down when his father would take the family on outings. When their father died the car had been sat in the garage just rusting away. Jack had asked Billy, what he wished to do with it. 'Scrap it.' had been his answer. Jack had then asked if he could have it. Billy had asked if he were mad. So Jack had ended up with the wreck. During Jacks time with the Swindon police force he had worked on the car rebuilding it nut and bolt, over a period of six years. When it was complete it looked like a brand new car, only it was sixty years old. From its gleaming spoked wheels, to it burnished leather seats and custom made soft top.

Then just a few weeks after it has been completed, he had been deliberately run off the road and the car had been totalled, Jack had been lucky to survive the crash. Now some years later he was ninety nine percent, the way through its third incarnation and second total rebuild.

"Thanks Janet." Billy said and walked over to the double wooden doors of Jacks garage. After opening the door and entering. Jacks feet were sticking out from underneath the jacked up car.

"Hello Bill." Jack said sliding out from under he beloved MGA

"How did you know it was me Jack?"

"Janet would never have sent anyone else out here, knowing I was working on dads car."

"Ohhh Well I think it probably runs a lot better than when dad had it." Billy said.

Jack stood up and first wiped his hands on his dirty overalls and then opened a small fridge that was sat under his workbench.

"Beer?" Jack asked taking two bottles out of the fridge. One of which he handed to his brother, who took it and popped the top off in the side of the bench.

"Looks nice again." Billy said

"Yes with a bit of luck I will get it finished by the end of summer. Fred from Boston Auto Body Repairs has set some time aside to paint it."

"I thought you said you could not get the right paint?"

"I did but Fred Shail, found a company to make some up just from a fleck of the original paint. Fred may only have one eye, but that one eye is better them most other finisher's two eyes. Besides I trust him as a friend. So what is it you need from me this time Billy?"

Billy feigned hurt

"Aww why would you think I need something from you Jack?"

"Because Billy. You are here without Jenny, I do presume that she is not in the house with Janet?"

"Yes OK I am here without Jenny. I want you to do some checking for me please Jack."

"On what or whom?"

"Our glorious benefactor. I worked it out yesterday he has shoved almost a quarter of a million of his money, into our home and business." Billy said

"I thought he was some sort of tree hugging, planet saving, animal loving, philanthropist."

"Yes all that is true at least on the face of things, but given the way the previous Vet died it got me wondering, if that is all there is to the Perkins."

"The police investigated that murder and they seemed to think it was a drug deal argument gone bad. They have a warrant out for the murderer, one of my friends at Boston nick, seemed to think that it was a Russian, who has already fled the country."

Billy took a swig of his beer and looked almost like he believed that, but he could not convince himself that was all there was to it.

"I would still like you to get the full low down on our benefactor, Like where did he get his money from, are there any other projects like ours where he has totally paid for everything. Also what interests does he have in Pakistan, South Africa, Bahrain, The Gold Coast, Russia and China, these are just some of the places were we are starting to get our waifs and strays from."

"Are there problems that have come to the surface?"

"No not really Jack, I know that you used to talk about having a policeman's intuition. Well call it a family trait. Yes all the animals that we get are injured in some way and all have had surgical procedures for one problem or another. But there is something just not right about the way he is throwing money at us. You know the big field at the bottom of our land? Well John just went and bought it, then just gave it to Jenny for somewhere to exercise the dogs. he even sorted a full three meter wide walkway, that goes all the way around it."

"OK I get your concern. I still have some friends in the Swindon Police Force. I will give them a call and get back to you with as full a write up as soon I can. By the way its gonna cost you a dinner." Jack said and they clinked bottles and drank their beers.

10
Clean Bill Of Health

After his brother had left, Jack closed the garage door and went back into his house. He showered and dressed in casual clothes and went into his lounge and opened his telephone and address book. Having found the name he dialled the number.

"DCI Short"

"Hello Jean."

"Jack?"

"Yes Jean. How's life treating you? I see that they finally gave you the promotion you deserved."

"Yes Jack. They made me a full Inspector just after you left and the 'bean counter' quit to follow politics So DCI Weathers took his job and I got DCI Weathers job. So what gives for this blast from the past then Jack?"

"I need a favour and it might be a big one." Jack said

"Any favour for you Jack you know that?"

"OK Not sure where to start with this. My brother and his wife have a dog sanctuary and this bloke has invested a lot of money into their venture, and we are talking a lot of dosh as in the hundreds of thousands."

"Well surely that would be a good thing?"

"My brother is worried that its too good to be true and to be quite honest with you Jean, I do share his concerns."

"Why not ask the locals to help you, I am sure they would if you asked?"

"Perhaps Jean, but I would like to use your other half's connection with the FBI and Interpol." Jack said referring to ex DS Alex Gordon.

Alex had come into Swindon police from from the training college at Hendon. She and Jean were a couple. But Alex had worked with the FBI during Jacks last case, which had been the Swindon Serial Killer. Alex Gordon had contacts that no one else seemed to have.

"What's the name of the guy you want information on."

"John Perkins and his wife Natasha Perkins. They claim to have set up animal rescue centres around the world."

"What do you want to know about them Jack?" DCI Short asked

"I want to know, how he got his money. He claims to be a philanthropist and that he made his money in digital finance." Jack replied and continued

"His wife, I think is Ukrainian. I think she was married to a rich Russian and then divorced. Perkins claimed that he was a financial advisor to Natasha and told her to invest in BitCoin when it first came out and that they made millions from doing just that. Then they got married."

"So what makes you think he is hookey apart from being married to a Russian oligarch's cast off."

"Put put it this way Jean. The Perkins 'claim' to love cats and dogs but they have other to do the donkey work. I suppose that it could be because of their busy lifestyle but something just does not fit the bill. One more thing and it may not have anything at all to do with anything at all. The Vet who was working for Perkins, was actually murdered in front of me. That would be about three weeks ago. We had been out for a meal as a family. We had a drink in a pub and the Vet was involved in an argument over money. The later the same night in the restaurant the Vet was involved in another argument in the kitchen of the place where we were eating. We had then finished our meal and were walking back to the car and I saw another man literally cut the throat of the Vet in front of us. His killer is still at large. The local force seem to think that he escaped the country. So you can see why I want this fellow checked out"

"OK Jack leave it with me I will try and get back to you later today. Its been real nice chatting. Talk soon." DCI Jean Short said and hung up the phone.

As soon as Jean had ended the call with Jack she called up her life partner Alex Gordon.

"Hi Babe. Don't tell me you have to work late again." Alex said as she answered the phone.

"No nothing like that Alex. I want to pick your brain and contacts." Jean said

"Sounds interesting. What do you want?"

"Its a favour for Jack Hamilton."

"For Jack he can have everything." Alex replied.

Like Jean, Alex had been on the serial killer investigation, which had ended with two police officers dead and the culprit Shot by Jack Hamilton and Senior FBI Agent Mark Carter. It had been a case of suicide by cop.

"Can you use your contacts and find out everything you can on a Millionaire John Perkins and his wife Natasha. Perkins is a British national and his wife we think is Ukrainian but she could be Russian. Find out where the money comes from and any skeletons in their cupboards." Jean said

"Do you have any more details, as that is not a lot to go on?" Alex asked

"I don't have much more from Jack apart from the are now living just outside Boston."

"USA or UK?"

"That would be the Lincolnshire one." Jean answered.

As soon as Alex Gordon, had hung up on Jean, the first call she made was to Senior Agent Mark Carter at the FBI Training centre in Quantico USA. Alex gave him all the information that she had to hand and requested that he do a full search. Mark had come over and helped to end the murderous spree of the Swindon version of the serial killer Edward Theodore Gein. Jack and his team had shared a lot of their own intel with the man from the FBI. Mark said that he would use his position as Senior Training officer and have his students do all the hard work looking into the Perkins, then he would correlate into a single file.

That call ended and it was onto Interpol. Even though Alex Gordon was no longer a serving officer the very mention of Jack Hamilton, was enough to ensure the assistance of probably the best police resources into the criminal world and to that of international crimes.

Alex had one call left to make and she was not even sure if the person she was calling would still be alive. Or even with the internal secret police force. Still she dialled the man's personal telephone number.

It rang four times before it was answered. The line had been answered but no one spoke. Which meant that Alex had to speak first.

"Sergi?"

"Da?"

"Come on Sergi, don't be a pratt. I know that you already know who this is just by my voice and you personally gave me your private number."

"Alex so good to hear from you."

"See I knew that you recognised the number. I am betting that you have it listed as Boris or something like that." Alex said and she could hear Sergi trying not to bust a gut laughing.

"So! Tell me, Alex my dear friend from England police training. What is it the Federal Security Services of Russia can do for you."

"Well apart from a kilo of Beluga Caviar and a bottle of Stolichnaya Vodka you mean?"

"That for you I can do. Now tell me what you really want to know?"

"A man called John Perkins.""?

"So is not Russian man?"

"No Sergi he is British, but his wife may be Ukrainian or possibly Russian. Her name is Natasha. We think that she was married before to an oligarch and then divorced before she was married to John Perkins." Alex answered

"So tell me my wonderful friend, the why?"

"Because he seems to be throwing a lot of money at one animal charity."

"So now in England this is crime?"

"It might be depending on why he is doing it."

"So if I tell you about Natasha Krasnov."

"Sergi I never gave you her previous surname so how do you know this lady?"

"About eight years ago a good friend of a friend of mine Fedor Petrovich Krasnov. He was powerful and rich man but a Cossack. So could never really be a Russian. Still he was also friend of Putin. He was bastard to Natasha and would beat her in public. Putin tell him no more and to divorce. So he divorce her and for she to leave from Russia. But she stay and then Fedor his accountant he married her that is John Perkins. Then they leave together"

"Is that not strange that a Russian Oligarch has a British accountant." Alex asked

"For Russian yes it is odd, but he was Cossack and they want to trade with the world. So to have a western accountant not that unusual."

"Sergi you keep referring to Fedor Petrovich Krasnov in the past tense. Was his death suspicious?"

"All Oligarch deaths is big suspicious. But was not state sponsored, if that is what you think?

Because he did not remarry then Natasha she could get all the money except his finances have been locked by my government. He was friend to Putin." Sergi said. Then he continued.

"Mr Perkins has a lot lot of wealth of his own it is not from Natasha because she got the divorce money but in order to keep that money she had to reside in Russia. When she left Russia she left with no money."

"What about Bitcoin?"

"See Alex you do know something, I think."

"Honest Sergi I only have what I have told you. Mr Perkins said that his wife invested the divorce settlement in Bitcoin and that is how she is now so wealthy."

"No my friend Alex. All her assets are frozen including any digital funds. But we can not touch Mr Perkins as he is one of your citizens. Also like in the United Kingdom, John Perkins he has animal shelters and several rescue centres. I think perhaps he loves animals. But like you, we would like to know just where his money comes from. For you though Alex I will ask others to look harder and I will send you the Vodka and Caviar." Sergi said and the conversation ended.

Alex had written down all the responses from Sergi and it raised more questions than it answered. If the person with the real money was not Natasha but was John, then like Sergi she would like to know where his got his funds from. Still at least he had not done anything illegal in Russia. Plus he did invest in the care of animals.

So it was a shady, but clean bill of heath from the Russian FSB, as Alex was working on the basis of her report for Jean, the phone rang.

"Hello Alex Gordon speaking"

"Now then Alex, How y'all doing in the land of tea and fish with chips." The slow southern drawl of Mississippi born, Mark Carter said

"Fish and Chips" Alex corrected him.

"When I was in England is was sat in Jacks car just about to eat my fish and chips with mushy peas and we had to dump them for an emergency. If memory serves me right it was to save your girlfriend Jean Short."

"I will tell her she still owes you a Fish Supper. So what have you got for me Mark?"

"Not so much what I have got for you. When we started to ask questions about Mr John Perkins some powerful people want to know why the interest? Care to tell me what the interest is?"

"If I could I would but truthfully I was just asked to make an enquiry. Jean was asked by Jack.

"On the surface Mr Perkins is squeaky clean. He pays his bills and is known world wide as a man who loves to save animals. Set up a lot of rescue centres around the USA imports rescued dogs from all over the world. Even pays all the Vet bills. "

"Mark you say my enquiry ruffled feathers, who's feathers precisely?" Alex Asked

"One of our less than honest senators with more powerful friends than I have"

"Well if he is less than honest cant you arrest him or something and just find out why he is so interested in Mr Perkins himself?" Alex asked

"Politics my dear Alex, Politics. Put it this way we are not looking at Mr Perkins but we are looking at a senator who wants to know why we are looking. I will keep in touch" Mark said and ended the call.

Alex was still writing the report for Jean when the telephone rang again.

"Hello Alex Gordon"

"Ahh Miss Gordon, I understand you want to know about John Perkins?"

"Yes, who is this?"

"Never mind who I am, suffice to say this, I crossed swords with him once. He is not at all what he seems."

"And what does he seem to be?"

"Like Gods gift to do gooders."

"OK so tell me about him then."

"I had a kennel and he came to me and offered to help me get bigger and better."

"And?" Alex asked

"Well I declined, so the bastard set up his own kennels right next door to mine. Even had his own Vet. He shifts animals in bulk, that is not rescuing. That is a big business model. So he wiped us out."

"That does not sound like too bad a thing to save animals in batches rather than one at a time.?" Alex said

"But every rescue centre has to run at a profit, no matter how small a profit. Even those that are run by charities. Banks don't accept a negative account. Because he does not care about profit he wipes out genuine rescue centres unless you work for him."

"Well thank you for your information I will bear it in mind. By the way who told you I was asking about Mr Perkins." Alex asked

"I mean I cant say as he has a Court Order against me officially saying anything about him to anyone."

"That does not answer my question. Who told you I was asking?" Alex asked again and the line went dead.

She looked down at her phone and it said number withheld. She would have Jean check it out later and made a note of the exact time.

The long and the short of her days work. so far was that Mr Perkins whilst not always liked by everyone seemed to have a clean bill of health.

11
Building Completed

Jack relayed all the information back to his brother, including the stuff that had come from the FSB and FBI, that although John Perkins was not everyone's flavour of the month. He had been a financial advisor to Natasha and her ex husband. And there was no proof that he had invested in bitcoin for Natasha, he himself did have large holdings in digital currency. He was also know widely throughout the world as an animal loving philanthropist. Even if he did step on toes to be bigger and better than most others. Still that was not a crime. Jack laid Billy's mind to rest at least for now.

All the new kennel blocks and catteries were now completed. The exercise area looked like some giant kind of garden and play-zone for dogs. With its tunnels and see-saw planks. Oversize balls and tugging ropes all set on AstroTurf, making it look like a grassed over area. This was all surrounded by a wide pathway that followed the eight feet high, chain link fence. Each cattery now also had it own fifty foot long enclosure. In short, The Marjorie Cat and Dog Rescue Centre was the crème de la crème of animal rescue centres. There were some small dog or cat hotels, that may have been better but they were not for injured or sick animals or for those animals who were looking for new homes.

John had called the night before to let Jenny know that they would have seven cats coming in from Bahrain and eight dogs were due in from South Africa. As they were arriving at different times and in different airports. Billy and the new extra Handyman both had to drive down to London John went to Gatwick for the dogs and the new guy Mike Stanford went to Heathrow for the cats.

Back at the rescue centre Jenny was taking the two new kennel maids through their duties and showing them where everything was. The two experienced girls were looking after the few animals that they still had waiting for new homes. John said he would be here tomorrow and Natasha was over at Newmarket looking for some horses for their stud farm.

John had said that they needed to expand from cats and dogs to re-homing horses. He had said that a lot of racehorses simply get shot at the end of their racing life. These would mainly be from the USA and from the Arab nations. He had even employed his own equine Vet who had taken over the surgery that Mario once used, although they had vastly extended that surgery at the rear and installed bigger doors suitable for horses.

Natasha had asked Jenny if she would like to be a part of a horse rescue centre. Jenny had declined, not because she did not like horses just her time was fully taken up by her own rescue centre. Even the offer of more staff and money could not persuade Jenny to change her mind. As such the Equine Rescue Centre was at the Perkins Farm.

Billy arrived back at the rescue centre before Mike and handed the dogs over to the kennel maids, who in turn booked them in, before taking them one at at time to their in-house Vet, Kareem and his wife Fatima.

Everything went like clockwork, dogs in, wounds redressed, photos taken and then advertised on the webpage which now had over 100,000 registered homes looking for specific animals. Word seemed to have got around that, if you did not mind your animal with a small scar, then you could get a beautiful cat or dog from The Marjorie Cat and Dog Rescue Centre and there was a good chance that you might even get a rare breed. All the animals had been neutered which stopped those attempting to make a profit by breeding with these rescued animals.

The cats arrived just as Kareem had finished checking the dogs, once again there were several rare animals including a beautiful grey long haired, Ragdoll, Birman with almost fluorescent bright orange eyes. Jenny pointed out to one of the kennel maids, that in this country, this cat would probably sell for anything up to £3k as a kitten.

Over the coming weeks the animals kept coming and most were only in the rescue centre of a couple of weeks. The voluntary donations from happy families was almost at a level where the rescue centre could become self sufficient. There was even more money coming in from a major cat food supplier who had an advertisement on the rescue centre's website and social media pages.

Almost six months after Kareem took over as their Vet, they lost a dog. It had just been collected with a batch of dogs from Pakistan. It was not Kareem's fault, it had happened on the journey between Gatwick and the rescue centre. Kareem said he would conduct an autopsy and let Jenny know how the reason for the dogs death just in case it was anything contagious. The dog in question had been a female Bully Kutta or Pakistani Mastiff. When Billy had opened the van on arrival at the rescue centre, the dog had been dead for about an hour and there was a lot of white foam around the mouth. None of the other dogs seemed to be affected by anything similar.

After checking over all the other new arrivals Kareem and Fatima did their postmortem. When they had finished Kareem wrote his report which said that the dog had died from septicemia as a result of an infection in the wound caused by neutering. When John learned of this he went crazy shouting at Kareem in Arabic. Then he called another person on the phone and again shouted in Arabic. Shortly after a black van appeared at the rescue centre and they said that John had called them in order to take the dog carcass for incineration. The paperwork they carried matched the dogs own paperwork. So Jenny had the Vet hand over the body of the dog.

Some days later a Black Range Rover like the one John owned, arrived at the Kennels and two men in business suits got out and asked where John was. There was something about them that raised the heckles on Jenny's neck. There was just something about the way that they asked, made her dislike them immediately. Jenny pointed them down to the Perkins farm. As soon as they had left Jenny called Natasha and told her about these men. Natasha had told her not to worry they were here about the horses.

The following day John came to the rescue centre and his face was swollen and even though he wore his Rayban sunglasses they did little to hide the fact that he had a pair of black eyes and his nose was split.

"Jesus, John, what the hell happened to you?" Jenny asked him.

"I was standing behind a horse when I should have been standing at the front of him, and he pushed me up against the back wall of his stable." He replied

"Now you should know never to get behind a horse especially a horse that you don't know. Have you been to the hospital?" Jenny asked

"Don't worry Jenny its not as bad as it looks."

From the way that john moved it actually looked like it might have been a lot worse than he was saying.

"I just came to say we have a cat that is coming in from Myanmar, it is a Burmese female. Can either Billy or Mike pick it up from Heathrow." John said

"Mike is already down in London at Gatwick I will call him up and ask him to get over to Heathrow." Jenny said.

Billy who had been down seeing his brother Jack, arrived back just as John was leaving the rescue centre in his Range Rover. John seemed to ignore Billy's wave at him or perhaps he did not see the wave. Still, he had to speak to Jenny.

"Hi Babe, I need to ask you something?"

"Now that sounds all mysterious and like bad news." Jenny replied before planting a big wet kiss full on his lips right in front of one of the young kennel maids.

"Eww you two need to get a room and do old people really do that sort of thing!" the girl said

With that Jenny pulled billy closer and kissed him deeper and longer. The girl looked embarrassed and took off to he duties.

"Now lover boy what is it that is so important that you cant tell me you love me before anything else?" Jenny asked

"You know that Pakistani Mastiff that died a couple of weeks ago?" Billy asked

"Yes of course I do I remember any animal I have ever had that has died. I remember the Cat and of course I remember a Dog from just a short time ago. It died on the way here from sepsis according to Kareem."

"And the black van that took him away to be incinerated?" Billy asked.

"Yes what about it?"

"John arranged all that. Right?" Billy said before continuing.

"Don't you think it all happened so fast? Dead, autopsy, and burned up all in the space of two hours?"

"Sure it was fast but you know John, he is bull headed and likes to use his money to make things happen fast. Look at the way he bought the field, got planning permission and even started the new kennels here all in the space of two days." She replied. And then asked in a more worried tone.

"Billy why are you asking me this?"

"Because I think something is terribly wrong with the way we are getting all these animals from around the globe. Don't you think that the animal rescue community would have heard about John Perkins before he came here? Also why us? Why not use somewhere that was already big enough to handle quantities."

"Who else could take the numbers that we handle?" Jenny asked defensively

"I don't know Jenny but I checked with the animal crematorium. The woman who runs it said she has never cremated a Pakistani Mastiff. Further to that she never had any dog for cremation on the day that the two men came for the dogs body. Also she only owns one van and that is a silver Transit Box Luton van. So she does not know who took the dog but it was not her." Billy said.

"Well perhaps John has a contract with a different animal cremation company. Anyway why did you go there to ask her questions?" Jenny asked her husband.

"I don't know Jenny just something feels all wrong." He replied.

"You know what Billy I think you are Jealous of the fact that I finally got this place up and running perfectly." Jenny said pulling away from her embrace with Billy.

"No Jenny its not like that at all. It is because I love you and worry about you." He replied

Then all of a sudden, what had been a discussion, became an argument and then became a screaming match and ended with Billy going to stay at his brothers for the night.

Before Billy left for Jack's he called Mike up and agreed to have the cat delivered to Jack's house. Jack wanted to see if there was any wound under the bandages that each animal had when it entered into their care.

Mike arrived about an hour later and waited while Jack took the cat inside Jack's home and removed the bandage and dressing from under the cat's belly.

The front left shin had been shaved and there was evidence of a place where either an injection had been made or a catheter inserted. There was a small wound that had four stitches in. So much for his theory of stolen animals. That is what Billy had thought. As most of the dogs and cats were rare breeds. He gave the cat back to Mike with its dressings replaced and asked him not to say anything to Jenny. Mike promised to say nothing.

Jack who had been present when Billy removed the bandage and dressings, waited until Billy returned to the house.

"So what were you looking for?" Jack asked

"Well I thought that Kareem might have been taking the microchips out of the cats and dogs and replacing them with new ones. That way if the animals were stolen then there would be now way to track them."

"Really Billy? I think you are becoming a little bit paranoid. I had my sources check out John Perkins and his wife Natasha. Both their backgrounds came back clear. There is nothing there, he has never been convicted of anything more than a parking ticket."

"Jack you used to say the best thing a police officer had in his professional toolkit was a coopers nose."

"And that is right Billy, but you are not a copper and neither am I any more. The best thing you could do is to make things up with Jenny in the morning."

"Jack I just know something is wrong and I know I am right about it. My gut tells me that we have got ourselves mixed up in some terrible deal. I just don't know what it is. This is a big ask I know Jack. Is there any way that you could have John followed to find out what he is up too?" Billy asked.

"I'll tell you what Billy, let me talk to one of my old contacts again and I will get him checked out again. But leave this to me don't try to do anything yourself. Promise me that?" Jack said

"All right I promise."

"And one more thing Billy. Promise me you will fix things with Jenny."

"I promise I will try."

The following day Jack called up DCI Jean Short once again.

"Hello Jack, what's up?"

"I know you did me a huge favour in doing a background on John Perkins. My brother just cant shake the feeling that something is seriously amiss. Since we spoke the last time the Rescue Centre has doubled in size and its intake of rescue cats and dogs has almost tripled." Jack said

"But surely that is a good thing lots of animals getting loving homes." Jean replied

"On the surface of things yes. You know my old man was a copper?"

"No I didn't Jack but it does not surprise me as you always did have an excellent coppers nose."

"Well it could be my brother might also have inherited that particular gene. Who do you know could do a private eye bit of work?"

"Why don't you do it yourself Jack?"

"Because I know the man and he knows me. I need someone outside of the circle. I want him followed 24/7 if I can. I will pay for it. You know my word is good Jean."

"What you are saying is you want someone you can trust not to stuff things up?"

"In a word Jean? Yes."

"Tell you what Jack, I am due some leave and I know Alex would love to see you again. What if I were to be on holiday around Boston?"

"I cant ask you to do that Jean, you have your own work to do."

"We have nothing major on at this time, just some stuff that drugs squad can handle. See you tomorrow morning." Jean said and ended the call before Jack could protest any further.

"Thanks Jack, for not just blowing me off and saying I am paranoid." Billy said

"I never said you weren't paranoid. Anyway you know what they say?"

"What."

"Just because you're paranoid does not mean that the whole world isn't out to get you!"

"Funny Jack real funny!"

12
Getting The Team Back Together

Billy had returned home that morning and made his peace with Jenny by way of a lot of grovelling and promised to just get on with his work. Which is exactly what he did.

Later that morning three cars pulled up on Jack's driveway. Jean Short got out of the first car, followed by Alex Gordon from the following one and in the third car was someone Jack had most definitely not expected to see. Tom Patterson who was a civilian employee from the Technical Department of Swindon police. Jack had not seen him since the Swindon Serial killer. That was around four years ago.

"Well don't just stand there Gawking help me unload some of this equipment, Tom said pressing his key-fob and opening the boot of his 4×4 Jeep Compass."

Jack greeted all of them and invited them into the house while also helping Tom bring in multiple aluminium cases from his car and stacking them to one side of Jacks Kitchen. Jack had already warned his wife that there might be some old friends from the police force coming to visit, but he had said nothing about Tom. This was on account of it was news to him as well.

"So I kind of expected you two, Jack said point to Jean and Alex but to be quite honest I never expected to you see you, like ever again Tom. In a nice way of course."

"Of course but you are going to need me Jack, especially if what the girls are saying is true and your man is a globe trotter." Tom said over the cup of coffee that Janet had placed in front of him.

"You see Jack, in the real world of policing the uniforms need us invisibles to get your evidence, and sometimes, through some quite nefarious methods. Hence I borrowed some equipment from the storeroom. Well actually I signed it out to DCI Short."

"You did? Did you? Well in that case don't break or lose any of it or its your job that will go and not mine." Jean joked with him. And then continued

"Jack we have all taken two weeks annual leave. And we brought three cars as it is a lot easier to track someone in multiple cars. Tom is going to act as a base for us is it OK, if he stops with you. Alex and I will be at one of my friends in Spalding so that is not too far from here right?" Jean said

"You know you all did not have to come and help. You know that we might be chasing a dead horse or a complete nothing." Jack said

"Tell me Jack, you called me so what does your own gut tell you about this guy Perkins?"

"I have not one shred of proof but he is just way too smarmy and way to rich to not have a murky background." Jack replied

"So where is this bloke now? Is he in the Country?" Tom asked

"Yes I think he is at his farm. It is next door to my brothers place. The actual house is about half a mile from Billy's home."

"OK, what car does he drive?"

"What difference does that make Tom?" Jack asked

"Jack how long have you been a civilian?"

"About four years now, why?"

"Well I hate to tell you this boss but in technology terms that is like light years behind. So what car does he drive?"

"One of those new flash Range Rover Sport models

"Right then, I can tell you where and when he is, anywhere in the UK or if he drives out of the country. It makes it easier to tail him from a distance. Do you have a mobile phone number for him?"

"I don't but I am sure Billy does."

"Right will I need that as well and any land line number for his home or business."

"Jack. Alex and I are going to head over to Spalding. We will be back later and take you through what we have planned." Jean said and they both left.

"Right Jack are you gonna find me a nice quiet place to set up my stuff?" Tom asked

"Sure Tom, what do you need?"

"Nothing at all Jack, apart from a dry spot with an electrical hook up."

"What about internet don't you need a connection or something?"

"I brought my own Jack, I use satellite connection. Its more private, if you get my drift."

"Nope but I will take it as read that I understand nothing about your side of things Tom. Do you need a room in my house?"

"Do you have a garage as that might be better I don't sleep much, so I can work undisturbed and also not disturb you at the same time. Also no one will know I am here." Tom replied

"OK whatever suits you best. Let me help you with your boxes of toys."

"Oh by the way this is for you." Tom said passing Jack a telephone.

"Thanks Tom I already own a mobile phone."

"Not like that you don't Its the latest in Satellite phones. Each of us will have one. Keep it charged." Tom said as he passed over a charger to Jack.

Later that day, the two girls returned from Spalding. Jack took them over to his garage where Tom was sat at the workbench sipping a beer and wearing a pair of headphones. Jack tapped him on the shoulder.

"I see you found my beer fridge?"

"Yep good beers too, Desperado nice one Jack!."

"You still have that old rust bucket?" Jean said pointing to the MGA.

"That's no rust-bucket in fact I would say that if you can find any rust on it I will give you a tenner," Jack said feigning hurt.

"OK Tom please tell me that all that stuff on my workbench does actually do something."

"See that map and the red dot that is moving?"

"Yes."

"Well that is Perkins Range Rover."

"How or don't I want to know?"

"No its all legal sort of. He has a new Range Rover right?"

"Yes."

"Well all new Range Rovers come with a factory fitted tracker as part of their low-jack systems. So I just entered his name into the DVLA database It gave me his registration and then I looked in the Range Rover security database and it supplied me with a tracker code."

"Barely legal, I think that requires a court order?" Jack said

"Lets just pretend we have that OK, besides we are not officially here. Now do you want to see something really special, well actually hear some thing special?"

"What?"

Tom pressed a key on his laptop and turned up a speaker that was sat next to the larger computer screen.

"….and the way that we get them to help us is to put them in a position whereby they cant. Also where are we on the next horse shipment" Perkins voice could be heard.

"You know what happens if this all goes sideways, this time it will be more than a slap you get. You do understand what I mean by that.?" said a Slavic sounding voice. Then it went quiet before some music started to play.

"You hacked his phone?" Jack asked

"No need too. He is using a hands free system on the Range Rover. It has a microphone built into its electronics. Strangely its part of their own security system so I just hacked that. Far less security on that than trying to hack into someone's phone these days especially iPhones which is what he has and he has the latest generation. You would be lucky if the NSA of the USA could hack it let alone us. So we hack the car. Now Jean or Alex or even you Jack can tail them from a mile or so back and I can be in touch with our sat phones if he stops somewhere or picks anyone or anything up. I have a little bit more of that conversation, but I think you got the bones of it."

"Yes I did and it tells me one thing"

"What's that? Jean asked.

"Our man Perkins is not the head honcho! Good work Tom. I will need the telephone number of the Vet at your brothers and also the one at the Perkins farm."

"I am sure we can manage that. I will talk with Billy and get you those numbers."

"Don't any of you want to know where the other person on Perkins call was calling from?"

"Goes without saying Tom, so surprise me." Jack said

"Moscow, to be precise, from inside the Kremlin."

"Are you sure about that Tom?" Jack asked suddenly aware that they may well be stepping on the toes of some really big hitters. Also who else would be listening in on that call.

"Jack it was a simple trace. Much easier than most people think, especially on international calls. It was made on a mobile phone, using an international network but using the car to hear it all made things that much easier. If he uses hands free in his car we can hear both sides of the conversation. And we will be able to pinpoint him, when he uses his car. As soon as I get the Vets number then I can do the same with his."

"First see if you can get a handle on who he was talking to in the Kremlin."

"If he is using a FSB phone, it will not be so easy they use their own network. A lot of wealthy Russians like to use iPhones and the later the better. So they use them on less than secure networks. How do you think your brother would feel about us tapping his phones?"

"I don't think my brother would mind but Jenny now she would throw a hissy-fit so we will not tell her and whatever you do don't get caught! So can you track and follow by one means or another both the Vets and both of the Perkins? Actually probably best that I don't know, just bring me the information that you can."

"Yes, Yes and OK no problem" Tom replied and continued after another swig of Jacks chilled beer.

"I will always be in direct contact with Jean or Alex, I will record everything just in case it is required at a later stage, although I am guessing it will not be officially required."

"Just drink Jack's beer and shut up Tom." Alex said jovially and then on a more serious note.

"What happens if we find evidence serious criminal activity?"

"I guess we will cross those bridges as we get to them. Alex just how trustworthy are your contacts in the USA and also in Russia?" Jack asked?

"Well you already know my contact in the USA."

"I do?"

"Sure its Mark at the FBI"

"Ohh OK and in Russia?" Jack replied

"Well that one is a little more complex, it is more of favours owed to me. I was able to identify one of their FSB agents, who was trying to interfere with the Gas prices for his own profit. It turned out to be the son of the man that now owes me this big favour. I kept his sons name out of the mix, which saved his sons life. Theoretically I could still drop the bomb on that one." Alex said

"But you wont?" Jack replied

"But I wont. No." Alex said and closed that line of conversation.

"I will follow up on any UK based criminal activity and make sure the correct authorities are brought up to speed where, when and if required. If that is OK with you Jack." Jean said

"OK Jean can you thank Senior Agent Mark Carter when you can?"

"Well how about now you old salty dog" a slow souther droll of the man from the FBI with Mississippi tones.

Jack turned to see Mark Carter standing like he had first met him, Suitcase in one and a Samsonite Briefcase in the other.

"Hello yourself I hope you brought some of that coffee you have made for you, by your friend with the coffee shop?"

"You already know, I never leave home without my Mississippi Delta Grounds. I believe that I am on vacation so, as that will make things a lot easier, with the British Authorities." Mark said dropping his bags and grabbing Jack in a bear hug.

Mark looked around and then said

"Looks like you got the little old team back together for a reunion party I guess."

13
Follow The Money

"The first thing they teach us at Quantico when we are learning to become fully fledged members of the FBI, is that there are basically two types of crime. Ones where money is not involved and ones where it is. So we already know that in this case a lot of money is involved in the setting up of these rescue centres. Now I had a peek inside the personal bank accounts of Natasha and John Perkins. They have a lot of property around the world currently valued in the Billions of dollar, yet looking into their bank accounts there is only around one million dollars." Mark said

"And that is odd how Mark?" Jack asked

"Well if you own Billions in real estate then you tend to have bank accounts to match their wealth theirs does not but they seem to have a cash flow of around fifty million per month. It looks like half of it goes into bitcoin the other half goes to some offshore account the owner of which I am trying to track down. The end of the month balance always seems to be around one million" Mark said

"Well $50 million a month is a hell of a lot of money from a man who probably shells out around half of that on good deeds around the world going on how much he has spent on Jenny and Billy's place. So where does it all come from?"

"All I can tell you is that it comes in from Bitcoin and that is about as untraceable as things get without having access to the computers or the pass codes of those who are paying. Bitcoin goes from one person to another and then from the recipient into their bank for real money by them cashing out their bitcoin through banking systems even through something like PayPal. What you have to understand about Bitcoin is that it does not actually exist. It is just data. If you lose your password then you will never recover your bitcoin. With banks there are lots of ways of proving who you are and that you own X amount of money."

"So what you are saying if I have a handle on this, is, that his money comes from unknown sources and then into his bank from bitcoin into dollars and then out from his bank back into untraceable bitcoin?" Jack asked

"Not quite Jack. Bitcoin first has to be changed from data in currency like US Dollars or GB pounds. That is done through digital traders. These digital traders take a buyers or sellers fee in digital currency then they transfer to your bank in real money. They are like traders on the stock market. Only they are playing with your money and they set the value levels"

"So how do we stop it? Or take the money back?"

"Well we could if we can charge him with the proceeds of crime act, which is pretty much an international law. Or if we get his access codes, we then change those codes and lock him, her or them out of their bitcoin." Mark said

"Is that even legal?" Jack asked

Mark shrugged his shoulders.

"Most criminals will never admit to having been locked from their accounts as invariably they probably owe monies from it, to other not so nice people. Remember that the tax man is the powerful weapon in your toolkit. AL Capone was responsible for all sorts of murder and mayhem. He was never prosecuted for a single murder yet there were dozens attributed to him. He was eventually jailed for income tax evasion." Mark said

"I can get in. If I can get close enough to his laptop or if he uses mobile banking via an app on his iPhone." Tom said

"I always thought that iPhones tell you they cant be hacked and that even the FBI can's get access to them." Jack said

"A little disinformation, that we put out there to encourage crooks to use their iPhones when conducting their activities. We never tell them we hacked their phones. We even apply for court orders to force Apple to release their access codes, knowing full well they will deny it. Real sneaky don't you think?" Mark said

"Don't suppose you could share those codes with me?" Tom said

"I guess I could Tom, but I am afraid then I would have to kill you and Jack has seen the size of my gun" Mark said

"Too much sharing of information there" Alex said with a wink.

"OK lets set things up proper, I will do the first week on nights and Alex can do the day shift, then if we are still here, I will swap with Alex. You boys sort out what you are doing, for now I am going to grab forty winks." Jean said

Back at the rescue centre the kennels were barely cold when another animal would take its predecessors place. Donations now matched the outgoings of the centre, yet John still paid for all the running costs. The result being that bank account for the rescue centre was extremely heathy. There was no need for Jenny to take anything from it because John was still paying her wages and those of Billy. In fact all the staff wages came from John. Without fail the funds were transferred in on the first of each month.

Jenny did not seem to question the where or the why of all this money being diverted into an account, that bore her name. Billy though worried more and more as the centre, had become more about John's money than it did about Jenny's love for her animals. Still nothing at this point actually seemed to be illegal. That was until one day Billy had collected a group of cats from Myanmar, he had transported them back to the rescue centre and had handed the cats over to the kennel maids after which he took the transportation crates to the crate cleaning area.

The girls were all busy, with the new intake, so Billy had decided to clean the crates himself, before breaking them down and packing them for return to the Myanmar Rescue Centre. Where they would be reused for more cats bound for the UK.

Having first jet washed all the cages Billy was removing the clips from around the edges of the crates when he found a small stone that was stuck between two edges of the crate. Billy was initially going to just throw it away. On initial inspection It really did just look like a dirt bit of gravel or a broken piece of dirty brownish glass with bits of sand stuck in it. There was something about this 7mm sized stone the struck Billy as different. Absent-mindedly Billy put it into his shirt pocket and carried on with his sanitation of the crates, before bundling them together ready for John to collect for the return shipping.

The next morning Jenny was putting a load into the washing machine which included the shirt that Billy had been wearing the previous day. As she always did she checked in the pockets of his clothing, as previously he had left all sorts of items in his pockets, when he discarded his dirty laundry. So it was no surprise when she could feel something in the breast pocket of his shirt, she just assumed that it might be a nut or a bolt from something Billy had been working on. She emptied the stone out onto her palm and looked at it. It was shiny and dull at the same time and quite ordinary looking. However if Billy had put in his pocket, it would have been for a reason, although she could not fathom that reason. So she put it on the kitchen window sill and carried on with her daily duties. Jenny also forgot about the mystery stone.

Then one day Billy noticed the stone in the kitchen window. The sun had caught it in its rays and the stone seemed to breath a light, like the kind you see in the depth of glowing embers. Billy had been watching a television program the night before and it showed some small meteor particles some were smaller than the stone he owned and some were the size of tennis balls.

When cut and polished they looked quite nice. Many people used them as pendents and even for use in rings. Billy thought that would be a nice present for Jenny if he could get someone to mount it in a piece of jewellery. He had to go into Lincoln today to collect some feed for the animals. So once again he slipped it into his shirt pocket, and headed out the door.

Just after billy had left John arrived at the rescue centre. After saying good morning to Jenny, he went to see the Vet, who was down at the kennel block. Jenny was just about to go down with a pot of coffee for the kennel maid, when one of them appeared at the kitchen door.

"Jenny I think you have better come down to the kennels, there is a huge argument going on something to do with one of the cats that came in the other day. I am worried either the Vet will kill John, or he will kill the Vet. Jenny put the coffee pot down and ran to the kennel block. Even before she got there she heard the disputation, now it would seem there were three voices in the argument. There was a woman's voice almost screeching. That voice belonged to Fatima.

As jenny opened the door into the Vets surgery, John had Kareem pinned against on wall, while Fatima was doing her best to protect her husband by getting between the two men.

"What in the name of fuck is going on?" Jenny shouted as she entered the room. And then continued

"Not only are you terrorising the animals, you are scaring the hell out of my kennel maids. I could here you all, from almost my front door. Whatever this is all about, I cant see any reason for the violence that I can not only hear in your voices, but that you seem to be showing to each other." Jenny shouted at the threesome.

"John would you care to explain yourself?" She asked

John released his grip on Kareem and stepped back, allowing Fatima to now put her body in front of her husbands.

"I am so sorry. Jenny please accept my apologies. It was something and nothing that got a little bit out of hand." John said

"I don't give a toss what it was about." Jenny said closing the door that the kennel maids were gawking through from the open doorway and then she continued.

"This is still my home and my rescue centre and I don't care whatever beef you two may or may not have caused the pair of you, to kick off at one an other. So I would be grateful if any future altercations are carried out far away for my property."

"Like I said Jenny, Kareem and I did not agree on something and it just escalated, for which I am extremely both regretful and sorry, as I am sure Kareem and his wife are." John said

There was something in his voice that seemed to not ring true about that statement. Jenny looked at both John and Kareem, but decided to leave things as they were for now.

John made his excuses and then left.

"I don't suppose either of you would like to tell me what was going on there?" Jenny asked Kareem and Fatima. Neither of them answered and they both just looked at the floor. So Jenny went back into the kennels closing the door of the Vets office behind herself.

"What exactly did you hear? Of the argument?" Jenny asked the kennel main.

"I think john said something about one of the cats being short, well that is what it sounded like. Except that does not make any sense at all, I probably misheard. I think that Kareem said no, that they were all the right weight. Then Kareem and Fatima were shouting in Arabic. Like I said none of it made any meaning but I thought it best to come and get you to stop them from fighting." The young girl replied.

"You did the right thing in coming to get me. I am sorry I left the coffee up at the house get the other girls and come up and have your lunch with me OK?" Jenny said and walked back to the house.

Billy had parked up and was strolling through the centre of Lincoln looking for the small shop which his friend worked in. His was a proper jewellers, where they make real items from scratch. It was not one of the regular high street names that most people assume are jewellers. All those shops were are retail outlets for mass produced crap, and mostly overpriced crap at that.

A bell above the door binged as Billy entered, a young lady was behind a glass display case, in which there were a variety of necklaces. On one wall, there were several inglenook inset shelves. These had large stones, that had been cut in half to reveal coloured crystals inside. Billy knew only a little about them but he did recognise some smoky quartz along with amethyst.

"Can I help you sir?" The woman said looking up from a magazine she was reading

"Yes. Is Phillip in?

"He is just out to lunch but he should be back soon if you wish to wait? Or perhaps it is something I can help you with?" She asked

Billy reached into his pocket and pulled out the small stone and laid it on the glass topped counter. The woman picked it up and looked at it, then got a magnifying glass with a light built in and looked at it again.

"What is it?" Billy asked and continued before giving her a chance to answer the first questions.

"Is it a bit of a meteorite or just a bit of glass burned into sand?"

"I am sorry it is not something I recognise, but I don't think that it is anything from outer space."

"You don't? Why not?

"Well most of the stuff that falls down to earth come from space right? Which means that it comes down through the earths atmosphere right?"

Billy nodded his head but said nothing. The woman continued looking at the stone and talking at the same time.

"So entering our atmosphere causes friction that results in heat, a lot of heat as such, there tends to be a lot of carbon deposits from the burning and I don't see anything like that. So I would guess that this is more earthly than outer inner or outer space"

"Ohh" Billy said.

"As for burned glass in sand, again I am afraid not, again for similar reasons I can't see signs of burning."

"So just a rubbish stone then?" Billy asked

"I cant say, what I can said is I have never seen a stone like it, and I have been collecting odd examples for years. Phillip might be able to help, it might be worth something or it might just be a worthless piece of sea-glass. Perhaps someone brought it back from Cuba, that is where most sea-glass comes from. Its caused by antique bottles being broken up in the sea and then being washed on the sandy beaches again and again so you get a matt finish mixed with a shiny glass like finish sometimes with bits of sand stuck to it." She said and handed it back to Billy.

Around ten minutes later, Phillip returned to his shop.

"Well hello stranger, what brings you in from the backwaters to the metropolis that is Lincoln."

"I thought I would drop in and see an old fossil, who likes to play with other old fossils and such." Billy said reaching out for Phillip's hand.

"Fancy a catchup and a coffee." Phillip said

"Sure I might as well I came here hoping I had a bit of a meteorite that could be made into a ring or a pendent and it turns out that it might be sea-glass or something" Billy said following Phillip into the back of the shop.

There were polishing tables and along with diamond cutting discs and other tools. Nothing appeared to be laid out in any order and it was a wonder that Phillip could find anything in here. Phillip cleared a space using his arm as a brush and put two cups down before filling them from a hot jug of coffee.

Billy told Phillip how Jenny and he were now back together and that the rescue centre was now massive as well as making money for them. Anyway he had found this reddish coloured stone in the bottom of one of the crates and if it had been worth anything at all then he would have asked Phillip to make her a bespoke piece of jewellery out of it. At that point Phillip asked to see the stone. Billy took it out and placed it in his friends outstretched hand.

Like the girl had done before Phillip looked at it and then placed it on an electronic instrument and viewed the stone on a computer monitor, about a magnification of five times the actual size. Then he increased the magnification so that the stone now almost filled the computer monitor. Billy could now clearly see that it was not glass but what looked like bands of coloured crystal like structure that ranged between red purple and almost black. Phillip went and collected a book from the back of the shop and started to thumb through the pages, before finding the one he was looking for. Then cross referring it with the image on the computer screen.

"Where did you say you got this from Billy?"

"It was in the bottom of one of the import crates that I was cleaning."

"I don't suppose that came from Myanmar?"

"Now just how in the name of hell did you know that?"

"I think this little stone that you have here is something called Painite"

"Ohh so its not worthless then? So could you cut it and set it in a ring then?" Billy asked

"Well Yes I could, but let me just have a closer look at it to see how it would cut." Phillip said and started to take measurements with a micrometer and then he set it upon a set of scales before wrapping it in some tissue paper and putting into a small box, before placing it on top of the book he had been reading which was now on the untidy worktop.

"The uncut size of this Painite stone is just a little under two caret in weight. Cut and polished the size would be a tad over one caret."

"And what would that cost to have done, including a yellow gold setting?"

"Billy I think perhaps you should sit down."

"You are going to charge me for your labour after thirty years of friendship?" Billy asked

"No Billy for you my work is free you just pay for materials which will only work out at around £200."

"So why did you ask me to sit down like it was going to hurt?"

"Because Billy if I am right and I ninety nine point nine percent sure that I am. Painite with this colouration is worth around fifty to sixty thousand pounds a caret!" Phillip said and continued as Billy did as he had been bid and sat down on the swivel chair in front of the workbench.

"And you tell me this gem was just laying there in the bottom of a crate"

"Yes mate and I almost chucked it in the bin."

"It is probably one of the rarest gemstones in the world and so far it has only ever been found in Myanmar. All I can say is your wife is a lucky lady. I might and it is only a might at the moment, be able to make a matching pair of earrings with the left over piece from the main stone after cutting."

"Thanks Phillip, make what you can from it, Jenny has always appreciated your work. Give me a call when its ready please."

"Will do."

Billy walked back out of the shop like he was floating on air, in an almost dreamlike state he finished his business in Lincoln and drove home.

14
More Violence

Weeks later and Billy got the call from Phillip to say that he had completed the work that he had been doing for him using the Painite. So later that morning Billy made his excuses from work and headed over to pick up the dress ring and earrings which he had commissioned for Jenny.

When he got to the shop Phillip was standing behind the glass display case waiting.

"Come through to the workshop Billy." Phillip said.

Billy followed him into the rear workshop

"Mary can you take an early dinner break, and can you lock the shop door when you go out please? In fact if you could take the afternoon off, as I will be tied up for a bit. Thanks Mary"

The assistant was more than happy to have her lunch break early, she had wanted to do some clothes shopping anyway. Phillip watched her on the security monitor and waited until she had locked the door and left the shop.

"Normally I would not bother to enquire as to the history of a stone, but in this case I really must do. You see there are only two other jewellers who have ever had a Painite stone, good enough to equal and true brilliant cut facets in. Also as far as I am aware there is only one small part of the world. where this stuff even exists, that being Myanmar. You told me that this was in the bottom of one of the cat crates? How do you suppose it got there?" Phillip asked his friend.

"To be quite honest, I kind of thought that somehow a bit of gravel got lodged in the bottom of on of the crates when at some point it had been set down on the ground, then it got wedged between the side and one of the clips." Billy replied

"I am sure that you have heard about blood diamonds?"

"Sure Phillip they are diamonds from conflict zones where they are used to buy weapons and the like. Although I am not sure how to tell one from any other diamond."

"The reality of that Billy is that you cant, especially when it comes to a cut stone. The only way to be sure would be to ask for proof under the Kimberly Process. That is like a paper trail that follows a stone from a mine in its rough stage all the way from export to import. Then from the cutters to the jewellery makers and down to the retailers." Phillip said

"So are you saying that the stone that I found is like that? and that it should have had a certificate. How can that be if it was just on the ground and then got picked up on the bottom of a shipping container. I mean that stone was not used to buy guns or anything like that. It was just good fortune." Billy answered

"That may well be so Billy, however both the British and American governments have banned the import of Jade, Rubies and Painite from Burma and in particular Myanmar. Now whilst you and I know that this Painite came innocently from Myanmar, others do not and if you start letting people know what it is and where it came from there is going to be a whole lot of misery brought down on you." Phillip said

"So what do I do about it?"

"Well I have set the stones and if I were you I would call them Rubies or Garnet. From my personal protection I am going to say I set two small and one larger Garnet, if that is OK by you?"

"Well I am happy to say that. So mums the word I guess." Billy said and shook his friends hand.

On return to his home Billy got on with his duties, in a weeks time it would be his wife's birthday and he would give her the present then.

Jenny had kept quiet about the argument between John and Kareem as she did not want Billy going off half cocked and make matters worse between the Vet and John.

Billy was working on building a covered walkway around the entire Kennel and cattery blocks, this would make it easier for the prospective new owners to view the animals without having to actually enter the buildings. The Idea being that they would build a small outdoor cafe that would cater to their clients. It would also have a covered walkway to it, to encourage the prospective new owners to hang around a little longer and to be able to see all the animals. The would-be new owners were encouraged to take dogs to the recreation area and spend some time with the animal.

Billy had already built a similar area for the cats which had an eight foot brick wall, with glass windows built into it surrounding for the cats and hopefully new owners to see them. This too had a large play area for the cats and allowed possible owners to not only view the animals but to interact with each other. Jenny thought this extremely important for potential new owners and animals to have a chance to bond.

Billy was whitewashing the exterior walls of their house one day when two black Range Rovers pulled up in their car park. Not that it was unusual for folks to arrive in these large 4×4's but it was peculiar for two of these identical cars arrive together. The men that exited the cars did not look much like most of the families that came for cats or dogs. These were the type of men who came looking for people rather than puppies and kittens. They had an air about them, which said don't even think about fucking with me. One of the four men came to the reception and spoke to Jenny.

"Hi is John about?"

"And you are?" Jenny asked

"Just tell John that we are here to see him."

"Excuse me? This is my home and rescue centre so please do not come here and start barking orders at me." Jenny replied

One of the other men joined his friend at the reception desk.

"Trouble Charlie?" he asked his friend

"Not unless this daft bitch wants to make it." He replied and then continued talking this time to Jenny.

"Now be a good little girlie and run alone and get your boss, before I lose my patience with you."

The man's attitude was starting to frighten Jenny, which of course was his intention. So she picked up the telephone and called Johns home and waited for it to be answered. It was answered by the housemaid.

"Hello this is Jenny over at the rescue centre. Can I speak with John please." Jenny asked

"Just one moment please." then there was a long pause.

"Hello Jenny what can I do for you today?"

"John there are some men here looking for you." She said and then Jenny turned her back to the two men at the reception desk and lowered her voice.

"They are not very nice men John can you get over here fast please?"

"I will be right over Jenny. Don't worry I will sort this out." John said and the call ended.

Some ten minutes later John's own Range Rover pulled into the car park next to the two black ones. Then he came into reception. He spoke quietly to the two men and they left the reception area and walked to the far side of the car park. As soon as they did that, then Jenny ran to the side of the house that Billy was currently painting. She told him about the men and how they had called John her boss. Billy accompanied his wife back to the reception area. Just in time to see the two more men from the other car walk over to where John was talking to the men who were with John.

Their body language said everything that they could not hear. They were definitely pissed off at John for something. The voices were starting to be raised and other visitors to the rescue centre were staring to look towards where the argument was going on between john and the four men.

Parts of the conversation Billy heard

"By next week at the latest or else." One of the aggressive men said

"But it was not our fault, it must have been the Vet in Burma."

"Well I don't care if it happened on the fucking moon. I know I did not get what I fucking paid you for." The leader of the men said as he grabbed John by his Jacket lapels.

Billy had seen enough, he could not let the argument become physical. So he walked over to where John and the four men were standing.

"Gentlemen this is a family orientated centre, so if you could please lower your voices and stop swearing. There are young children around." Billy said to the group in general.

"Beat it before you regret it." One of the men said to Billy.

Billy was about to reply when John spoke.

"Sorry Billy these men should have come to my home to talk with me. If you men would be so kind as to follow me I will show you the way." John said.

Billy could see that whilst John was taking the argument away from the rescue centre, he was also afraid of these men. As they walked to the cars one of the men got in beside John in his car and the other three got into the cars they had come in. John drove out first and the others followed. Billy returned to where his wife was at the reception.

"Billy those men thought that John owned this place and they scared the hell out of me. Did you hear what they were talking about?"

"No not much of it just that I think he owes them something and something to do with Burma. I think he must have some business there. Something had gone wrong or was not right with what ever it was that these men had ordered. I am sure John will sort things with them. Don't worry Jenny I will talk to him and try and find out why these people thought he owned this place." Billy said to his wife and calming her down.

Three days later John came to the rescue centre and he looked like he had been run over by a herd of cattle. His lip was split and he had stitches above his right eye which was showing purple bruising around it. He had a bandage to one of his hands. It was obvious to Billy that John had received a beating at the hands of the thugs that had gone to his home. Still that was not really Billy's problem

"I am so sorry that you had to witness that argument." John said

"I don't think witnessing it bothered Jenny as much as they came here and effectively said that this was your place. They said you were the boss of Jenny and to be quite honest John if it happens again we will have to sever ties with you. I am not having thugs coming here and threatening my wife and the staff here. Jesus John, there were young families here at the time. You know we are happy to accept all the animals that you rescue. Whatever business you have with these men is just that, your business. So I would appreciate it, if you have any more visitors like them then if you could give them your address john and not ours."

I really am sorry Billy. It was a business deal that went sideways on me and unfortunately they were not the normal people that I work with, They did not fully understand the risk of investments. Sometimes stock goes down and sometimes it goes up. There are never any guarantees in stocks and shares. They bought into an investment in one of my companies in Burma and it went a bit south with some of my own stock. Unfortunately I allowed investors in who did not understand the risks involved. I personally lost money on this investment. I actually lost more than they did. And they used violence to attempt to to resolve the issue."

"OK. But make sure that anyone who you deal with realises that we are just a rescue centre for animals from around the world and that Jenny is the boss here, she only works for the animals and not for you, me or anyone else."

15
Moving On

Jenny's birthday bash was a fantastic day they had all gone over to Lincoln for a slap up meal and then to a concert at The Lincoln Lawns, before heading back home to Jenny's where they had quite a few drinks. Billy had called a taxi for Jack and Janet and they all said goodnight. After checking in on the kennels and cattery they headed up to bed.

Billy had covered the bed in petals and in the middle of heart shape that had been outlined in rose coloured petals there was a small leather heart shaped box. Jenny saw the bed and turned to hug her husband.

"What is in the box?"

"Well as you have lost all your super-girl powers including your x-ray vision, I guess the only way you will know is to open it." Billy said as he kissed his wife.

Jenny picked up the box and opened it.

"Ohhh my God Billy they are beautiful. Are they Rubies?" She asked knowing full well that Billy would never buy junk, she also recognised the craftsmanship of their life long friend Phillip Burrs. Jenny had attended some craft courses that he had led some years ago. Billy had actually gone to school with Phillip so they were proper old school friends. His silver and gold work was always Celtic in origin.

"You wish darling. They are Garnets from an old stone I found. I actually thought that you had chucked it out until I saw it on the kitchen windowsill." Billy said truthfully, well at least about finding it.

"I wondered where that had gone, I almost threw it away. What beautiful colours they shine like fire." Jenny said putting the ring on her right hand and the stud earrings in her ears.

"You like them?"

"I love them darling. I will never take the ring off, its so beautiful." She said dragging her husband to the bed.

"Make love to me all night long darling." she said and for the greater part they did.

The next morning billy had to drive to collect a Great Dane that was coming in from Russia via Heathrow Airport. All Billy knew was that, it was less that eighteen months old and that a Vet in Russia had saved the animal which was going to be destroyed due to a broken limb. The paperwork he had showed an X-ray of the dogs leg what had a metal plate holding the lower leg bone together and it had also a metal replacement for the shoulder joint. Looking at the X-Ray Billy was surprised that someone would do that much work to save the animal and yet not keep it. Still it would have a good home through Jenny's rescue centre.

Dog collected, Billy headed home, he was about ten miles from the airport when he noticed a black Range Rover behind his van, not that it was that unusual God knows that it appeared to be the most common colour for these things. It was most popular with the wealthy but also with drug dealers and the like. Basically they were the cool symbol of wealth.

Years ago it would have been a Rolls Royce. Now only old rich folk drove them they were out of vogue. Only when he pulled into a service station and stopped for a coffee and a burger, did it begin to bother him. The very same Range Rover was parked three rows down from where Billy was parked. The driver was sat at the wheel doing nothing else.

Billy finished his burger and left the service station. Perhaps it was just coincidence that the black 4 X 4 had pulled into the service station the same time as he had. Lets face it he thought about one in twenty cars on this road would probably pull in for fuel or food or both.

Billy drove down the motorway and there it was again sitting just three cars behind. Billy changed lanes so did the Range Rover. Billy changed back and the black car. Billy saw a police car and pulled alongside and the Range Rover dropped back out of sight. This made billy think that he had been imagining things. He never saw the Range Rover anywhere else on the way home. He would talk to Jenny later.

Back at Jack's, Tom had set up all his gear that included laptops for a variety of different uses including one, who's sole task was to record any and all messages. Those included voice, text and now even keystrokes from John Perkins computer as well as the two Vets and Natasha's devices.

Jean was using Toms Jeep Compass and was currently almost a mile behind John, who was making his way to a meeting in Manchester. All that was known about the individual that he was due to meet is that his first name was Grigoriy. So far they had no second name for the man. They had arranged to meet in a hotel on the outskirts of Manchester. They had a meeting arranged for 8pm in the restaurant of the Lowrey Hotel. One thing for sure Jean was not dressed for that swanky place.

John had called the guy up to say that he was about an hour away from Manchester, but that everything was now fixed the mistakes had been sorted and that he himself would make up for the previous shortfall. Tom had really wanted to be there as he would have been able to use a parabolic microphone or bug their rooms. Jack had told him not to worry there would be plenty of time for him to use his electronic toys.

As Jean was only dressed in denims and sweatshirt along with a pair of well worn trainers she could not follow John into his dinner meeting. Also as it was valet parking she had to park up further down the road without a clear line of sight to the hotels restaurant.

Jean parked the car and took a DSLR Camera with a telephoto lens fitted. She might not be able to hear the mysterious Grigoriy, but she would at least be able to get a picture of him as he was meeting Perkins. After grabbing his picture jean went back to her car. The Low-Jack system on Johns car would activate the tracking system when he got into his Range Rover. Jean decided to snooze in her car.

She was woken by a tapping on her window. There was a police officer standing next to her drivers door. Jean buzzed the window down.

"Yes officer is the there a problem?"

"Is there a reason for you sleeping at the side of the road?"

"Sorry officer I got tired driving so pulled over to grab forty winks, instead of driving dangerously while half asleep"

"May I ask where you are headed and where you have come from?"

"I was going from Swindon to Lincoln, but decided to pop into Manchester. Is that a problem?"

"Is this your car?"

"No it belongs to a good friend of mine and before you ask I am insured to drive it."

"Have you been drinking Mam"

No officer just coffee and driving."

"Can you come and sit in the back of my car while I check your details out."

"Officer is this really necessary, I have broken no laws." Jean said

"We have had reports of solicitation in this area so I am just checking, do you have any proof of Identity." He asked and just as he asked that, the ten inch tracker screen that belonged to Tom burst into life.

Jean had enough of this and reached into her pocket and pulled out her police ID in its leather folder. Just then John pulled out in front of her and like most folks when the see flashing blue lights and someone pulled over, they look. John noticed the car and the woman driving it.

"Son you had no reason to check me or the car out, I was doing nothing illegal. As far as soliciting goes did you see me attempt to even make a conversation to anyone else but you." She said handing over her warrant card.

"Please accept my apologies Mam. I did not know you were a police officer." The constable said

"Now I am not saying I was, but just suppose I was on an undercover operation. You do realise that because of you, it would have blown my cover."

"I am sorry Chief Inspector. I was not aware of that." He said and handed back her police ID." She buzzed her window up and looked at the red dot on her screen.

Johns car had not travelled far before it stopped again. He had stopped right next to a block of flats on one side and a City park on the other. What it did not show her was which of the two he had gone into. John had seen her white car with the police behind her, so her cover was effectively blown. She started up the car and headed back to her temporary home in Spalding.

The next morning Jean and Alex met up at Jack's and she passed over the little that she had learned along with the picture of Grigoriy. Tom took the picture and scanned it before doing a facial recognition search in the internet. They all sat and watched as thousands of faces flashed by at an incredible rate.

"So how many faces does this software recognise then Tom?" Jack asked

"Well there are around nine billion folks on the earth and around two thirds of them have at least one picture on the world wide web in some form or another. Police records, passports, driving licenses, social media accounts, even school pictures. So I guess about six billion." He replied

"And how many can the program scan in a minute?"

"So it takes 360 millisecond per picture but we can cut that in half by just selecting men and then again buy selecting white. Then select an age group of say thirty to fifty so we can reduce that down to around half a billion so if we scanned them all before we found him about eight days. But we can work that he his probably or Russian or Ukrainian given what we know so far ten one hour max."

Two minutes later the computer stopped and Grigoriy face was matched side by side to the photo that Jean had taken.

"Grigoriy Petrovich born in Kyiv, August 4th 1981, son of Fedor Petrovich Krasnov, occupation Personal Assistant to The Deputy Chairman of the Dumas Upper House. And that is all the information that it gives, no address, no background nothing just his name, date of birth and position." Tom said

"From what my friend Sergi told me real Russians look down on Cossacks, so how did he get so high up in the Dumas, also I am sure that was the same surname of the Oligarch that Natasha was married to, but there is no mention of a child in her background. So if this is the Oligarch's son? Then who is the mother?"

"We should warn Billy and Jenny."

Jean said to Jack,

"No not yet. This Perkins bloke is obviously mixed up in some crazy shit, first we have to make sure that there is no way that this can blow back on Billy and Jenny. So for now we gather more information." Jack said before continuing.

"Mark, where are we on getting some extra supplies from your friends in the US Embassy?"

"Still working in things there Jack. I have some toys from a friend who works for the CIA, those should be with us tomorrow."

"Do I want to know what you are getting from the embassy Jack?" Jean asked

"Probably not but Mark tells me that the stuff he is getting from the CIA, will help us keep better tabs on Perkins." Jack replied.

"Right I am out of here I will use your car if that is OK Jean." Alex said grabbing her car keys

"You know what they said Alex, what's mine is yours." Jean replied and blew her a kiss.

Billy arrived back at the rescue centre with the Great Dane, which had almost a full length cast on on one of its front legs along with a large dressing on top of the same shoulder. Billy took the dog straight into the Vet. Kareem said that he would take his own X-Rays before deciding on his treatment plan. This was probably the most damaged animal that the rescue centre had taken in so far. The vet said that once he had taken his own images of the damage to the dogs leg and shoulder, then it could go straight to its kennel. Kareem said he would then see the dog again tomorrow. So Billy waited while the X-ray was done and took the dog to its new temporary home.

16
Surgical Intervention

First thing the following morning, the Vet came into the reception area of the rescue centre, specifically to talk to Jenny. However she was on the telephone, checking on one of her cat placements. While he waited he looked to be reading through the medical notes on one of the animals.

"Yes Kareem, how can I help you?" Jenny asked him.

"Mrs Hamilton, the Great Dane that came in yesterday, which had been involved in a road traffic accident prior to being sent over here, he has some problems."

"OK?"

"The plate in his leg and artificial shoulder joint have been incorrectly installed and if I don't do something about that very soon, then I am afraid that he may soon develop a serious bone infection. It is not something that I can just treat with antibiotics. I am going to have to replace all the metal work. Getting the shoulder joint and making the leg plate is simple enough. The operation itself is not complex or difficult, although it is very time consuming and will require a large blood transfusion. I would like to operate today providing I can get the blood. It would be best if we could get some blood from a larger veterinary practice as they would have this in stock. I was wondering if you could contact your old vet, and ask him if he could supply some blood for transfusion?" Kareem asked

"Oh my, would it not be better to just take the dog down to him we have enough finances to pay for any operation." Jenny said

"Joint replacement is what I specialised in my surgery in Bahrain, so for me it is fairly routine. Also it would be better not to move the dog around too much." He answered

"OK I will call him and see what he has." Jenny said and picked up the telephone and dialled the number from memory.

"Boston North Vets." A woman's voice said

"Hello it's Jenny for The Marjorie Cat and Dog rescue Centre. Would it be possible to have a quick word with Alasdair please?" Jenny said

"Just one moment I will put you through."

There was a short delay and the Alasdair's thick Scottish accent, came on the phone.

"Hello Jenny and how are you and all your animals doing. I hear great things about your centre and the good health of your animals. So how can I help you. You have not lost another Vet have you?"

"Things are good Alasdair. Apart from my in house Vet Doctor Kareem Hussain has to do some surgery on the shoulder of a Great Dane and he tells me he will need some blood for the operation." Jenny said

"Yes I am sure he would they there is always a danger of nicking something, I would be happy to assist if he wishes?" Alasdair said and Jenny passed on what he had said to Kareem.

"No that will not be required as my wife has assisted me on many of these operations. Please just ask if he has four units of whole blood, DEA One Positive, that I can have. I can have it replaced in forty eight hours." Kareem said and Jenny passed that on to Alasdair, who said that he would send it up to her this morning. They said their goodbyes and the conversation was over.

"Its done Kareem, I will let you know when the blood gets here." Jenny said and Kareem went back to his surgery.

The blood arrived some thirty minutes later and Kareem asked one of the kennel maids to bring the dog back up to the surgery.

Some six hours later and along with three units of blood used, both the metal plate and the shoulder ball joint had been replaced. The dog was still under the influence of the anaesthetic so they kept the Great Dane in a cage at the Vets surgery. Fatima said she would stay with the dog all night long to ensure that there were no complications.

Jenny popped in to see the dog before going back to the house. The dog was sporting a new full leg cast and was sleeping soundly. While she was there she looked at the X-Ray that the vet had taken of his own work. They did look a little neater than the previous X-Rays.

The plate on the leg was smaller and thinner, and the Shoulder joint was now a ball and cup joint. On the side of the bench next to the stainless steel operating table were the previous bits of blood smeared metalwork. Jenny left saying goodnight Fatima.

"Hows the Great Dane doing?" Billy asked Jenny over the dinner table

"Kareem replaced all the metal work and from the X-Rays which I saw, it was a lot better looking than the previous Vets work. Fatima is looking after the dog tonight. Kareem said it might be a day or two before the dog is well enough to go back down to the kennels and around ten days before he will be able to walk properly on his own. Plus it would be another three weeks before he even thinks about taking the cast off, then a week or two before re-homing." Jenny said

"That all sounds good. By the way I promised Jack I would help him out tonight, so I hope you don't mind." Billy said

"Why would I mind Billy, he is your brother. Besides I have some paperwork to catch up on we have been so busy of late. You go and have a pint with Jack say hello to Janet for me."

After dinner was finished Billy drove his old VW Beetle to Jacks. Where several cars were parked outside his garage. Billy went to the house, then he knocked and entered, before walking into the kitchen. He had expected to see at least three or four people there. There was just Janet.

"Hi Janet, is Jack around or has he gone shooting rabbits with friends?" Billy asked thinking that was the reason for the extra cars parked outside, next to Jack's BMW.

"Yes jack is here, he is out in the garage with some old friends from his police days, don't ask me what they are up to, as Jack has not told me that yet."

"Do you think he would mind if I went over and interrupted him?"

"I don't think so Billy after all you are family, just promise you will pop back in here before you go."

"Of course I will, right I will go drag him out from under dads old car." Billy said and left the house before walking the short distance to the garage doors.

Billy entered via the small personal door set into the big double doors. As he entered he was surprised to see that two large monitors had been set up over Jack's workbench. Along with that there were numerous other technical looking items, actually on the bench along with several laptop computers. There was a tall man in a dark blue suit with blonde hair and an all over buzz cut, which from behind almost made him look military. There was a woman standing next to a man who was working on one laptop. The man on the other laptop, had his hair tied back in a ponytail. The woman turned around a spoke to Jack who was on the other side of the ponytail man.

"We have an identity on one of the people that Johnny boy has called in Pakistan. It is Noomyalay Faridun Mohammad. He is on the watchlist for Interpol along with the FBI. Added to this, I see we have a flag that says that the CIA are aware of this man and that he has links to one of the most powerful warlords in the Kandahar region of Afghanistan."

"So why would our man want to be involved with a warlord?" Jack asked, before seeing his brother standing behind the four of them, as all four pairs of eyes suddenly swung to Billy.

"Well Jack? Do you think there is something you want to tell me? I am guessing that all of this has to do with Perkins." Billy asked

"Ohhhh Ummm Hi Billy, so how long have you been standing there?" Jack asked

"Long enough to know that this has something to do with Perkins, and not in a good way, going on the last bit I overheard. So would like to enlighten me?" Billy replied.

"All right but before I do let me introduce you to these kind people, who are helping us look into the affairs of your mister John Perkins. That young lady over there, is retired Detective Sergeant Alex Gordon. The Young man with the computers and other electronics, is Tom Patterson he currently works as technical support for Swindon Police. Now we come to the tall man in the fancy cowboy boots along with a Brooks Brothers suit and the military haircut. That is Senior Agent Mark Carter of the FBI. We do have another member of our little team but she is currently working or perhaps sleeping. I am sure at some point you will run into her. She is Detective Chief Inspector Jean Short. Now each one of these fine people have at one time or another and in some, way saved my life. So the fist thing that you need to know is that we trust every thing they say and do. Got that?" Jack said

"OK that I get, but do we have an explanation for all that and whatever else is going on." Billy asked waving his hand towards all the highly technical equipment on and around, Jacks workbench.

"Billy you asked me to look into John and to find out why he spends so much money on your home and rescue centre?" Jack said before continuing.

"Well at first I thought that he was just what he described himself, that was until we dug just a little deeper." Jack said

"So all the stuff he does is illegal?" Billy said

"At the moment that would be kind of previous for us to make such a broad and sweeping statement, by the way Hi." Mark Carter said reaching his hand out. Billy shook the man's hand it was firm and honest. Billy noticed that he made full eye contact while shaking hands.

"Billy I believe that there is something very strange going on. At the moment though, we just don't have the evidence that will hold up in court. Now imagine if we get it wrong and Perkins is completely innocent. If we accuse him of something he has not done. Not only will it be the end of the careers of my friends here, we could be sued for every penny we have and that includes our home, my smallholding and of course your home, kennels and the cattery. So please do not even say anything to Jenny or to Janet, she thinks that I am helping Alex write her memoirs."

"Fine by me just can you keep me in the loop so I can protect Jenny and everything she has worked for." Billy said.

Over the next hour and a half Jack told billy all the stuff they had on Perkins. Which was not enough, everything on paper showed him to be an animal loving entrepreneur. Then came the question that Jack had been afraid to ask.

"Would you mind if we put a bug on your telephone and on the kennel as well as the vets?" Jack asked his brother

"I have no objection but for Christ's sake don't let Jenny know. As there is no way on this planet, that she would allow that. She still thinks the sun shines out of Perkins arse." Billy said and then went on and told about the arguments that had transpired over the last couple of weeks involving the Vet and the visitors.

He also told them about being followed by a black Range Rover. Jack made some notes and then offered Billy a beer from his fridge.

17
Mules for Cats & Dogs

The following day Kareem had packaged up the old metal plate and shoulder ball joint. After telling Jenny that it would sent to a Laboratory in London, to see why the metal had been the cause of the infection in the Great Dane, if in deed that was what was responsible for the infection. He gave her the package and told her the courier would be here to collect sometime this morning.

Jenny felt the weight of package and could feel the two bits of metal banging against each other in the box. Jenny had always thought that titanium was a relatively light material what was in this box was very heavy. They must have been big bits of metal. She put it on the reception desk for collection.

Billy was now making his own notes on any animals that they collected. He had not seen the black cars following him. So, he may have just imagined it.

Billy had allowed Jack's team to put bugs on the telephones and trackers on both the Vans along with their private cars.

"Just to be safe" Alex had said

The little bit which he had overheard, led Billy to believe that is the CIA were involved, then it was not a big stretch that drugs might be involved in some way. After all it was a well known fact that they had dirty hands in Columbia in the Contra fiasco, not to mention Air America. Is this what was happening again? Or was it the sale of drugs, to fund terrorism. The more Billy thought about it the more he realised that Jenny had inadvertently stumbled blindly into some serious shit.

"Alex put a sheet of printed paper, into Jacks hands. It gave the full rundown on Grigoriy who it looked like he was a suspect in his fathers murder. From the information on the sheet he read, it claimed that the young Petrov had been a son, made outside of his marriage, but as his father had imposed such serious restrictions on him after the son had come to the attention of the FSB due to his involvement in certain criminal activities. It was not only suspected that he had been involved in the murder of the Oligarch, but that somehow he had obtained his login and password details to his cryptocurrency.

Suspicion and proof though were not the same thing even for the FSB. The son was now one of the richest men in Russia and he still had ties with Putin. It is well known that Putin, made his money while working for the KGB, during the fall of communism as it was called in 1989. He had muscled his way into the oil and gas industry and literally made any opposition to his rule, disappear, never to be seen or heard of again.

The young Petrov had surrounded himself with ex KGB, FSB and ex Alpha Group soldiers, these ex soldiers were the equivalent to US Delta Force or the UK's SAS. In short he was pretty much untouchable. The FBI had him on their books for orchestrating murder and mayhem across the world.

On the face of things, Putin feared no man in Russia. Secretly though he would give Grigoriy Petrov a wide berth. Others though were saying quite the opposite. They claimed that he was just the tool of his puppet master Putin. He was bad news, not just to anyone but to absolutely everyone. Like Putin he had stolen by one means or another, his wealth and power. Like Putin he lived within the Kremlin.

At the bottom of the page there was a list of people, that John had spoken to in the last week. By using international numbers and the voice recognition match provided by Interpol. Petrov came back as the man that John Perkins had spoken to within the confines of the Kremlin.

"Right, that's it, Jenny and Billy have to cut ties immediately with John Perkins." Jack said

"Jack, we had a telephone call from someone who had previously been involved with Perkins in a similar way, he set them up as a fancy Kennels. When things started to go sideways, apart from all sorts of unprovable threats, John had a gagging order placed on him. That man is now in hiding, from the people who are the real money behind John. Which by the looks of things, that would be Petrov. And if Putin is afraid of this man, then we should tread extremely lightly and not do anything rash or half cocked. And if Put is the man behind him then rather than tread lightly we have to float around him. I say we try to take John out of the picture, without involving Billy or Jenny. Legally of course I am not talking about doing anything Putin style with John." Jack said

It was almost two weeks since Jean and Alex had come to Jacks with Tom and Mark. And not a lot out of the ordinary happened, until one day the two black Range Rovers pulled up at the Rescue Centre and four large men came into the reception.

"Can we see the Vet" One man said

The young kennel maid who was behind the desk asked them to wait while she went and fetched the Kareem, which she did. As soon as Kareem came through the doors he saw the men and ran back into his surgery and locked the door behind him. With that the men ran behind the counter despite the protestations of the you girl.

One man put his shoulder to the door which gave in easily under his weight. They ran into the surgery and then immediately back out.

"He has gone out the window" One of them shouted and then continued.

"He's round the back, you two go that way we'll take this side" He shouted going out the reception door.

They chased the Vet down to the tree line, where they caught up with him. One of them punched him in the face and Kareem slumped to the ground. Two men picked him up and dragged him back to their cars, before bundling him in and driving off. The whole thing took just a few minutes.

As soon as Jenny heard about what had gone on she immediately called Johns number.

"I told you what would happen if we had more trouble with your friends." Jenny said

"I am sorry Jenny I don't follow, what are you on about?" John replied

Jenny the set about telling him the events which had just transpired. John though, this time denied any knowledge whatsoever and said he would make some calls and get back to Jenny. She told him that he had just fifteen minutes to give her some answers or she would be calling the police.

Less than ten minutes later John's Range Rover pulled up at the front of the rescue centre. John got out and almost ran into the reception area. Jenny met him there equally flustered with Fatima by her side and the young kennel maid who was manning the front desk.

"Can we go into your office Jenny?"

"I suppose so." Jenny replied stepping aside to allow both John and Fatima into her office.

"Beth can you go and help the other girls out with their chores" Jenny said to the young girl.

The young girl left and walked down the passageway to the kennel block. When the girl had closed the hallway door behind her, Jenny entered her own office proper and shut the door before going to her chair behind her work desk.

"OK one of you had better tell me what the hell is going on here, or I swear I am calling the police." Jenny said

"Please Jenny, don't do that or they will kill Kareem." Fatima said.

"Who will kill him and why?"

"The men that took my husband, did so because they think he stole something that does not belong to him. I swear to you Mr Perkins, that Kareem has never stolen anything, ever. He had always done his work for Jenny and for you as he promised you he would." Fatima Said.

John had still said nothing. Jenny continued to ask them both questions.

"What is it that they think he has stolen?" Jenny asked Fatima while staring at John.

No answer came from either of them. Jenny reached for the telephone on her desk and started to dial the emergency number for the police. She had punched in two nine's and was just about to hit the third nine, when John held his hand up and shouted

"Stop, I will explain."

Jenny placed the telephone back down into its cradle.

18
Truth or Dare

"May I?" John said indicating to the seats that were in Jenny's office. The chairs were there for prospective new dog or cat owners.

"By all means, after all like everything here, you paid for it. Just remember though it is still my home and business. So what ever you have to say better be bloody good." Jenny said sarcastically

John and Fatima sat. Fatima looked at the floor and John wrung his hands like he did not know where to start.

"First off I need to tell you these men do not work for me. How should I say this in a way that not only you will understand but that you will see why we can not involve the police." John started to say

Jenny stopped him in his tracks by slamming her had down hard on her desk.

"I really don't give a shit who they work for John. They effective came into my home and kidnapped one of my staff members. And try hard to remember that I do actually have a degree in animal husbandry so I am not altogether stupid. If you like, you can even use big multi syllable words, without the fear of me misunderstanding." Jenny said with as much acid in the tone of her voice as she could master to match the words themselves.

"I am sorry Jenny I meant no disrespect, I just need you to understand that these are really bad men and if we involve the police they will kill Doctor Hussain. The men who took him work for a very dangerous man. He had something that was sent for the doctor to collect. However it never reached the doctor in the first place. That is the reason those men came here before and again today. They will only release your Vet when they either get what they were expecting or cash to its value. I already told them that I would give them the cash, but today they said they wanted both the cash and the missing item.

173

"What the hell are you talking about, what item. We only deal in cats and dogs." Jenny shouted at him

"Well that is not entirely true." John replied and then continued.

"The Burmese cat that came to us from Myanmar it was supposed to have a precious stone with it. But when Kareem checked it was not there. We think that the people in Myanmar stole it before it could be exported with the cat." John admitted

"What the hell are you talking about John? What precious stone?" Jenny said and unconsciously covered the dress ring as suspicion gradually swept over her.

"Are you really sure you want to know all the truth?" John asked. Jenny motioned for him to continue.

"The first thing you have to know is I am not the top dog in all of this. The cat was supposed to have a stone inside it when it left Myanmar and Kareem was supposed to retrieve it and then give it to me and I would give it to another man. The precious stone was worth over fifty thousand. So you can see why the men are upset." John said

"I don't give a shit about you trying to smuggle stuff through my rescue centre as far as I am concerned I am severing all ties with you John. So I don't want any animals from you and I don't want any more of your money." Jenny shouted at him

"Its not that simple Jenny you see everything is in your name, I never imported the animals they were all in your name. What do you think the police will see when they look at your bank account and then look at how much things have cost here. They will take it all away from you. Your home and the rescue centre. They may even come here and use force. I initially helped a man who had money problems. But it backfired on me. He is a very powerful and dangerous man, with massive resources. It was he, who arranged to have Mario murdered. All because a package ruptured inside the dog and it spoiled the shipment. Which was one hundred thousand dollars worth of LSD inside the dog in a container. That was just one animal. How many animals have you had through your doors since I came on the scene. That is right Jenny hundreds of animals and every single one of them was carrying a package of something valuable. Drugs, Jewels, Rare Metals or anything that was worth over ten grand an ounce. All the rescue centres around the world that we use are actually owned by you, at least on paper that is. When you signed some of the contracts like the one for the extra land, you were also signing for ownership of the other rescue centres. So I am afraid on paper it is you who are the Mr big in all of this. Even on paper I work for you. Kareem and Fatima work for you not me, there is a bank account with your name on and that is used for laundering funds into bitcoin."

"How do I know that you are not just telling me more lies.?"

"Why do you think you sent the plate and joint to a laboratory?" John asked

"It was Kareem that asked me to."

"But you employ him and the metal you packaged was Rhodium. Two kilograms of it at six hundred and fifty grand per kilo so that dog alone brought in one point three million. Now that was just one dog. The lowest value of any animal you have received has been the one that went missing. Most of the other animals carried between a hundred grand and three million dollars worth of merchandise. You are probably the worlds most prolific and richest smuggler in the world. See the account that was set up in your name to launder the money had so far washed about 10 billion. Remember you don't just own the Marjorie rescue centre you own centres in dozens of countries on all seven continents."

"Billy will kill you for this." Jenny said

"No he will not, because the people above me need this to continue. If Billy interferes with that, they will simply replace him and you. By replace that would mean a nasty accident would befall you or perhaps something like what happened to Mario."

There was a knock at the door and Jenny shouted. "No now!"

The door opened and Natasha entered.

"I take it you have told her the truth?" Natasha said.

"Good that will save me having to do it. Now I need you to go over to Manchester and fetch Kareem back. I have sorted the problem with Grigoriy. I am sorry that this happened Fatima. But we had to be sure it was not here that our package went missing." She said and John got up and left without another word.

"Are you his boss?" Jenny asked her

"Lets just say I am a boss, not your boss, but like you are the boss of the kennel maids. We need to move on past this Jenny. Fatima your husband is safe so could you give me some privacy with Jenny?" Natasha said.

Fatima stood up and wiped her eyes and left the room closing the door behind her.

"We are truly sorry for this Jenny, It was not meant to be this way. Things just sort of spiralled out of our control. The man behind all of this will always have clean hands because of the way that he operates. He owns none of the animal centres, or even the animals. He makes sure of that. All the money that he makes is sent as cryptocurrency and his finances never see a bank or even an accountant. He does not pay tax, like you do. So because you are the one of the final destinations of the animals, before they are cleared for new homes. The financial trail as well as the smuggling trail begins and ends with you. So take my advice do not make a big thing of this because it will only backfire on you. Let me tell you what you have illegally smuggled into this country. You have from Pakistan brought in the purest heroin. There is pure cocaine and crack cocaine from Columbia. From South Africa you have smuggled in Blood Diamonds along with The Rhodium from Russia, Painite from Myanmar, even though part of that shipment appears to have gone missing. Lots of rare earth metals from China and its associated regions. Tanzanite as the name would suggest from the Manyara region of Tanzania. Black Opals from Australia. Rubies from Burma and the list goes on and on. I am sure you will have guessed how these gemstones, rare metals and drugs are in some-way incorporated into the wounds of the animal from that specific location. Because you already have these smuggling routes assigned to you you cant stop this. If you wish to go to the police. Then that would be your choice but there is only one name they will find on the transit papers from being rescued into centres around the world to getting to you here in Boston. That name is yours. They will arrest you but then the real people behind this will extract their revenge. I can tell you honestly they will send people to kill everyone and everything you hold dear. They will burn it all down to the ground and then they will start up again somewhere else with someone who runs a small rescue operation. Also I cant help noticing that beautiful ring you are wearing Jenny, where did you get it?"

"What? Ohh my ring Billy had it made for me as a gift. It is just a Garnet and he had matching earrings made for me. They were made in Lincoln by a Jeweller friend."

"I hate to tell you that ring is not a Garnet" Natasha said, while holding Jenny's hand.

"Yes it is Billy found a pebble and had it made for me, he told me so."

"He may well have found the pebble and had a Jeweller make it for you. But it would be a very stupid Jeweller who could not tell the difference between a Garnet worth about £800 to £1,000 and a Facet Cut Painite that is worth £70,000 to £150,000. You are a lucky lady indeed. Our employer has already punished a man in Myanmar for the theft of this stone so you can enjoy wearing this very expensive set that you have." Natasha said and Jenny snatched her hand back covering the ring with her other hand.

Jenny sat there stunned, not so much about the ring, but more about the smuggling, how was she going to tell Billy..

"I have told you the complete truth about what you were doing albeit without your knowledge. I have also told you what will happen if you dare tell any authorities. The man who is the boss of all this if highly connected and uses bad people to help him keep control of everyone. You know they have beaten up my husband twice, not because anything that was his fault but in order to make sure that he keeps others in line. People like you. My husband is not like these men he does not use violence. So this is the truth. You need to talk to your husband to decide what to do next. I have told you the repercussions of going to the police. My advice is take the money that we are giving you to run your centre and say nothing to anyone. Give these poor animals a good life now.

19
The Truth
The Whole Truth
&
Nothing But The Truth

As soon as John and Natasha Perkins had left Jenny's rescue centre, she called Billy and left a message for him to come home as soon as he could. Almost two hours later Billy arrived with new animals for the kennels and Cattery. As all of the kennel maids had gone home, Billy logged them all in, next he settled them in their respective enclosures, before going up to the house.

Jenny immediately told her husband. all the details that John and Natasha Perkins had told her, leaving nothing out. When she had finished she threw the earrings and dress ring onto the kitchen table.

"You told me these were Garnets that you had from the stone you found. Did you know that they were made with Painite?"

"No not when I found the stone but later yes I did, but Phillip said I should say they were garnets because of their value and where they came from. I genuinely did not know they were part of a smuggled shipment. If I had I would never have asked Phillip to make them into jewellery for you." He replied before continuing

"I had my suspicions about John and I even shared them with you before now, which is why I have already asked Jack to look into John and Natasha Perkins. We should pass this information over to him and see what he suggests."

"What are we going to do Billy?" Jenny asked

"We do nothing at the moment. We just play along and let Jack and his friends look into this and see what they can do. Jack will never allow any harm to come to you or me, you know that." Billy said as he put his arms around his wife and held her close in a protective and loving embrace.

Billy told Jenny that it would be best if he spoke to his brother on his own but he asked his wife to write down as much of the conversation as she could remember. Billy took the sheets of paper and drove the short distance to his brothers home.

"You should read this Jack" Billy said handing over the pages.

Jack read them slowly one page at a time before laying them down on his dining table. Janet came in and offered Billy a cup of coffee.

"What's up with you Billy? Has Jenny kicked you out again?" Janet asked seeing Billy's serious looking face.

"What? Oh no nothing like that, things are all good on that score." Billy replied

"OK if you say so, just you looked a little upset." she said

"Oh right, No it is just work stuff getting me down is all." Billy replied.

"I think it would be better if you told Janet the truth Billy, she already knows something is up, because of my visitors." Jack said and then Billy recounted everything leaving nothing out.

Janet sat down at the table and held her husbands band.

"Do you want me to go and see Jenny while you work things out with Jack?" Janet asked

"If you don't mind Janet. That would be a weight off my mind, she needs a shoulder to cry on and I need to be here at the moment, tell her we will fix this."

Jenny picked up the keys to Jack's BMW and snagging her coat off a hook by the back door she left. Billy and Jack walked over to the garage, where Mark, Tom, and Alex were sat at the workbench. Billy started to recount what had gone on at the rescue centre, when Tom held his hand up to stop him.

"Ahhh Billy we already know I bugged Jenny's office and that of the Vet. We were just debating how to tell Jack, but I guess that is moot now." Tom said.

"It has filled in a lot of blanks for us as well" Mark Carter added.

"If I let Sergi know he might be able to help out a bit, with some more information. One of the things we should not do at the moment, is to let Interpol or the British authorities know. As they will go in and take the Perkins out and that would mean that those above Perkins would have to clean house and that would include Billy and Jenny." Alex said

"I don't think we can handle this on our own we need more than just the five of us" Mark said referring to Jack, Alex, Jean, Tom and himself. He continued

"I am sure that I can get myself assigned to the US embassy in London again, which would allow me to gain a couple of US marines and a little firepower." Mark said referring to the last time he had cause to work with Jack.

That had been on the serial killer case which had happened some years previous. On that occasion Mark had been able to carry a personal firearm. His choice had been a massive 50 cal Desert Eagle hand gun, which was closer to a canon that it was to a pistol.

"How would that work Mark would the US embassy allow you to simply borrow a couple of their marines?" Jack asked

"Well I could give them a bit of the story especially the titbits about someone close to Putin who might have placed himself in a position where he could be blackmailed, at least for now. Its always good to use someone like that. Obviously I would work anything like that out with you Alex." Mark said

"What I meant was, where are they gonna live while we sort this out?" Jack asked.

"Jack these are Frogmen. They will sleep standing up or under water if you ask them to. Basically they will sleep on the floor of your garage or in their cars. But they will be able to provide protection for Jenny and Billy. I think I can also persuade some of my colleagues from the FBI to sit in on this with us. Simply because it will give us a big in, to this form of smuggling. I am sure that they probably have their dirty hands on kennels in the USA as well as the UK and many other locations. When we break all this up, as we will jack, we will have to close all the locations down at the same time. That is when we will send our files, to Interpol and others. But for now I would say Billy's best and safest bet, is for them to play along as if they are still in the dark and not to openly ask too many questions." Mark said and even with his slow southern drawl it was said in a hurried manner.

"What do you think Alex?" Jack asked

"I think that I will be OK, but Jean will have to return to her Job with Swindon police unless she can work something out with the UK serious Crime units, or perhaps with the anti-terror unit. I will talk to her when she gets back here." Alex replied

"Tom, we are gonna need you as well." Jack said

"Well I was supposed to retire in three months anyway, I am sure I can ask my boss to allow me to do it early without loss of my pension." Tom said

"Who's your boss Tom." Jack asked thinking he could pull some strings.

"Ahh That would be Jean, so I cant see any problems there, apart from the fact that I have twenty grands worth of their high tech gear." Tom replied

"Not a problem I can get all that out of date stuff replaced immediately with newer and better stuff." Mark said with a wink to Tom.

"Right, Billy get back down to your wife and we will fix this. You have my word on that." Jack said to his brother.

Billy drove the short distance back home and assured his wife that Jack and his friends had a handle on the situation. Whilst Jenny believed him she was still worried. She could not shift that worry. Jenny had seen Natasha in a completely different light.

The following morning the Vet was returned to the rescue centre, he was somewhat bruised but other than that, his injuries did not appear to be too serious. Fatima held on to him, in a fashion that showed just how afraid she had been, that she might never see him again.

Jenny called them both into her office, in the full knowledge that her office was bugged. She told Kareem that she knew everything about what was going on and after what had happened to their previous Vet, she advised that they all continue to play along and not do anything stupid or rash.

Knowing now that John and Natasha were not the top dogs in any of this, rather they were just slightly bigger cogs in the same operation as the Marjorie Rescue Centre was.

Even if John had not told Jenny that, she would soon have guessed. Especially after the two beatings John had suffered at the hands of those men who came in the Black Range Rovers. They too, were probably not at the top of the food chain either. It was like some kind of pyramid scam. Apart from those who actually gave a home to the rescued animals, everyone else were part of the smuggling crimes.

Jenny was a completely innocent animal rescuer, who had been caught up in the operation. But her financial records for the centre and her own personal account which was now incredibly healthy as well as the value of her property, would make her look as guilty as any of the others in this scheme.

Jenny had her doubts months ago and Billy had warned her there was something wrong with all the money that John Perkins had thrown at Jenny's rescue centre. Jenny though had ignored all her own concerns and found a way to discount Billy as him being jealous or some other excuse.

There was still something that bothered Jenny, had John and Natasha told them the truth, or was it just their version of the truth.

20
Putin's Friend

When Jean arrived back at Jack's garage that evening, Alex filled her in on the situation. Jean had felt that it was better for her to return to duty as the Detective Chief Inspector that she was. She said that Tom should stay on as Technical Assistant to Jack and she would square the circle on that, in this way Tom would not lose any of his pension and he could retain hold of the equipment until the stuff from the FBI arrived.

As Alex was a free agent she could do as she wished, but Jean gave her blessing nonetheless. Mark said he would have to go to the Embassy in London but that he would return in a couple of days. His advice before leaving was that Jack should keep the circle of those who knew the truth, a small one. The more people who were involved in the investigation, then the greater the propensity for things to go belly-up. So it was agreed that until Mark returned, then Jack's team would do nothing but monitor the situation and keep records that could be used when the time came to dismantle this criminal organisation and pass it over to the UK's Organised Crime Unit, along with the FBI, Interpol and the FSB.

Over the next few days, Jack spent much of his time down at his sister-in-law's rescue centre. Just to make sure no one came looking for Jenny or Billy in the way they had for Kareem.

The Ring and Earrings that Billy had given to Jenny, Jack had suggested that they keep at his home as Billy had genuinely found the stone, even though it had been sent illegally from Burma, the criminal organisation had given the stone, up as lost or stolen before it reached the UK. So Jenny gave it to Jack for safe keeping. Jenny forgave Billy for not telling her the real value of the stone, after all he had taken it to Phillip thinking that it was worth perhaps a few hundred pounds at best.

Three days later from the big reveal, Mark arrived back with four rather scruffy looking men, who he explained, were in fact Frogmen of the US Military elite and they rarely looked like servicemen, unless there was a requirement to do so.

Their long hair and beards made them look like local farm workers, so there was less chance of anyone taking notice of them while they were here.

What they were here for, was protection, if and when required. Each man had a large holdall with them. Jack was betting that those bags contained the tools of their trade and that did not mean spades and shovels.

These men put their bags down and then left the garage returning a few moments later with large plastic flight cases which they stacked next to the workbench.

"Some new toys for you Tom" Mark said then he walked over to Jack and the two men left the garage for a more private chat.

"I have spoken to some people at the FBI's Organised Crime Unit. They have been aware of something like this happening in several US states, but that they only know of a few occasions where animals have been stopped by the US Border Control. The American authorities have agreed not to make any arrests or to stop any animals that they discover with one contraband or another, until we have enough information to take this all down from the top. Like your brother Billy and his wife, all the actual re-homing part of this operation, the other centres, appear to be innocent stooges in all this. Because every part of this is compartmentalised then if one rescue centre is discovered to be running some contraband or other, then there is no blowback to those above them. Because it just becomes a case of he says she says but without proof only those at the bottom get burned. The FBI have said in the past. where they have already raided kennels in the USA that were operating as Jenny's. When caught and awaiting their court date, then witnesses have an uncanny habit of disappearing or taking the entire blame themselves. Thus the chain is broken and they just start up somewhere else. In 1980 around 2,000 animals were imported to rescue centres in the UK, by 1990 that had only risen to around 3,000 now by 2020 that had soared to around 300,000 dogs and almost 600,000 cats. Most of these animals come from Eastern Europe and from North America although there has been a significant rise in animals being imported from the Middle East and South America. So we now know that there are in the region of 2,000,000 animals a year imported via rescue centres. Jack, Its not just cats and dogs, there are zoo animals, pigmy pigs, sheep, goats, lama's and now even horses. This is the new growth industry for criminals. Because it involves many countries that Interpol have no jurisdiction in, they are pretty much free to operate. What I have also been able to find out is that some of these animals, are first sent or one country, presumably with one contraband or another and then they are shipped on with something else sewn into them. It is a bit like a criminals spiders web. So in order to shut it down we must first find exactly who is at the top of things and then put in place a method of taking all these places down at the same time." Mark said

"Surely that will be an impossible task, I mean if these countries have immunity from Interpol, just because they have not signed some deal or other then how do you close them down?" Jack asked.

"Well that is my other bit of good news for you. It is only because the USA has around one hundred rescue kennels like your sister-in-laws, that the CIA has a bit of a reason to join in this fight. I don't know if you know this or not Jack, but the CIA are not allowed to operate within the confines of the USA, they can only be used on foreign soil. As such when the time comes, we will use them to help us shut it all down. However whilst we do have some contacts within the Russian FSB, I feel it would be a mistake to use them at least for now. It is well known that Putin keeps tabs on all those who surround him. Putin is probably more paranoid than Kim Jong-un. So we will use our own people, to try and follow this to the top man or woman. Having spoken to some of my sources in the CIA, they doubt that those at the top will go down without a fight. Which again is the reason we have to go after the top and work our way down to the Perkins of this organisation. What I personally have to do, is get all the various policing organisations around the world, to act as a singular police force without telling who and where, until we are ready to complete the orchestrated raids. That though, will be my problem. Having spoken to the my own boss and to the head of the CIA, It will be my job to coordinate everything, which is why I have brought Tom, some new toys. He will be able to have access to the FBI's central computer and through that, he will also have access to most police systems throughout the world, including Interpol. Jack if you could keep watch over the Jenny's Rescue Centre as well as the Perkins, as at this moment in time we are unsure, just how deeply the Perkins are involved, or how high up or down the tree of iniquity they are."

Over the coming days there did not seem to be any change in the way things were happening, then one day a large van pulled into the rescue centre. The van bore plates that claimed to be from Poland, along with an EU sticker on the back. The driver jumped down from hi cab and walked into the reception area, where Jenny was sat behind the desk working on some paperwork, for prospective adoptions.

"Hello can I help you?" She asked

The man tall, but not skinny. He placed a clipboard on the counter, Jenny picked it up and had a quick look, it appeared to be written in some Slavic or Cyrillic language, so it meant nothing to her.

"I am sorry, what is this?" Jenny asked

"You sign." The driver said in a heavily accented voice.

"I don't think so. Not until I know what I am signing for." Jenny replied and handed back the clipboard.

"You sign I give and I go Yes" He repeated

Jenny came out from behind her desk and took the clipboard with her, complete with its pen that had been taped to a length of string, making sure that the pen was always attached to the clipboard. She walked out to the van, which turned out to be a large Horse Box van capable of holding at least 6 horses. Jenny put her hand on the side panel and could feel the weight of horses shifting the position of their hooves.

"Horses?" She asked the man

"Da loshadi Da"

"Loshadi?"

"Da loshadi is Horse Da."

The conversation was becoming hard work so Jenny decided to take it to simple levels.

"You Polish?" She said pointing to the driver

"Net, Russkiy"

"OK so you are Russian?" Jenny lead the conversation

"Da"

"Russian Loshadi?"

"Net Rumynskiy"

That just took a blank stare from Jenny, the man took out a smart phone and spoke into it and the metallic voice on the telephone said

"Romania"

"OK So you Russian. Horses Romanian?"

"Da Da"

"OK But here is dog and cat"

Another blank look

Jenny Pointed to the kennel block

"Woof woof, me eow me eow" Jenny said imitating the sounds of cats and dogs.

"Net loshadi, net loshadi"

The driver scratched his head and then went to his cab coming back with a slip of paper. He passed it over to Jenny. There was one word written on it 'Hatawa' Jenny look and shrugged her shoulders before giving it back

"Natasha" the man said

"Oh OK you want Natasha Perkins?"

"Da Perkins dacha"

Jenny had heard the word Dacha before and knew that it meant a house in the country or second home of rich Eastern Europeans

"OK Perkins not here." as the conversation was going nowhere fast Jenny decided to call the Perkins home. First the housekeeper answered and then she was put through to Natasha.

"Hello Jenny. How can I help?"

"There is a Russian here with a van load of horses, which are either from Romania or Russia and I think they are meant for you."

"Yes can you send him down here?"

"I could If I spoke Russian, would you like to talk to the driver?"

"No that's OK Jenny. I think it would probably be best If I popped over and then had him follow me back to the farm. Tell him to stay put."

"You tell him, I don't speak Russian." Jenny said passing the telephone over to the driver and not giving Natasha any chance to refuse.

"Da?" The driver said then there was a short conversation in what Jenny presumed was a Russian before the driver passed the phone back to Jenny, by which time Natasha had disconnected the call.

"Please wait here." Jenny said, while miming, waiting.

"Da I zhdat'."

"Whatever" Jenny said with a smile

About ten minutes later Natasha arrived in her husbands white Range Rover along with Alexi who was their Chef also their Butler, Driver and Bodyguard to Natasha, when her husband was not around.

Natasha got out of the car and first she said hello to Jenny before walking over to where the driver was leaning against the side of his van smoking a foul smelling hand rolled cigarette. There was a quick conversation, which Jenny presumed was in Russian. Then Natasha called Alexi over and whispered something into his ear. Alexi got in the drivers side of the big van, before the original driver got in the other side. Natasha said that she was sorry that the van had gone to the kennels when it should have gone straight to the farm.

"It is a Romanian stallion that I have bought for stud" Natasha had said.

Before getting back in her husbands car and driving off behind the van, now being driven by Alexi.

Billy had a tendency now, to leave most of the collections and deliveries, to Mike, the new driver handyman. This then allowed him the time, to keep an eye on other things at home. It also allowed him the chance to go over to his brothers and get updates on everything else. That is where he was today.

"Billy how do you feel about having a couple of new hands on deck at the kennels?" Mark had asked in his usual slow southern style

"Not quite sure on how that would go down with Jenny really, especially if you are referring to having a couple of your fellow Americans, who look like extras from 'The Hurt Locker' or 'The Green Zone'" Billy said pointing to the group of four bearded men who were busy playing some card game.

"Billy the more I learn about these people, the more I worry about you and your wife's connection with them. You saw what they did to the Vet and also to John, Those people, were much higher in the smuggling operation, than either you or Jenny. Do you really think, that they would not use force to ensure that you keep the supply chain moving. I am sure that because it is such a busy kennel and cattery, that there must be more ground-work, as well as helping out with other jobs. Have a word with Jenny, but my honest advice, to which I am sure Jack will back me up on, these are not the sort of people who will think twice about hurting you, or worse." Mark said.

Billy looked to his brother, like he was waiting for permission to say yes, which is exactly what he was looking for.

"You want my advice Billy, convince Jenny. Because as all of this comes to a head, as it will sometime in the not to distant future. Then on top of that, there is a danger of things turning at the least unpleasant and at the worst downright bloody dangerous." Jack said.

One of the men who had appeared to be taking no notice of the conversation, as he was playing cards with his compatriots suddenly stood up and spoke.

"Hi friend, trust me we are real good at being what people think we are when we are not. I can be a toilet cleaner or a dog walker or even a gardener to the outward eye. Any one of the four of us can do that. But inside we are battle hardened soldiers. Each of us has completed at least eight tours in Afghanistan. Some of us have even worked in places like a North Korean Death Camps. The point being we are very good at blending in without getting caught. We have skills that not only keep us alive but also those who we have been assigned to protect. All four of us have done close protection work, in the most dangerous places, that this planet has to offer and we are still here as are those we protected. My advice to you, is take the offer. But Sir, it is your choice." The man said and then sat back down and continued to play cards.

Tom had been listening in, on what had been going on back at the rescue centre. He had also been watching it fortunately out of Billy's line of vision. Jack though had been watching. As Alex slipped on a pair of headphones.

Jack wanted to tell his brother everything that was going on with the investigation but felt Billy and Jenny would be that little bit safer, for being a little less informed.

"Billy my honest advice is find at least two of these men some work at the centre." Jack said

"OK I will see what I can do, but Jenny is the boss of the rescue centre and what she says goes." Billy said and then left his brother to do what ever detective work he had to do.

When Billy had left, Tom took off his headphones and turned around on his computer chair.

"There was a Russian down at the rescue centre just now, he said he was looking for the Perkins place, but he only spoke in Russian. I did a full facial recognition check on this guy. He is indeed Russian. But he is bringing up flags all over the place. His passport that he used to enter the UK yesterday says his name is Leonid Ivanov, yet his name on the FBI database is Calin Volkov. The CIA have him listed just as Fedorov. But the most interesting thing is a photograph taken by the TASS Russian state sponsored news agency, which shows the same man as a personal aide to Vladimir Putin. Now that is pretty fucking high up the monkey puzzle tree if you ask me. So what would he be doing over here.

21
When Is A Horse Not A Horse?

When Billy arrived back home and Jenny had told him about the big Russian, that had come there with a horse. Billy had explained his worry about the mess they had found themselves in. Then he told her about the friends that Jack had that would look out for them to ensure they came to no harm. Jenny agreed to meet with them to talk it over, that was as much as she would agree too without actually meeting everyone.

Billy called his brother and arranged for Jenny and himself to come over and meet with Jacks team and also to find out what they knew about the Perkins.

Billy and Jenny ate their dinner in almost complete silence. Jenny tended to become introverted in times of stress and Billy like a lot of other men was never sure how to talk to a woman when they were like that, as it always seemed to end up in an argument. After dinner they drove to to Jacks.

First going into the house and talking with Janet and Jack, Jenny found out that Jack had explained everything to his wife and would also do so, to Jenny and Billy when they would meet with the rest of the team who were in Jack's garage.

"Lets first get the introductions done. This tall refined gentleman is Mark Carter of the USA's Federal Bureau Of Investigation. The young lady sat at the workbench id Alex Gordon she is ex detective with Swindon Police Force. The long haired git at the bench is our resident geek Tom Patterson. He is basically our invisible eyes and ears on things. The four gentlemen on the floor are Brian, Buddy, Zack and Orville. They don't have any other names and I am not even sure if those are their real names. What I do know is, that they are the absolute best in close protection and undercover operatives." Jack said and each said Hi as Jack introduced them.

"It is truly a pleasure for me to finally make your acquaintance mam. I have heard so much about you from Jack. Besides any woman who loves cats is top floor in my books, better than a chilli dog at the super bowl." Mark said

"Pay him no heed Jenny, he is slick as Mr Sheen furniture polish and he is full to the top with flattery. But Mark has connections like you would not believe, he also was the other man who stopped the Swindon serial killer. Not to mention he also saved my life. He is a modest American, though you might find that a hard thing to believe, that in itself should tell you all you need to know. I am the one who connect the dots on the stuff, the rest of them find out." Alex said

"We are here for you in any way, you would like us to help. Mark is modest we are not. If I promise to protect you then that is what I do, as do my collogues. My honest advice Mam is let at least two of us work at your centre, I know your husband and his family would sleep better for it as I am sure would Jack and the rest of his team." Zack said

"Wow I am in awe gentlemen, I really don't know what to say. I did not know that there were so many people looking after Billy and myself. Billy said the Jack had friends working on it behind the scenes but he did not tell me much more than that. I don't know if I should be more or less scared." Jenny said

"More scared is always better then less scared Mam. Fear keeps you on your toes and stops slip-ups. Learn to talk slower mam, it gives you more thinking time when others are talking to you, again it will help you not to give the game away. That not only protects you but those around you too." Zack replied

"Do you want me to bring her up to speed Jack?" Tom said

"Well surely that is a question you should be asking me?" Jenny said

Tom looked at Jack who looked at Billy, then back to Jenny.

"OK but I will make a deal with you."

"What is that?"

"I tell you what we know all the way, but only if you accept Zack's offer." Tom said

Jenny agreed and over the next two hours Jenny sat back as a combination of Jack, Alex, Mark and Tom laid out what they knew and what they suspected. Nothing was left out including just how dangerous the situation could become.

At the end of it Jenny agreed to have two of the 'Frogmen' to work at the kennels as kennel hands and general gardeners to keep the grounds looking good they would both stay in the old residential caravan at the rear of Billy and Jenny's house. As an extra part of their cover Jenny would even tell John and Natasha that she had taken them on and then she was sure that the Perkins would probably pay their wages.

The final part of bringing things up to date was, what had happened earlier that day with the Horse box and the Russian Driver. Tom called Jenny over to look at a computer screen which showed the back of the Perkins home. The video showed the white Range Rover arriving and then the van with the Russian and Alexi.

The Russian went to the rear of the van and dropped the tailboard before opening the double doors and entering the van. He came back out with a horse on a bridal and tether then led it to the stables, before returning to where Natasha and Alexi were standing

Natasha held the clipboard and pen that Jenny had held previously some hours earlier. Then Russian then entered the Van and came out with another horse and he repeated the process another four times until six horses were stabled. All of the horses seemed to have one injury or another, just like Jenny's cats and dog did.

"Natasha said it was just one horse, not six. I knew from the feel of the van when I placed my hand on the side, that there was more than one beast in there." Jenny said

"Remember one thing Jenny?" Tom said

"What is that?"

"You are not aware of any of this, as far as you are concerned there was just one horse delivered to Natasha today." Tom replied

"Tom do you have my place bugged and under surveillance?"

"Yes but not for the same reason as we do for the Perkins. We have John and Natasha under our eyes and ears to collect evidence. We have Billy and you under surveillance, in order to protect you." Tom said

"And we will" Zack said and added

"So which of us, would you like to be your dog boys?"

Jenny chose Zack and Buddy and then she and Billy left in his VW Beetle.

The following morning as advised by Jack, Jenny placed an advert in the local paper and on their website for "Two Gardener's and General Labourers" required for large Kennels and Grounds. She did this on order to create a bit of a back story to have the two

'Frogmen' in situ at the centre. For most of the day the telephone rang constantly and emails flooded in, some were from individuals others from agencies and some were even from landscaping firms offering their services.

Jenny and Billy held genuine interviews, again this was something that Jack had told them to do to bring an air of believability to things. Obviously they chose Zack and Buddy. All the documentation had been supplied by Mark and it showed them to be a pair of brothers who had been working their way around Europe for the last few years. Their passports showed that before last year they had worked in France, in a few vineyards. Since arriving in the UK they had both worked on a petting farm in Nottingham, which had recently closed due to Covid-19, followed by a downturn in the economy. The nail in the coffin for the petting zoo was an outbreak of Bird-flu. So they had seen the advert and Billy and Jenny had give the jobs to the two men, with their excellent references.

Later that day Zack and Buddy arrived in a beat up old pickup truck that was almost as much paint as there was rust. That said the engine sounded healthy. They parked it next to the caravan and then put all their bags into the mobile home. Even later that day Zack and Buddy went around the property secreting weapons away in places where no one else would see or even think of looking.

That night and out of sight of everyone except Jenny and Billy the two Americans taught some basic life saving skills to their hosts. Moves like how to break someone's hold from around your throat, and how to parry a knife attack. These lessons would continue every night for the next few weeks. Billy already knew how to use a rifle and a shotgun. So Jenny was taught the basics, even though Zack said that if him and Buddy did their job correctly then there would never be any requirement of Billy and Jenny to use their newfound skills.

A few days after Zack and Buddy moved in there was another delivery of horses to the wrong address again. It was a different driver from the previous delivery from Romania. That said it was pretty much the same sort of thing, with the exception that this time John came over with Alexi to guide the driver of the horsebox down to his farm.

"I looked at the paperwork that the driver gave you" Zack said

"And?" Jenny asked

"Well apart from the fact that it was written in Russian. The address was to your Rescue Centre, and not to the farm. Yet the driver asked for the Perkins farm."

"Probably just a mistake?" Jenny replied in a half hearted fashion.

"Or that the paper trail leads directly to you and not to the Perkins. Lets face it those import documents had your name and address on and not Natasha's or Johns." Zack said

"What would be the point of that?" Jenny asked

"Well apart from from the obvious, like who would get the blame when things go belly up. It could also be that they are getting ready to skip and burn the trail." Buddy said

"I think what Buddy is saying is that they might be laying the groundwork to clean house."

"I thought that this worked as a pyramid type thing, that the only way to close everything down was from the top."

"That is true, but perhaps someone at or near the top is giving out warnings of some kind."

Buddy said

"But you said when they burn things down people like those at the bottom disappear." Jenny said worriedly.

"Yes that would normally be the case, but normally those at the bottom don't have a pair of US Frogmen to look after them" Buddy said and then he and Zack high five'd each other, adding.

"Oorah!"

Tom had been looking at the cameras placed at the Perkins farm and noticed the new arrivals of the injured horses, which was not dissimilar to the previous delivery. Then he noticed something odd and decided to scroll back on the video recordings of the Perkins farm.

"Jack what do you make of this?" Tom said

"What you got Tom."

"Actually very little, just something a little bit odd. You know a few weeks ago when the first delivery of horses. We thought that the driver had parked up for the night in the stables and then driven off the next day?"

"Yes and?"

"Well what do you make of that?" Tom said pointing to the screen

"Its the Horse box. That was parked up and then left the next day."

"Yes. Now look at this." Tom said as he scrolled through the previous recordings to the view from just now.

"Another horsebox?"

"Yes Jack but look at the building behind at the edge of the door does that look like the edge of the previous Van?" Tom said

"Can you zoom in on it" Jack said

Tom zoomed

"So when did it arrive back?" Jack asked

"I am not sure it ever left. Is there a back way into the stables?"

"I don't know Tom but we need to get some cameras inside there rather than looking from the woods. Can you not fly a drone over the top" Jack asked

"I could but they might see it, it would be better to be inside as we could get clean audio. Parabolic microphones are OK but they pick up a lot of other background noises. Can we get Brian or Orville to go in and place some stuff, also to have a good snoop around the place."

"Lets ask them." Jack said and walked over to where the two frogmen were sleeping on camp-beds.

He was just about to wake Brian to ask

"Sure we can go tonight, what do you want and where do you want it?"

Tom and Jack explained what was required.

"If it is the same sort of thing as last time there should be a dozen or so horses down there and you know what Jack?"

"What?"

"Apart from when they arrive, I have not seen a single horse walking in the yard or in the fields next to the Perkins home. So they must be keeping them stabled? Why would they do that?" Tom said

"Makes them easier to catch?" Orville said and continued.

"For when they have people come to see them for re-homing like at Jenny's place"

"But I thought the Perkins were running some kind of stud farm?" Brian said

"We only have Natasha's word on that." Jack said.

Later that night Jack dropped the pair of blacked up frogmen off near a wooded area to the south of the Perkins farm. Then said he would see the two men later or if they needed picking up for them to call.

Around four hours after being dropped off Jacks telephone buzzed.

"Pick up from the Dee Zee." then the line went dead

"Mark what the hell is a Deezee."

"Hell Jack that a simple one it's a Drop Zone."

"Ohh Right. I best go then." Jack said and drove off to collect the two Americans.

Jack pulled off the road at the point where he had previously left the frogmen. And waited. Jack waited for half an hour and was just about to return home, when his telephone rang.

"Do us a favour mate kill the internal lights of you car. And we will be with you in a minute."

Jack reached over to the rear of the car and remover the lightbulb above both passenger doors and then did the same in the front placing all four bulbs in the small try next to the gear stick. As if out of nowhere both the back doors opened and then closed.

"Take us home Jack." one of them said.

Once back in the garage the men removed their night watch caps and backpacks, which had been used to carry the surveillance equipment.

"The Perkins farm is like Fort Knox man." Orville said

"How so?" Jack asked

"He has trip wires in the woods, cameras along with motion sensors. We had to walk all the way around until we were almost at Jenny's place then we went in from the bottom field. I guess they expect to have trouble come at them from the front. We got in the back of the stables. Here is the really fucking weird thing. No horses."

"What do you mean No horses, I saw them take delivery of six animals today." Tom said

"I said there were no Horses but there was a huge walk-in freezer. I took a peek in there and there was a shitload of vacuum packed butchered meat, that I can only presume was Horse-meat. There was all sorts of equipment in the Stables. It mostly looked like butchery equipment. Then there was a large safe. But it was a relatively old one, so was simple to look inside and it was full of these." Orville said, whilst removing an object from his pocket and passing it over to Jack.

"A computer chip?" Jack said turning the seal package in his hand.

"Lets have a look at that?" Tom said and Jack passed it over.

Tom looked at the chip under a magnifying light. Then started typing stuff into his computer.

"OK Got it what you have there is a XQR6VFX130-1cf1752V manufactured by the American company Xilinx. They are used in the aerospace industry as well as Nuclear power stations and also some use for high end military weapons. They are worth in excess of $100,000 each. They are worth more than their weight in diamonds."

"OK but who would buy these?"

"Enemies of The USA and its partners, did you find anything else?

"Yes a couple of dead folks who I presume were drivers or they could be some of these folks that had an argument with Perkins, they were in big sacks ready to be disposed of. Both had their throats slit. I would guess from what you have told us about This John and Natasha Perkins that they would have used someone else to do their dirty work. So we need to be on the lookout for that person. From the way the drivers were killed I would guess that the murderer has certain professional skills, the type of skills. The sort of skill-set that we possess. As such I would guess, something like Spetnaz."

"I would guess that would be Alexi, unless there are folks there we don't know about" Jack said.

"You know what they say about follow the money? I think first we should follow those Micro chips, because whoever is using them could be a much more serious challenge to the world rather than their smuggling operation. Also how the fuck did they get their hands on them without ringing alarm bells at either the FBI or the CIA. I need to look into this further before we do anything else Jack." Mark said before opening up his own secure laptop.

"Tom you can activate those cameras we have two in the courtyard, each should give you a one eighty and there are four more inside the stable blocks, we stuck a pair of sensor mikes to the kitchen window and the same on the back windows. They are pretty invisible so unless you knew what to look for then you wouldn't notice them. So now you have full eyes and ears on the place." Orville said

Tom logged on to his computer and entered the pin codes of the cameras along with those of the flat near invisible condenser microphones.

"Wow where can I get some of those Mikes from?" Tom said

"I believe they might have come from the CIA, and they are gonna want them back at some point.

"I can see why, they are crystal clear. I can hear their TV better than my own."

Hey guys I just some information from my friend in the Kremlin, you need to hear what he has told me." Alex said

"Do tell all." Orville said

OK remember when my contact told us about this guy called Leonid Ivanov or Calin Volkov or Fedorov, no matter what name he uses. Putin is genuinely afraid of this man. He used to be in the background of things but now it seems he wants to be the next Russian Premier, in order to do that he first has to be Richer than Putin and he has to amass an army of people around him who are ready to die for him. Se he must first become the richest man in all of Russia. Or at least convince those around him that he is. Then he must have the power over smaller nations who will allow him to utilise their resources. One of those nations is South Korea. It is the top nation for making parts for nuclear reactors and we have seen increased shipping of selected parts to ports within Russia."

"Do you think this guy is planning to blow up Russia or something?" Jack asked

"Not on the intel that we have at the moment. What we do know is that a singular individual has managed to increase their wealth to that approaching Putin. That kind of wealth has the power to make changes. Normally in Russia when people who are in the inner circle of Putin, they have a habit of having heart attack or sometimes fatal accidents. Others just disappear along with their families. For the sake of arguments lets just call this guy Fedorov, as no one seems to know for sure what his real name is. The point is we are not the only ones interested in him. He has come to the attention of most Western countries along with their security agencies." Alex said

"Why would their security agencies be bothered about some guy in Russia. Surely getting rid of Putin would not be a bad thing. After all look at his stance towards Crimea and Ukraine as a whole. I am sure they would sleep better without that despot?" Tom said

"Sometimes things work better with the despot that you know how to ben rather than the despot that breaks when you apply pressure. The UK,

USA and the likes Know how to handle Putin. They have people who work for them in Putin's government. A sudden change could affect the world in untold ways, both financially and for global security." Mark said

"How does all that fit with the smuggling of precious stones and micro chips." Jack asked

"Well you know those chips are valued at $100K each. How many of them did you see at the Perkins?" Mark asked Orville

"Dozens of them, too many to count."

"So they are probably conducting the physical business side of thing on UK soil. They smuggle in precious stones and rare metals to swap for the smuggled Microchips. That being the case we need to find out fast, where these chips are going and what they are liable to be used for?" Mark said.

"One thing is for sure they are not running a stud farm for horses.

22
Deep Frozen Assets

"Alex where are we with the details of the Kremlin link on this?" Jack asked

"I have heard nothing from Sergi in the last two days, it could be that nothing has changed since the last time we spoke." Alex replied

"Tom what have we got from all those cameras down at the Perkins place."?

"Alexi seems to have installed a generator into one of the Horseboxes other than that not a lot. The strange thing is that Mr and Mr Perkins don't actually seem to talk to each other. They don't even eat together unless they have guests. Even then they don't talk about anything illegal. It is like they know they are being watched and recorded."

"Is there any chance that they know we are on to them and are deliberately playing to the camera, so to speak?"

"Of Course it is possible Boss but I would say highly unlikely, or they would have moved the horseboxes into plain sight. I think that the Perkins marriage is a marriage of convenience, in some way which I have yet to figure out." Tom replied.

"Do you want me to go down and give the place a once over in daylight?" Orville asked

"No lets just see how things play out for a bit longer. Then we might." Jack replied.

"So are both the Perkins and their staff at home just now?" Jack asked

"According to what we can see and their mobile phones yes." Tom replied

"Do we have any info on the two drivers that came with the horseboxes."

"I am assuming that they are in hiding at the Perkins, or that the Perkins are hiding them somehow as we have not picked them up on the cameras. Also there are no other mobile phones pinging the towers."

"Come on people we must have more to go on than we did almost a week ago." Jack said

"Jack I understand your frustration at this but we need to be patient, if we go in mob handed at this point the only thing we will achieve is that the Perkins will be in the wind and all the others will get burned. It will look to the authorities that Billy and Jenny are behind the whole scam. And If I am honest Jack even though we know they were duped as were all the other Kennels that the likes of the Perkins, set up. The evidence will only show the Kennels to be guilty of money laundering at best and support of terrorism at worst. I don't know about here in the UK but in the US that carries a twenty five year service. I am sure given time you could prove their innocence, but that would take time. During that time your brother and his wife would be in jail and their genuine business would be ruined. I am waiting to hear from a CIA operative who is embedded inside Moscow. He is following up on something that might break the whole damn thing wide open or it might just be nothing." Mark said

"What are you not telling me Mark, We are all friends here and I have never known you to hold anything back from me." Jack said

"Jack I am not holding anything back from you, Like I said I am waiting for an operative to give me some information. He is an ex FBI guy I worked with years ago before he crossed over to the dark side. As soon as I know something then you will too."

Back down at the rescue centre, there seemed to have been a marked increase in the number of animals coming in from all over the world. The kennels and catteries were constantly full. Had Mark not arranged for the two Americans to come and help out, Then Jenny would probably employed two more people anyway.

The two frogmen, had blended in well. They carried out a variety of tasks and Billy noticed that at any given time one of them would always be just seconds away from Jenny or the main office. They did actually tidy the grounds and keep the borders neat and weed free.

One day Billy had taken a casserole that Jenny had made, up to their caravan. He knocked and entered without thinking about who and what these men were. On opening the door Billy almost dropped their dinner, as a pair of powerful looking handguns were pointed fair and squarely at his chest. Billy did the right thing even though he did not think about it at the time he froze.

"Jesus man I could have killed you just then. Did your mother not teach you to knock and wait for a door to be answered." Buddy said

"I am sorry I did not think, I was just bringing you some dinner that Jenny made." Was all Billy could say.

"Well don't just stand their with your dick in the wind, get inside." Zack said as they both lowered their guns.

Billy entered and put the casserole down on the table and then closed the door. All the curtains in the residential caravan were closed making it almost like night inside, it was only then Billy realised that he had also been lit up by the beam of a torch. Zack turned on the internal lights as Buddy turned the torch off. Both men then placed their guns on the table next to the crock-pot that Billy had placed there.

"I would not let Jenny see those guns she would freak, if she knew you had them here." Billy said

"Listen man, we are here because Mark Carter knows that at some point we will be needed. He did tell you that we were here to protect you. You already had one of your Vets murdered in front of you. You have had another beaten and sent back to you and even the Perkins guy has received two beatings. There will come a time when people will stop using just warnings. And then some rather nasty types are gonna appear and try to clean house. We are the best in the world at what we do and we have stayed alive because of the tools of our trade. I for one intend to go back home to my wife and daughters when this gig is up." Zack said and then continued and pointed to his gun at the same time.

"And this, is what ensures that for me. It is also what will ensure the safety of you and your wife. I know you have different gun laws in the UK, so seeing these might be a bit of a shock and we understand that. You will not see us with guns outside of this mobile home, Unless there is actually the requirement to use them. So just knock next time and wait. By the way, say thank you to Jenny for the food beats the hell out of MRE." Zack said and then seeing the quizzical look on Billy's face he added.

"Meals Ready To Eat, they are military field rations. They either heat in the bag on their own or you just add water to them. Half straw and the other half preservatives and salt."

"Ohh OK If you guys need anything to eat or drink just ask." Billy said while glancing around the caravan. He noticed one of the two holdalls belong to one of the men was spread open on the floor. There were several loaded magazines along with rectangular blocks wrapped in some wax type paper covering. A gas mask along with several large cylinders. Buddy closed the bag with his foot.

"Sorry I did not mean to pry."

"No worries man. Just be cool about it all. OK?" Zack said and Billy left.

Billy was not sure if he should be more or less worried after seeing the thing ha just had. Billy did though feel better protected. He would not bother letting Jenny know about the guns as she would only worry more than she was.

The following day there was movement down at the Perkins Stables. The horsebox that had been retrofitted with a generator was now being loaded up with a dozen or so chest freezers. They were loaded on using one of the small forklift trucks that were always in the concrete stable-yard. Then one of the missing drivers appeared. John Perkins handed the man an envelope and the driver got in the Cab of the Horsebox before driving back out from the stables and up the driveway towards the main road.

"Jack look at this?" Tom said indicating to the large monitor at the back of Jacks workbench.

"Right so one of the vans are leaving."

"Not that Jack. This." Tom said while selecting an area of the screen with his mouse and then dragging it outwards. The vehicles numberplate came up and jack absent-mindedly read it out aloud V00RVV.

"And" Jack asked

"That van came in registered as a PP99986 and was registered to Poland and was registered to the Russian Driver. So now it is re-registered with a year 2000 British registration. Let me just check that on the DVLA database" Tom said

He clicked away at the keys of his keyboard.

"It is registered to John Perkins Farm. The only way that could have happened so quickly is for him to already own that registration number already registered to him and then have it transferred, which would also make it legal for the UK roads." Tom added.

"Can you check and see if he has had any other recent vehicle registrations or new ones added or transferred?" Jack asked and again Tom clicked away

"I have one he F00CME it was transferred from a Range Rover to a Bedford 7 ton Horsebox today." Tom said

"And the Range Rover?"

"Scrapped apparently an insurance write off."

Thanks Tom, not that any of that gives answers to any questions.

"Orville can you follow that van and get a peek what it is that is inside the freezer, I mean apart from the horse-meat. You can take my BMW."

"NP but keep the Beemer, I will take Marks lease car if that is OK with you Mark?"

"Sure just bring it back in one piece please." Mark said and tossed over the keys to a silver, two year old Ford Mondeo.

Orville drove off and kept in contact with Tom. It took him about thirty minutes to catch up with the horsebox and he stayed an average of 6 cars back following the van down the M1 motorway and then around the M25 outer ring road for London. Then the M3 down to Southampton. When the van parked up in a car park near the docks.

Orville waited and watched. He had cracked his window open in order that the car did not steam up. Nothing shows someone is watching you like a car with misted up windows, especially if there is only one occupant in the car. Orville wound his seat back as far as it would go so that his head was now on a level with his steering wheel. If anyone noticed him it would look like he was getting some shut eye before catching a ferry or boat. It also might look as if there was no one in the car especially if viewed from the front. Orville sat he watched and waited.

The driver of the horsebox opened his door and climbed down and then locked the van and walked off in the direction of all night cafe, which was about one hundred yards away. He waited until the driver was in the eatery, before exiting his own car the vanity light he had removed even before he had left Boston. He walked casually as if he too was going to the eatery. A large tractor unit came in and parked just behind the horsebox. Then its driver pulled his curtains and its internal lights went out. The driver was probably waiting for a trailer coming off a morning ship, so was getting some sleep to allow road time for his pickup.

Orville reached the back of the horsebox, he bent down and untied then retied his bootlace. The truck had completely blocked any vision of the van from the all night cafe. Moving swiftly he made his way to the side door of the horsebox, picking its lock in seconds. There were two banks of chest freezers each had a padlock. Again these posed no problem opening one it appeared to have bags of frozen meat, he removed some and found that there was a layer of cardboard under. Quickly clearing the top two rows of packaged meat he lifted the cardboard. One quick picture with his mobile phone and then he replaced everything as it had been, then exited and relocked the door and walked casually back to his own car, before sending the picture to Tom.

23
Wash Day Blues

"Your gonna want to see this boss and you too Mark." Tom said looking the picture that Orville had sent him.

"Bloody Hell. Is that real?" Jack said

"I would say it looks to be as pure as Jack Daniels over ice on the bayou" Mark said with his usual slow Mississippi way.

"Do they even have bayou's in Mississippi?" Alex asked.

"Oh yea of little knowledge. The Mississippi delta has some of the best bayous in the whole of the USA. Don't let all those movies about the Floridians let you think they are the only ones with gators and swamps. Our skeeters are bigger too."

Both Alex and Mark studied the photograph,

"So we have to assume that each freezer contains the same then we are talking a massive shipment." Mark said.

"What do you want Orville to do?" Tom asked Jack.

"Ask him if he can fit a tracker to the van at least until I can get my buddy in the CIA to follow it with a satellite. Then tell him to get back here as fast as he can." Mark said.

Tom relayed the information over to Orville, who said that he had already stuck one on the back of one of the freezers and had it logged into Toms system. All Tom had to do was to enter the IP address of the tracker into his system, which Orville had texted to him.

"In that case tell him to come home, as it looks like we will needs all hands on board." jack said.

"If what we have seen is just part of a shipment being sent into central and eastern Europe, then that could seriously impact on all financial institutions of of the world. In a word financial terrorism." Mark said and added

"I would say what ever scheme they are running is close to its fruition, then we are going to have to find out just exactly who is behind it."

"Could it be state sponsored?" Jack asked

"All things are possible, I suppose. One thing is for sure they are not bringing that lot in inside animals." Alex said pointing to the picture.

"What if the animal thing is just about the finances. You know the ability to make other things happen." Tom said

"I need to do some checking with my embassy Jack and its not something I can do over the telephone. I don't want to make any wild guesses, especially seeing the possible twist that we have." Mar said

"Do you want to borrow my car?" Jack asked

"Depends on how soon Orville can get back here?" Mark replied

Having checked with Orville who said he would arrive back in about 3 hours, Mark decided not to bother taking Jacks car. They spent the time brainstorming. In light of the new information they had just received it was debated as to weather Billy and Jenny should remain in situ or be replaced by either members of Jacks team or members of the FBI. In the end it was decided to leave Billy and Jenny in place but keep the security around them.

Jack decided it would be best if he were to go and see his brother and talk things over before things finally came to a head.

"So the precious stones, drugs and precious metals are not what all this is about then?" Billy asked Jack

"It is what is known as a facilitator crime." Jack replied and then seeing the blank look on Billy's face, he continued.

"OK a facilitator crime, is a crime that is committed in order that another more serious crime can be either orchestrated or committed. So all these valuable items are being smuggled in, using the animals are being done to raise funds for another crime. Without going into the specific details, we have made a discovery that would lead us to believe that this is the case. We know that John and Natasha are actively involved insomuch as the horses that they rescued also came in with part that had been operated on. Obviously a horse is a much bigger animal, ergo they would have been used to smuggle larger quantities or whatever high value items they needed. We do also know that they slaughtered all the horses, in order to export the meat to France. That in itself is not illegal as we have since discovered that John owns half stake in a local abattoir he also holds an export license for meat for horse-meat." Jack said

"So he imports healthy horses to smuggle whatever it is he smuggles and then destroys the horses. Surely as they were bought as stud they would be high end racehorses? Would they not be worth a lot more alive rather than as a meat product?"

"Possibly Billy but dead horses tell no tales, no pun intended. No one would be able to prove if any joints had been made from precious metals or if the horse had been used to carry drugs or precious stones. When they are dead they are dead. So there ends the evidence of smuggling." Jack said

"So this facilitator crime, do you know what it is?"

"We suspect at this moment although we will not know that until we get to the top of the criminal tree in all of this. What we do know is it is much, much bigger then any of us realised."

"So John and Natasha are knowingly involved?" Billy asked

"We believe so but just how involved we don't yet know. But things will probably become much more dangerous for everyone involved. Mark is going down to the US Embassy this afternoon. I cant tell you everything because I don't know everything. Hopefully when Mark returns from London we will have a much better handle on things. My advice for now is to try and keep things as normal as you can. Try not to worry and especially, not to say too much to Jenny. If these people think we are on to them I am sure they would have no qualms about using deadly force to keep their secrets."

"Are you saying we are in danger?"

"No I don't believe so Billy, but I think it could become if you change your routines. You will be safe enough with Zack and Buddy watching over you, and Tom, has your home and grounds covered with damn near as many cameras as Buckingham Palace." Jack said and then walked Billy back to his house where Jenny had a pot of coffee bubbling away on the stove and plate of biscuits on the kitchen table.

Mark left for London at almost the same time as Jean turned up at Jacks place.

"Hello stranger what brings you over here?"

"Oh I have a few days off and thought I would come and visit my better half." Jean said whilst getting a big hug and kiss from Alex.

"You better com into the Garage as we have made a little headway, see if you can give us a different angle on things." Jack said as Alex and Jean walked arm in arm beside him.

After everyone was greeted Jack asked Tom to give Jean the low-down on everything they had discovered since Jean had left to return to her policing duties in Swindon.

"So we thought that this was about millions when it could conceivably be about billions or even trillions?"

"That's about the essence of things Jean." Jack replied.

As they waited for Mark to return Alex and Jean helped to correlate all the evidence into a singular file, ready for all the criminal investigation services around the world. When this was finally completed there would be no hiding place for those at the top, assuming that they did not burn the whole operation before the authorities knew about it. If that were the case then it would without doubt be the most audacious criminal act ever committed, especially considering just how many countries were involved albeit without most of their governments knowing about it."

"Alex?" Jack asked

"Yes?"

"Just how much do you trust Sergi"

"I would say that so far everything he has told me so has turned out to be truthful. Why do you ask?"

"OK what about the information that you share with him do you think that he would ensure that it remains with the remit of your circle?"

"You are obviously going somewhere with this Jack, spit it out?"

"If say what we are looking into has something to do with the upper echelons of the Russian government, would he be safe to share what we know with or would it get leaked to his masters?"

"Here is what I think Jack. Sometimes sharing of information can be counter productive. I know that we are looking into folks who hold the ear of Putin or actively support him in his policies. So in this case I would share after the fact rather than before it and then apologise to Sergi with some fine Scotch at a later date." Alex replied

"OK Thanks for your honesty, tell me you have your files complete and ready to send when the powers that be jump?" Jack answered just as Mark returned.

There were three other people with Jack making the garage a very busy place, given all the flight cases and bags that were already there.

"Jack I would like you to meet a few of my friends. The young lady if from the from the US Treasury department. Marie O'Malley." Mark said and the young red haired lady in a grey business suit stepped forward and shook hands first with Jack and then each of the rest of the team as they introduced themselves.

"This is Robert Millman of the Central Intelligence Agency along with his colleague Mitch Horowitz. Both of these gentle men will be working alongside you Jack, as this is still your investigation." Mark said and then she stopped Jack from explaining that he was in fact retired by saying.

"As you can see the Brits had such a good handle on this that they called the FBI to assist in their operation. They have been sharing with us since the dit-dot-go. This is not of course the first time that Jack and his team have work a case with the FBI. Jack in fact saved my life by shooting a man. I tell you this so you know you can trust Jack with your very life." Mark said

While the rest of the team introduced themselves Jack pulled Mark outside and whispered to him.

"Mark you know I am retired, I cant officially lead any kind of investigation. God knows if our government get wind of this little operation then I am just as liable to end up in jail, as the bloody criminals we are hunting."

"No one needs to know you are retired at least from our end of things. After all we cant officially conduct an investigative operation on British soil. So there has to be a Brit at the lead point. And When it all comes to a head and we crack the case I will be sure to point an applauding hand in the direction of Detective Chief Inspector Jean Short. I Shall also make sure that you are given due credit over the big pond. It will be good kudos for you all. Right lets get back inside DCI Hamilton." Mark said with a smile.

"Just before we go back in, what gives with the CIA and the Treasury agent, which is what she is, if I am not mistaken?" Jack said

"Well the CIA need to know where all the stuff coming into the USA is coming from and more importantly who is behind it. Yes she is a Treasury agent. You saw what was in those freezers. That was a lot of frozen assets heading to France. There is money laundering on a small scale and then there is this." Mark replied

"Fair enough, it will do for now. Lets get back in there and try to fix things." Jack said

24
Bernhard Cash Machine

"Right now all the introductions have been done I am gonna ask y'all to listen to what Agent O'Malley of the Treasury Department has to say and y'all might want to rest your weary rear in the saddle for a while." Mark said in his own imitable style.

"Hi and first off thank you so much Detective Hamilton for allowing us to come in on your operation. Of course anything that happens on UK soil will still fall under the jurisdiction of you Brits. What I am about to tell you might blow a lot of your theories completely out of the water. I did a quick read of the report that was provided by Alex Gordon. You theorised that these smuggling crimes were the small end of things and were, in your words, facilitating crimes. Since we received the pictures from the Seal team who are working with the FBI on the ground here. It pretty much proved your theory, however for about two years now my department has been working in the US and also in Argentina on an investigation into fake US Dollar bills. They range across the board from the one to the one hundred dollar bills. The thing about these fakes is that they are not as of yet turning up in the USA in any numbers, sure the odd one or two will appear now and then. The thing is of late they seem so have stopped dead." Marie said and stopped as Jack put his hand up.

"Surely if they have stopped then that is a good thing." Jack said

"Yes you would think that wouldn't you. The thing is this is the second large quantity of US currency that has come to the surface in the last week. What you don't know and that is because we pretty much kept a lid on things. What you may know or have heard about is that a small cargo plane crashed in Bolivia and burst into flames on impact. Well that was the story. Yes there was a crash. By sheer chance there was a team of US Marines on exercise with Bolivian Rangers in the The Cordillera Real mountain range. They were only a mile from the crash zone so they raced to see if there were any survivors. There were. But there were also four large crates of what at first glance appeared to be mixed denomination US banknotes. They secured the scene and held captive the survivors. After contacting my department via their own HQ we flew two agents and dropped them by parachute to the site. They were able to identify that these were in fact Bernard dollars. As soon as that was established the two survivors were handed over to US authorities and the wreckage along with its contents were torched until there was nothing left but ash. We think that the cargo that went to France is destined for whatever purpose that Bolivian one was."

"When you said that they were taken into custody just who has these survivors?" Jack asked

"That would be us." Mitch Horowitz replied, before continuing.

"So I am sure you are all well aware that we have certain small units based around the world, who look after American interests. We have a couple of those units in Bolivia."

"I guess you are talking about your Black Op sites that don't actually exist?" Jack said

"Something like that. So we have these two guys, one of whom is a Bolivian subject so is probably just a hired hand. The other man though is a Russian citizen. We are currently conducting our investigations on him at the moment. Which brings us to the now and I think it would probably be best if we have Marie explain what we think is going on at the moment. Marie?" Mitch said.

"Have any of you ever heard of a project called Operation Bernhard?" She asked and apart from the two CIA guys who obviously knew what was going on, there were blank looks and shaking heads.

"Right so lets start at the beginning. Operation Bernhard was an exercise by Nazi Germany initially to forge British bank notes. The original plan was to drop the notes over Britain to bring about a collapse of the British economy during the Second World War. The first phase was run from early 1940 by the Sicherheitsdienst or SD for short, under the title Unternehmen Andreas or in English Operation Andreas. The unit successfully duplicated the rag paper used by the British, produced near-identical engraving blocks and deduced the algorithm used to create the alpha-numeric serial code on each note. The unit closed in early 1942 after its head, Alfred Naujocks, fell out of favour with his superior officer, Reinhard Heydrich. The operation was revived later in the year, the aim was changed to forging money to finance German intelligence operations. Instead of a specialist unit within the SD, prisoners from Nazi concentration camps were selected and sent to Sachsenhausen concentration camp to work under SS Major Bernhard Krüger. The unit produced British notes until mid-1945. Estimates vary of the number and value of notes printed, from £132.6 million up to £300 million. By the time the unit ceased production, they had perfected the artwork for US dollars, although the paper and serial numbers were still being analysed. The counterfeit money was laundered in exchange for money and other assets. Counterfeit notes from the operation were used to pay the Turkish agent Elyesa Bazna code named Cicero, for his work in obtaining British secrets from the British ambassador in Ankara, and £100,000 from Operation Bernhard was used to obtain information that helped to free the Italian leader Benito Mussolini in the Gran Sasso raid in September 1943.

In early 1945 the unit was moved to Mauthausen-Gusen concentration camp in Austria, then to the Redl-Zipf series of tunnels and finally to Ebensee concentration camp. Because of an overly precise interpretation of a German order, the prisoners were not executed on their arrival, they were liberated shortly afterwards by the American Army. Much of the output of the unit was dumped into the Toplitz and Grundlsee lakes at the end of the war, but enough went into general circulation that the Bank of England stopped releasing new notes and issued a new design after the war." Marie said and stopped for breath.

"So if you don't mind me asking what has the forgery of old British notes got to do with what is going on now with the US banknotes. You already said that we changed the design and that was that. Right?" Jack said

"Correct however the US dollar bill has not changed much since its inception, sure there are new secrets being added on new notes but we cant retrograde that so any old notes are just that and there are trillions of old notes still out there in circulation. It is estimated that at any one time there is up to sixty percent of all US currency is held outside the USA, in currency exchanges, banks and the like, all around the world. So continuing. In early May of 1944, Ernst Kaltenbrunner, an SS Obergruppenführer which was a general in the Reichssicherheitshauptamt otherwise known as the RSHA, ordered that the counterfeiting unit begin to produce forged US dollars. The artwork on the notes was more complex than that of the British currency and initially caused problems for the forgers. Additional challenges they faced included the paper, which contained minute silk threads, and the intaglio printing process, which added small ridges to the paper. The prisoners realised that if they managed to fully counterfeit the dollars, their lives would no longer be safeguarded by the work they were undertaking, so they slowed their progress as much as they could. The prisoners considered this to have the tacit approval of Krüger, who would face front-line duty if Operation Bernhard ended. In August 1944 Salomon Smolianoff, a convicted forger, was added to the production team at Sachsenhausen to aid the counterfeiting of US dollars, although he also assisted in quality control for the pound notes. The Jewish prisoners working on the operation at the time complained to Krüger at having to work with a criminal, so he was given his own room to sleep in. In late 1944 the prisoners had counterfeited the reverse of the dollar, and the obverse by January 1945. Twenty samples of the $100 note were produced but without the serial number, whose algorithm was still being examined and shown to Himmler and banking experts. The standard of engraving and printing was considered excellent, although the paper used was technically inferior to the genuine notes. Finally the algorithm for the serial number was completed and full runs were ordered. The counterfeit money was transported from Sachsenhausen to Schloss Labers, an SS-run facility in the South Tyrol. It was put through a money laundering operation run by Friedrich Schwend, who had been running an illegal currency and smuggling business since the 1930s. He negotiated a deal in which he would be paid 33.3% of the money he laundered, 25% was given to his agents undertaking the work as payment to them and their sub-agents, and for expenses leaving him with 8.3%. He recruited what he called 'salesmen' in various territories, and built a network of some fifty or so agents and sub agents, some of these were in fact Jewish, deliberately selected because there was less chance that the authorities would consider them to be working for the Nazis. He informed his agents that the money had been seized from the banks of occupied countries. Schwend was given two objectives. To exchange the counterfeit money for genuine Swiss francs or US dollars, and to assist with the funding of special operations, including buying black market arms from the Yugoslav Partisans then selling them to pro-Nazi groups in Southeast Europe. Then a massive catastrophe struck. The War ended! Most though not all of the counterfeit money was collected and burned BUT the plates which were recovered were one full set. It was rumoured at the time that there was a second set of plates, which somehow fell into the hands of the Argentines. Some three years ago these counterfeit notes started to surface and like the first time, the only thing that was wrong was the Paper. It was better but still not quite right although you would need a laboratory to show this. This paper looked and felt like the real deal. They had even cracked the code for newer serial numbers. Then just as we were about to arrest the forger he died in a fire and the plates were once again lost. Now we know they are back in circulation and they are printing notes in numbers that we have never seen before. If they flood the US with this quantity of counterfeits, it will cause the dollar to drop in value on the international market. In short it could actually bankrupt the US economy as there would not be enough reserves in Fort Knox to cover the value of notes on the market."

"Let me get this right someone is deliberately buying these fakes with diamonds, gold and the likes" Jack said

"Yes that's right." Marie replied

"So why would you willingly exchange genuine high value items, for something you know to be fake and worthless?" Jack asked her once again

"To be quite honest we are not entirely sure what any individual would gain from this. Obviously the forgers are becoming insanely rich. Those buying the fake dollars cant be paying more than ten cents on the dollar in order to sell them on at anything up to thirty cents on the dollar. What I can tell you is that the actual smuggling of high value items is effectively a deliberate loss making operation. But not for the traders as these items are stolen in the first place. All in all as bit of a mystery" Marie said.

25
The Head Honcho

Marie accepted a mug of coffee from Mark ad let the magnitude of what she had just revealed to Jack and the others, to settle in.

"OK so I understand the interest of the FBI and the Treasury Department. I also understand the CIA interrogating the people they found at the crash site but what is the CIA doing here with you just now Mark?" Jack asked

"They are here because, they unlike me are allowed to operate outside the USA. I on the other hand can only officially work in an advisory capacity like I did with you before, on the Edward Theodore Gein copycat murderer. They can operate with the remit of International Law against terrorism. Unlike the FBI the CIA already have numerous offices and sites in most countries of the world even some of those that are hostile to the USA."

"OK So what is our next move Mark? Or do we have have to wait for other elements of this, to happen first?" Jack asked

"Marie?" Mark said passing it over to her to answer.

"As you now know the CIA discovered some large crates of this counterfeit money at the crash site in the Bolivian mountains. The value of that find was estimated at twenty to fifty million. The estimate of the funds in the freezers sent to France I estimate between fifty and one hundred million. This we think is the tip of the iceberg. I should really let the boys from the CIA fill you in on what they had learned since the plane crash in Bolivia." Marie said. Handing things over to Agent Mitch Horowitz

"Hi once again guys. Right so back to the crash in the Cordillera Real mountain range. We traced the plan back to the Jorge Wilstermann International Airport is a high elevation international airport serving Cochabamba, the capital of the Cochabamba region of Bolivia. The plane was a logged flight from Argentina. We since discovered that it was a layover stop. Before Buenos Aires international airport. The plane was registered to company in Switzerland. The aircraft effectively airport hopped from airport to airport until landing in Argentina. We are trying to ascertain if the cargo was loaded in Switzerland or any of the stops before it landing in Argentina. We actually thought that the money was coming in from Europe, even though the hearsay history that we have would point to the print plates being held in South America. We tracked the actual printing paper to a company in Germany. The thing about the paper is that is is pretty much unique to the US Dollar. I think I am right in saying that the paper used for US note, are a blend of twenty five percent linen and seventy five percent cotton. This paper has tiny red and blue synthetic fibres of various lengths pretty much evenly distributed throughout the paper. In the USA there is only one company that produces this paper and that is Crane and Co, who are a Massachusetts-based company. It is harder to get a roll of paper out from there than it would be to get a gold bar out of Fort Knox. So that meant that we were scouring the world for paper producers who would use linen and or cotton in their paper. The weight of each dollar bill is one gram so the weight of the paper used has to be factored in including the ink. We found a paper mill in the UK that had previously closed about four years ago. Now they make paper for the art world, who demand a paper that is approximately the same weight and quality as those used in the US Dollar. The company was purchased by a Russian Oligarch who has since died. But it is still managed by a Russian business consortium, with questionable back ground. Most of the workers are also Russians. Now whilst the production has increased exponentially, the actual sales of artists products has remained the same. So where is all that paper going and more importantly who is it that is buying it? When we know that we can shut the whole thing down."

"So what you seem to be saying is that these fake US Dollar bills are being made here in the UK and then shipped worldwide?" Jack said

"That is about the stretch of it. However it is no use us just going in and shutting down the paper works. We have to first find the plates. We are more likely to do that when we find the ink supplier. The ink is quite specific to the US currency. So the paper works is near Bulbourne and we have a couple of guys keeping an eye on things there. The ink used in modern US Dollars is what they call magnetic ink. so it can be quickly scanned like a barcode. The older the note though the harder this becomes, whilst it still contains iron it is in much smaller quantities. So these folks have gone for the mid ground. But we have to fine the ink producers or importers and then follow that to where the actual printing takes place."

"And you think that is also done within the UK?" Jack asked

"That is the theory that we are working in. and it is something that we we have to find with urgency. But it does not end there. At the same time we have to find where all the counterfeits have gone and retrieve them, and or destroy them."

"And all this has to happen at the same time?"

"In a nutshell Jack Yes."

"What was the name of the Oligarch?" Alex asked.

"Which?" Mitch asked

"The guy who initially bought and set up the paper mill."

"Oh yes right that was a man called Fedor Petrovich Krasnov."

"The ex husband of Natasha Perkins?" Jack said.

"Just how did this guy meet his end?" Tom asked

"I am not quite sure the info that we have on file is that he had gone through his divorce and was getting on with life. Then he was involved in a fatal car crash, which ended in a fireball. He was identified by his dental work." Mitch replied

"Is there any possibility that he could have faked his death?" Jack asked

"I suppose there is always a chance that could have happened. Except that most of his wealth ended up with the state, ergo in Putin's pocket. I cant see any oligarch giving up his companies and wealth, to become the owner of a paper-mill."

"Unless that paper-mill was worth all the money in the world." Jack said. Which sort of became the conversation killer.

That evening Jack drove down to check in on his brother and sister in law. After chatting to both of them about the kennels and catteries jack went and spoke with the two US Navy Seals and brought them up to date on everything. He asked them to be extra vigilant especially when any new faces came around.

Billy was really starting to worry about the number of animals they had been dealing with in the rescue centre. Jenny had reduced the time which the incoming animals would stay in the kennels before being re-homed. This time had been reduced from two weeks to just seven days. Jenny had worried that this was too soon, however the choice was either extend the kennels, which she really did not want to do any more than she had already, or turn down the animals and send then to other rescue centres. Which obviously would start to involve other innocent people. So to Jenny it was a Hobson's Choice.

As Billy and Jack were walking around the grounds of the rescue centre, they started to brainstorm.

"So if this big Oligarch, who was married to Natasha and was the man behind the fake money who is now dead, then who do you think is the top man on this money tree now?"

"At this point I cant be sure, perhaps it is Putin himself, or that nutter from North Korea or even the Chinese. Whoever it is, seems to have a real hard-on for fuck the USA up the ass." Jack said

Jack said goodnight to his brother and drove back to his home. Janet was in the kitchen when he returned.

"Just how much longer is this farce going on Jack. I married a 'retired police officer'" she said with imitation speech marks in the air using her fingers.

"I will be honest with you Janet I don't have an answer to that question other than, I know if the situation were reversed Billy would cross hell and high water to protect you and me. What I can tell you is I think that this thing that they are innocently mixed up in, is rapidly heading towards an endgame." Jack replied.

"Just how much danger are they in? I know that they have two very dangerous looking men working down at Jenny's centre and I have seen the men who are in the garage and they look like they eat nails for breakfast and I don't mean fingernails Jack. The other people who arrived today who are they and please be honest with me Jack. Jenny will not say a word and I am betting that is because you told her not to talk to anyone including me." Janet asked her husband.

"Janet darling, I have deliberately kept you out of this thing because I really did not want to worry you. But you are right we are married and that is a partnership. But before I tell you the full in and out of things. I need you to promise first that you will not go crazy and start screaming. Also that you will not repeat anything that I tell you, especially to Jenny as there are some things that she is not aware of and which we ourselves have just discovered. So if you can categorically promise me that? Then I will tell you everything."

Janet promised and poured them both a cup of black coffee.

Tom and Alex were taking turns at tracking the freezers and presumably the horsebox first as it arrived in France, then as it made its way down to Germany and to Berlin, where it stopped. Around the same time another load of horses arrived at the Perkins farm and the second horsebox filled with freezers, presumable loaded with meat and US Dollars. Orville was only able to get a tracker fitted under the Vehicle itself.

Due to the hidden high resolution low light cameras that Orville had fitted in the stables, they showed six horses being delivered and within minutes they were killed by Alexi using as Abattoir Bolt Gun. They were rapidly butchered and lumps of metal along with vacuum sealed plastic bags containing unknown items were removed and first the bags were rinsed with cold water to remove the excess blood. These bags were placed inside aluminium flight cases. The hides were sealed in bags along with the bones after butchering. The meat was packed and load on top of what seemed like an endless supply of large chest freezers. Which Alexi then loaded onto the horsebox and connected up a new generator to them.

Alex and Tom made their notes about these items, dates and times. In the morning Jack called a meeting to see what had happened during the night.

"Morning Boss." Tom said and continued

"The Perkins farm was a hive of activity last night and this morning. Between 6pm and midnight last night they had three van loads go out. Orville was only able to tag the wagons. And they seem to be going in all directions. Two went via France and one has gone from Felixstowe to Belgium. They are currently loading another two. Things seem to gone onto a higher gear." Tom said

"Where are the freezers being stored before they load them onto the vans?" Mark asked

"At the moment we can only guess, Orville is still down at the Perkins. He is trying not to get noticed. Tonight he is going to try and backtrack where ever it is that Alexi appears with the freezers on his forklift truck." Tom said

"Jack we need to have some of your security services on board with this, because if we find where they bought the freezers from. Then find the delivery drivers and ask them?" Mark said

"You know if we involve MI5 or MI6 they will take over the operation and shut you out." Jack said

"Jack you know you still have me and I can pull some strings with the Lincoln Police Force. Why don't you let me talk to their Chief and get back to you?" Jean said

"OK how long will that take?" Mark asked

"Give me five minutes" Jean said and took out her mobile phone a pressed one of the names on her speed dial list.

Jean spoke quietly and with a certain urgency, then she listened before talking again. Then said goodbye and smiled.

"Lincoln drugs squad are going to look into the purchase of the freezers, if Orville can get a brand name for them. If he can do that given the quantity of these freezers being used we should be able to identify the supplier. The Lincoln police has said they would be willing to have some of their manpower to help us this also includes one of the Armed Response Vehicles, should it be required. I have told them that will not be necessary."

"Go on Jean how in the name of hell did you manage that?"

"I told him I had an operation running with the National Crimes Agency. Which as you know Jack, allows us jurisdiction on an as and when basis. I should think within minutes of getting the name of the supplier we will have a location of these freezers that Perkins seems to have in abundance." Jean said.

"Jack I have some info." Alex said removing here earpiece and putting her phone down.

"What is it?"

"You are all going to want to sit down for a sec. You know how Sergi previously told us that Fedor Petrovich Krasnov had crashed and burned in his car, and then saying that he had been identified by dental work."

"Yes and now you are going to tell us that he is alive and well and living in Cuba?" Jack said

"No not quite. But he has told me that the dental records were faked. So it was not him that died in the crash." Alex said

"Did he tell you, where he thinks this Krasnov bloke might be?" Jack asked

"Indeed he did. Sergi seems to think that he is alive and well and hiding out here in the UK."

"Alex do we have any pictures of him?"

"I think so" She replied

"Now can you get me a picture of that guy who is an aide to Putin the one where Tass published it."

Alex went and printed off two pages and brought them to Jack.

"Now I am no expert but if you change the hairstyle of that guy with Putin and remove his glasses then does he not look like a ringer for this Fedor Petrovich Krasnov bloke?"

"Bloody right he does sir." Alex replied and kicked herself for not having noticed this before but then again none of the security services had noticed it either. Not Interpol, FBI, MI5 or even the CIA.

"We need to check with UK Border control and see if you can get a match for our Mr big!" Jack said and passed the pictures back to Alex.

26
More Frozen Assets

"Jack we have a lead now on the delivery agent for the freezers. They were delivered by an online electrical company, they have shared with the Lincoln police the invoice and delivery details apparently the order was delivered in three loads as they could only fit twenty of these large chest freezers in their delivery tracks at a time. The delivery drivers are all down at Lincoln nick ready for us to interview them." Jean said with a smile on her face. Knowing full well the buzz that Jack would get from being back in the saddle again.

"You seem to have forgotten that I am no longer a serving police officer."

"That's all tight Jack, they don't know that."

"fair enough." Jack said grabbing his Jacket

All three of the delivery drivers were interviewed and all there stated the same thing that they had offloaded the white goods at the old barn to the side of the stable block. Jean and Jack returned to the garage and arrived as Mark was in the middle of giving an update.

"Ahh Jack perfect timing. Interpol have give us a complete list of sites around the world and when the time is right all these places will be raided in unison, no matter what time it may or may not be,"

"Great thanks for that information. Where is Orville?"

"He is still down at the Perkins farm."

"Can you contact him and get him to go to the old barn and take a look inside the freezers there, or see if he can find where they are storing all the fake money."

"I can try but unless its an emergency he will not reply." Tom answered.

"We might have a line on where the printing is taking place. But we should not take any action on them until we jump on all the others. Our two friends from the CIA are gonna shoot off and hang around the printer and see where they are getting their ink from. So that will be a little more space in your garage Jack" Mark said.

Even though the two from the CIA were now in the process of packing up their gear and getting set to leave, Jack felt sure that they still had enough bodies to not only protect Billy and Jenny and that when the time came to close down the operation they would still have enough folks to take the Perkins farm.

Jack needed to talk to Billy and Jenny to give them the heads up that all the troubles should be over within and few days. Now that Janet also knew the full story behind what was going on, she could come with Jack and be a shoulder for Jenny to cry upon. Jack made his excuses and left the others to do what it was they did.

Billy met Jack in the small car parking area outside Jenny's

"So what worries do you bring me now Jack that you felt the requirement to bring Janet, who I suppose, is here for moral support?"

"Well yes that is one of the reasons but it is good news actually." Jack said as he followed Billy inside the house.

"Coffee Jack" Jenny said and then she saw Janet.

"Tea or coffee Janet" Jenny asked knowing that Janet drank both.

"Tea if you don't mind Jenny." she replied

When the formalities of brewing the hot drinks and the hello's had been done, they all sat at the pine dining table.

"So is there more bad news then?" Jenny asked

"Quite the reverse Jenny I come bearing good news this time. All your worries will be over in the not to distant future. We are about to close down all their smuggling operations, not just here or just the UK but this is a worldwide operation involving thousands of officers in hundreds of locations. They are ready to take the whole thing down. What they are waiting for is just confirmation on one or two things and we are in the process of checking the identity of the man who is at the top of this operation. Then hopefully things will go back to normal for you. If you are at all worried about anything or if you are fearful. Call me or go and see Zack and Buddy they will keep you safe. But in the meantime just carry on as normal, take in the animals and let Kareem do his thing, remember that Kareem and Fatima are as much victims is this as you are." Jack said and with that they finished their drinks and left

Unbeknown to Jack and his team or for that matter any of the policing agencies involved in this investigation, things were happening much faster with the criminal element in all of the smuggling operation. They had almost reached the completion of their own operation. The man who was Putin's ex right hand man and advisor had resurfaced in Romania.

He arrived at a farmhouse there in a convoy of black Mercedes G class SUV's. All of them had blacked out windows. The first vehicle skidded to a halt at the farmhouse door, kicking up a cloud of dust from the gravel driveway. The other five cars formed a semi circle around the first. All the vehicles were identical with their mirrored windscreens and blacked out windows.

They all sat low on their suspension due mostly to the extra weight of the armour plating. Apart from the first car each carried four large well armed men who like the vehicles were dressed identically in black combats complete with matching woollen caps.

When the men had closed all the gaps between the parked cars, did the front doors open on the front car. The man who had been in the front passenger seat opened the rear passenger door allowing its occupant to get out. The soldier in black combats, saluted as he held the door open and a tall well built man, wearing a designer suit, exited the car and walked to the front door of the farmhouse, ducking his head due to the low doorway. One of the soldiers followed him and then two other stood guarding the door. The other black clad men turned around in order to keep the protective circle looking out from the closed semicircle.

At exactly the same time Putin ended a meeting with his generals and left to go to his private office. A small lean man was sat in the outer office with an old style leather curved top briefcase. He stood as Putin past him by seemingly without even noticing him.

This man was the head of Russian financial affairs. He had been an accountant since leaving Moscow University almost thirty years previous. And had been in his post since the days of Boris Nikolayevich Yeltsin. He had managed to keep his post because not only was he good at his job he was the really good at his job.

Officially he balanced the books of the government, that was the easy part. The really clever part was to skim funds without anyone being able to prove it. Putin had been a billionaire before taking power, perhaps not in his bank account but in the businesses he had muscled his way into. Those were his hidden assets. His other hidden asset was his accountant. Vladimir Chekov.

A light flashed on the secretary's desk and she picked up the telephone before saying a few quiet words and then putting the handset down.

"He will see you now" she said in Russian

The accountant stood up and walked into the opulent office with its gilded Italian marble desk.

Since Covid 19 had struck the world in 2019. Putin had taken to having his meeting from end to end of the long table rather than across it. He was not going to be a victim of this plage that originated in Wuhan China. Many members of his staff had fallen victim to it. Whilst Putin did not wear a face mask, he demanded it of any person who he was in a room with. This was a routine weekly appointment, with his personal accountant. The national accounts were done on a monthly meeting with the other departments. The office was bugged and Putin knew it, because he had ordered it.

Putin said nothing but just held his gloved hand out and Vladimir Chekov opened his briefcase and withdrew an A4 sized hard cover accounting book. There was a page marked with a tag. Chekov handed the book to Putin.

The premier looked up from the book and shrugged

"When?" he asked

"Tomorrow Sir" The accountant replied

"Good, make sure there are no complications. I wish this to go smoothly. This will put Russia back on the world stage where she belongs as a leading player. The USA and the EU have held the stage for too long. Thank you Chekov. What about Krasnov? Is he ready?" Putin asked

"Yes sir. He is in Romania. His convoy travelled through Moldova last night and he is at the location as previously discussed. The man from England is due to arrive there tonight."

"Good thank you Chekov. I think perhaps you have deserved a dacha on the coast or in the mountains. No I think not." Putin said in a serious voice.

The accountant became worried. Was Putin going to make him and his family disappear in some lonely wood, as he had done so with so many of those who had either opposed this crazed leader. Or those who had failed him. Some times these failures had been of Putin's own making, not that it mattered the end was the same.

Then Putin burst out laughing.

"No I think you have earned to have a mountain dacha and a summer one by the Black Sea. You have done well. When this is complete I think you must also have the First Hero of The Russian Federation award."

"Thank you sir it has always been an honour to serve mother Russia and of course to you as our leader." the accountant said as Putin returned the book to his bookkeeper. The highest award that any person in Russia could have, was about to be awarded to him.

The meeting had ended and the accountant left the office. He had a plan too. That plan was to escape from Russia and to the safety of the west. He knew that as soon as Putin had made the changes he wanted then the only link between this international crime would be the man who kept the books, He had been followed for the last four weeks. He pretended not to notice them. The same black Mercedes just three cars behind. The same car parked down the street from his apartment inside the walls of the Kremlin.

About three months ago he had been in a restaurant eating with his wife. He had gone to the toilets, A man had approached him and told him that he knew he was the Presidents bookkeeper. This man had told him of a plot to wipe out the accountant and his family. They had information that could only have come from inside the office of President Putin himself. The man said he worked for the CIA, but that he had the cover as a street cleaner within the Kremlin.

They knew about an operation involving money laundering. The man had said he could save the accountant and get him freedom in the USA. He said to meet him in two days and he would prove that everything he had told him was true. Two days later they had met again in the toilets of the same restaurant. The man played a tape in which he could hear Putin saying he would get rid of the accountant the other voice was that of a dead man. It was Fedor Petrovich Krasnov. Who had supposedly died in a car crash.

The man from the CIA passed over four American Passports. One for each member of his family. Each one bore their names, but their last name was now Bernát. For this favour and the promise of a much better life he had made copies of some of

Putin's personal finances. But now they had that, they wanted more.

The man from the CIA had wanted a list of upcoming policies. Then finally they had asked for information on a plan that they had heard about to devalue the USA dollar. After that all he would have to do is to go to the American embassy with his family. And they would get them out of Russia.

This was good, as winter inside Russia was not all it was cracked up to be. The rivers and lakes would freeze. Inside the Kremlin apartments were always cold. The ancient heating system never really worked that well. They could burn coal and wood in the open fireplaces but the wood they supplied to him was always damp and would spit sparks all over the room unless there was a mesh guard in place, which reduced the radiated heat from burning coal and wood. The coal must have come from Siberia as like the wood it contained pockets of moisture and water and was difficult to light.

The accountant had thought that sometimes in the past, his life had been better outside the walls of the Kremlin, on his fathers smallholding that had been given to his parents to work. Giving almost fifty percent of what they grew to the state. But they had lots of wood from the forests that surrounded the farmland.

They could shoot rabbits, dear and even bear. They could fish for salmon and trout in the streams that flowed through the lands they worked. They had eggs, flour and lots of root vegetables The meat and fish his father would freeze to see them through the winter months. In the City there was always a shortage of one or more staple foods. Not so on his fathers farm. He should have stayed there and farmed like his father had. Life was simpler and safer being a peasant farmer compared to being a member of those that walked the halls of the glitzy palace of politics. Looking back the assets his father froze were much safer than the assets that he now now hid for Putin.

27
The Paper Trail

After the CIA guys had left so now there was a lot more space in the garage. They had kindly left some of their equipment, in the custody of Mark from the FBI. At least that is what they said, even though most of the electronic toys were being looked after by Tom, as he was the only person who really understood exactly how to use them.

Alex was on the telephone to her contact at Interpol and Jean was liaising with the Sunderland Police force who were all set for the raid on the Paper Mill. They in turn had been able let Alex know where the paper was being sent too for Printing and Cutting.

After thanking them Jean hung up, then she went over to where Tom was sat in front of his computer.

"Can you log into one of those satellites that the CIA gave us access too?"

"Depends on where you want to look?" Tom said

"How about the outside of Nottingham?"Jean asked

"Lets look shall we, exactly where do you want to look near Nottingham and please do not say Sherwood Forrest and Robin Hood." Tom said.

"A small industrial unit on Stoke Lane. I am looking for a container packing unit. Here are the satellite co-ordinates." Jean said as she passed over a slip of paper.

"Did you know you have the choice of four satellites that are over that zone at the moment?" Tom asked.

"Well use the one that gives us the best video quality."

"The that would be the Chinese Gaofen satellite. They are said to be the best image quality, probably why the CIA have the access codes. So what exactly are you looking for?" Tom asked

"We are looking for a large commercial area, probably with a large car park and only a few cars in it. There will probably be some kind of guard on the gate as well. They sure as hell will not be wanting any kind of uninvited guests." Jean said as Tom clicked away on his keyboard.

The image on the large monitor at the back of Jack's workbench showed a swathe across the middle of England. Then it zoomed in on Nottinghamshire and finally to the coordinates that Jean had given him.

"There" Jean said and pointed to an area on the screen.

Tom zoomed in so that the screen was filled with a complete industrial complex that first looked to be an abandoned factory. There were lots of large and small shipping containers most with their doors wide open. Tom directed the satellite's camera towards the gated entrance and zoomed down a little more. It showed a small hut with a roller gate next to it.

"Can you go infrared on that satellite?" Jean asked

"Sure" Tom said and clicked away. The screen showed the shape of two people sat at a table. It looked like they were playing cards.

"OK go back up a bit and see if you can find any other heat sources within that site." Jean said

Tom zoomed back out and found a group of six other people inside what looked to be an administration building.

"Perfect Tom great work. That is it. That is where they are printing the money at." Jean said and went over to where Jack was sat talking with Mark.

"We have the print factory. Its on the edge of Nottingham."

"And Nottingham police are on board with us?" Jack asked

"Yes same as those for the paper-mill and the Perkins and the thugs in Southend"

"Southend?" Jack asked

"Yes they are the ones who took Kareem and probably the same ones who gave John a good kicking. All the police units around the globe are going to strike their targets the moment we give the word. This is still your operation boss, even if the CIA or the FBI or even Interpol think its theirs It will be another Jack Hamilton case closed!" Jean said

Now everything was ready Mark said that if they needed any extra bodies then he would be able to get some support where and when required. After all as he and Marie said it was an attack on the American economy and their financial structure throughout the world. As such they definitely had a vested interest in ensuring that everything went off in a clockwork fashion.

Orville checked in from a ditch near the Perkins farm and said that the last six freezers were being loaded onto a horsebox with Hungarian plates. He also said that it looked like the Perkins were getting ready to leave the farm.

Alexi and his wife were loading suitcases into the back of a Ford Transit van. There were also some expensive looking cases next to the front door.

The satellite over the Printing operation showed there to be a flurry of activity. Boxes were being loaded into vans and there was now no guard on the gate.

The police in Pakistan were ready to close down three dog sanctuaries as well as a cattery. In Bahrain the police backed up by army personnel were going to do the same. The FBI had identified over one hundred and twenty sites.

Working with the local police forces and Army units the CIA had identified more than three hundred additional fake rescue sites, in all of the south American countries. Most of these were being run by well armed drug cartels. All across Europe, Interpol was working with local police and army units.

With modern technologies, when the word would be given then tens of thousands of police and soldiers would act as a single unit in thousands of places.

The power of the American dollar was bigger than any political power. World currencies were based around the US Dollar. Oil and Stock Markets, Bullion Markets and just about everything you could think of worked in some way on the US Dollar. It was the currency that was accepted in just about every country. Bearing in mind that almost 60% of all dollar bills were held outside of the USA. Few would know about the operation that had started with a niggling thought by the co-owner of a small Lincolnshire cat and dog rescue centre.

"Mark is it OK to send the rest of your seal team down to Billy and Jenny's place. I know there are two other places in the UK like theirs being used by the Perkins, but they are not family like Billy and Jenny" Jack asked

"Sure can. I was going to suggest that anyway. As we have seen the thugs come there before. I suspect that Perkins will try something there as well. If not him, then Alexi, or perhaps some of his cronies from elsewhere. This thing will end tonight."

Back in Moscow preparations were being made to recover the lost territories. Those that had disappeared prior to Putin becoming their leader. Putin had been born into the United Socialist Soviet Republic in the fall of 1952 at the height of the cold war. He had grown up with the USA attempting to dictate what his country could do. The Cuban missile crisis and many other crimes that the USA had twisted to put the blame on the USSR the American had interfered in Cuban politics and sent troops in only for them to be defeated in the Bay of Pigs. The American Air Force were defeated by the Cubans their army of Cubans who were supported by the CIA were crushed by the Cuban Rebel Army

Russia had offered a defence for Cuba a line of missiles pointed at USA Cities ready to destroy the USA. Nikita Khrushchev had been weak and had backed down to The USA President John F Kennedy, who had been the son of a bootlegger during prohibition, a common criminal in the eyes of Putin.

The dissolution of the Soviet Union began it's disintegration within the Soviet Union which resulted in the end of his country's and its federal government's existence as a sovereign state, thereby resulting in its constituent republics gaining full sovereignty on 26 December 1991.

In recent years the USA had put into place so many bans on import and export of goods to those countries that showed any kind of support for the Russia that Putin was leading into the new future. The sanctions placed were starting to bite especially after the region of Crimea had come back under the protective wing of Russia. Putin's plans to regain the Soviet Union were well underway.

Vladimir Putin lifted the old style telephone on his desk and placed a call.

28
The Big Take Down

All around the world Telephones rang and computers pinged as the message was sent out. Those that were poised to act would do so. Putin replaced the receiver.

His accountant calmly walked down through the shopping centre at Lenin Hills. They had parked their car in the underground car park. He had told his family to take nothing but the clothes on their backs. Then just to appear normal they had entered the Vegas Kunteso Mall and bought a few items which were placed in two Vegas branded carrier bags. In order that they did not arouse suspicion, they had only bought food items. They walked like many other families on Lenin Hill that day seemingly without a care in the world. There was a small cue of people standing outside the US Embassy. The accountant walked past with his family and then to a coffee shop that was less than twenty yards away.

The black FSB car was parked a little further down the road. Taking photographs of all those that entered or even those that went to the gates that were controlled by United States Marines.

The accountant sat down and ordered coffee for him and his wife and orange juice for the two children. He sipped his coffee and waited. Watching the cue of people in his peripheral vision whilst talking to his wife.

Now there were no people waiting to get in the embassy. The family picked up their shopping bags and returned back towards The Vegas Kunteso Mall. The men in the black Mercedes never even bothered to lift the camera until it was too late. By the time the family had handed over their new US Passports to the Marines on gate guard, their faces could not bee seen. The Marine looked at the passports he had been given and lifted the microphone to his radio, spoke for two seconds and brought the family inside the confines of the Embassy.

Another telephone was lifted in the USA. This telephone was located at The George Bush Center for Intelligence. It being the headquarters of the Central Intelligence Agency, located in the unincorporated community of Langley in Fairfax County, Virginia, United States, near Washington, D.C.

Some three seconds later another telephone rang. Also located in Washington D.C. this time it was at The J. Edgar Hoover Building located at 935 Pennsylvania Avenue NW in Washington, D.C.

Seconds later an international call was placed to INTERPOL General Secretariat 200, Quai Charles de Gaulle 69006 Lyon in France.

From there multiple calls at at the same time went out all over the world. These were sent to predetermined numbers and that included a call to New Scotland Yard. Police Station. Westminster, London. Specifically to their Organised crimes unit and also to the anti terrorism units. Over 10,000 police officers reacted within seconds of that first call. Most of those officers were armed. Another person who received a call, and that was retired detective Alex Gordon.

"Its happening boss." Alex said to Jack

"What is happening at the Perkins farm?" Jack asked

"We don't have anyone there any more sir as Orville and Brian have joined Buddy and Zack down at your brothers." Mark replied

"I think we really should get eyes on things there Mark. Jean can you run things from here?"

"Jack you are forgetting one thing. You no longer have any right to enter anyone's property. The same applies to you Mark. However if you two would like to assist me as witnesses then you can come with me. I am up to date on my firearms and have one in a lock box in my car. I am assuming that you have yourself on close protection duty at your embassy again Mark?"

"No y'all know I never leave my home without my coffee grinds from Mississippi nor would I leave without my trusty Desert Eagle 50AE." Mark said drawing a massive gun from under his well tailored Brooks Brothers jacket.

"Well I don't care what you say Jean I am not going down there unarmed. I will take my 12 bore." Jack said

"I am guessing you don't have a vest Jack? Not to worry I have a spare in my car. I assume you have one Mark?" Jean said

"After my last escapade with you two, damn straight I have a vest with me. So what is you plan Jean?" He replied

"Simple we go down and close their exit road and wait for the uniforms to arrive from Lincoln."

"How do you know that Lincoln bobbies are coming?" Jack asked her.

"Simple I just pressed this." Jean said referring to her police radio red button. And continued.

"So I would guess we have about a ten minute jump on the Boston police and around another twenty for the Lincoln Firearms unit to catch up with us. So we better get moving. My car and yours Mark." Jean said racing for the door. Closely followed by Jack who had to unlock a metal gun cabinet in his garage before taking his shotgun and a box of cartridges.

Jack sat next to Jean in her car. Looking on the back seat, there were two supposedly bullet proof and anti-stab vests. Mark followed in his hired car.

From the main road it was easy to see the Horsebox, along with a silver Ford Transit and the white Range Rover at the front of the Perkins farmhouse. Jean drove just inside the road leading down to the house. Where she had parked her car, due to a bend in the driveway, it was impossible to see the house, which by the same logic meant that they could not see her.

Jean jumped out and opened the back door of the car taking out and then tossing one of the tactical vests across to Jack. And she took the other and strapped it on. Jack did the same and then took his shotgun and loaded it, before putting as many cartridges as he could into his jacket pockets.

Jean went to the rear of the car and unlooked the boot before unlocking a gun box which contained a Sig Sueur 9mm pistol and two fully loaded cartridges. Jean strapped on a leg holster before putting the now loaded firearm into it. DCI Jean Short got back into the car and positioned it so that it was across the driveway, making it impossible for any car to pass without them falling into either of the ditches that ran down both sides of the road. Jean took the keys and walked to Mark.

"Can you place your car behind mine and get as close as you can, so the two cars are horizontal?"

"Sure can." Mark said now also wearing a tactical vest that had FBI on the front and on the back

He had his holster now over the vest and a further three magazines in a pouch attached to his belt.

They heard rather than saw the vehicles starting up down at the farmhouse. It was not long before their small convoy came into view. The Range Rover at the front followed by the Transit van and the horsebox bringing up the rear. On seeing the road blocked they stopped, at first confused as to why the exit to their private property was blocked. Then the realisation struck that this was not an accident but a deliberate attempt to stop them leaving the farm.

John and Natasha Perkins stayed in their car, but Alexi got out of the Transit and walked to the Perkins car. They were around one hundred feet from the blockade and although they could not hear what was being said, it was fairly obvious that Alexi was asking his boss what he wanted him to about the blockade.

A few seconds later the passenger from the Horsebox appeared and joined Alexi, it was the Vet that Perkins had hired for his horses. Alexi removed a gun from behind his back and gave it to John Perkins. Then both Alexi and the Vet returned to their vehicles. All three began to reverse back down the road until they were out of sight.

"What do you suppose they are doing?" Jack asked from behind the protection of marks car.

"Well if I were him I would first try to run the block." Mark said and then carried on.

"But he does not yet know the stopping power of the Desert Eagle. This baby here can take the block out of an eighteen wheel Kenwood or Mack Truck. So stopping them will be easy." Mark said

"Mark you do not shoot unless I tell you too. Have you got that?" Jean said.

"Yes Mam."

All three of them looked over the road from behind marks rented car and Jeans personal car.

"Jean what kind of insurance do you have on your car?" Jack asked

"Fully comprehensive why?" she replied

"You do realise if this comes under any of the terrorism laws that your insurance will not cover that?"

"Fuck well I never like the car anyway." She replied with a laugh.

Just then they all heard an engine revving wildly then they saw the Horsebox thundering up the driveway towards them and their cars. The big van smashed into the cars pushing then about five feet further up the road. All three of them had jumped clear just prior to the impact but were now on their feet as the Horsebox reversed to have another go at removing the blockade.

"Can I shoot now?" Mark asked Jean

"Yes but only shoot at the engine." Jean said.

The Horsebox rounded the corner again and Mark took careful aim and his hand canon roared three times. Then steam and oil spewed out of the front of the van the engine died. Alexi jumped down from the cab with a pistol in his hand and fired three shots in the direction of Jean and her companions.

Mark fired once more. Alexi's body hit the ground even before his brain had realised that his heart had stopped pumping. Not that there was a heart inside the empty chest cavity. The resulting carnage of being stuck by a fifty calibre round in the centre mass of his chest was instantly fatal. The round had first hit his sternum flattening slightly on impact, travelling at 1542 feet per second. It had exited Alexi's spine a millisecond later after first punching a gaping hole through the body, before the following shock-wave boiled what ever soft tissue matter there was left within the chest cavity. Death was caused by three things. Massive blood loss. Catastrophic damage to internal organs followed by rank stupidity. By thinking his small calibre pistol was a match for the gun that had already stopped the five litre engine block of his horsebox.

Back behind Jeans insurance write off of a car and Marks slightly less damaged rental, they waited to see what would happen next.

"What now Mark?" Jack asked

"Well if I were them I would try to flank us or I would make a run for it, but as they cant get up this road. Then it would be the later. I say we move down and use their horsebox as cover."

"OK Mark lets do this." Jean said and she led the way out from behind their damaged cars towards the van. Crouching low and running fast.

Jack quickly looked inside the large van. One of the freezers in the back had fallen over and there was frozen meat and bundles of cash all over the back of the horsebox.

"All clear here." He said and jumped back down to join the other two.

"Are there any roads out from the back of that place?" Jean asked Jack

"Not that I know of."

"Then they are gonna be on foot." Jean said and started to move forward following the line of the ditch at the side of the road.

A rifle shot rang out and Jean fell into the muddy ditch. Instinctively Jack and Mark hit the dirt at the same time.

"Jean?" Jack called out. No answer.

Jack and mark both slid down into the ditch and made their way to where Jean lay face down in muddy water. Jack rolled her over so that her face was now out of the dirty water. She groaned.

"Thank God Jean I thought you were a goner. Lets take a look at that wound." Jack said

Jack laid jean so that her back was against the front wall of the ditch offering her the most protection the direction of the farmhouse. The bullet had hit Jean on her left hand side where the vest joined. Jack rolled jean forward and found an exit wound. Whilst serious, providing they could control the bleeding it would not be fatal. Mark removed his tie and wound it into a ball and tucked it under Jeans vest at the back where the bullet had exited and then took a cotton handkerchief from his pocket and placed it on the front wound.

"Keep the pressure on that Jean and stay here. Your folks are on the way, Jack and I will follow these bastards."

"You better take this" Jean said with a wince. And passed over her radio to Jack.

"OK Jean stay here don't move and we will be back before you know it." Jack said then he and Mark, moved down towards the farmhouse keeping inside the waterlogged drain.

They made it down to the edge of the courtyard with its fancy ornamental fountain and pond. Perkins had a pistol as did Natasha, Alexi's wife was in tears screaming at Natasha, neither Jack nor Mark knew what it was she was shouting. At the end though it did not matter as Natasha turned and shot her maid from point blank range.

It was a small calibre gun with limited range, but at that distance it proved to be a fatal shot. Striking the woman in the centre of the forehead. Her body crumpled to the ground.

"Quickly this way through the house." John said as they ran for the front door. The original horsebox driver was at the door with his rifle poised, waiting for Jack or Mark to show their position. The Vet was beside him with what looked to be some kind of machine gun.

In the ditch, Mark motioned to Jack that, he was going to follow them through the house and that Jack should try and get somewhere around the rear of the farmhouse and stay under cover until Mark came out. Jack fitted the earpiece of the radio to his right ear and listened in on the police chatter. He pressed the red button again to give location and then headed towards the back of the house, leaving Mark in the ditch. Jack got to a good viewpoint and sat waiting. He watched the back of the house expecting at any moment to see Perkins and co, fleeing from the desert eagle of the FBI man.

"Get up real slow and drop the gun." John Perkins said.

Jack did exactly as he was told.

"Why?"

"Why what?" Jack answered

"Why did you have to interfere? We were on our way out of here and no one would have been hurt. You shot Alexi for what?"

"First you are breaking the law, second I never shot anyone. Thirdly. Alexi shot first.

"What does it matter to you if we broke a few laws. Your brother and his wife benefited from what we were doing. All those animals that we rescued and she found homes for these unfortunates. So we all made a little money."

"I think you made more than a little money, so when did you get the plastic surgery done? Before or after you divorced your wife Natasha? You are Fedor Petrovich Krasnov are you not?" Jack said

"My my, you have been a busy little man haven't you, who else knows?"

"Now if I told you that their lives would be in danger. So I think I will keep that to myself." Jack said

"How about I just Kill you now and take my chances." Perkins said and raised his gun pointing it at jacks head.

"On your knees and interlace your hands on your head." John said and when jack as done as he was told.

"Do you have any smart comment to make before I end your pitiful and worthless life?" John said.

Jack heard the gunshot, but felt no pain, then the weight of a man fell on top of him forcing him deeper into the muddy ditch

"Come on Jack stop playing around in the mud" Jean said from behind him.

Jack struggled out from under John who was laid dead face down in the drain.

"You know who that is Jean?"

"Ohh you mean who that was? Yes I knew it was Fedor Petrovich Krasnov. Alex told me just before we left yours. By the way you are welcome." Jean replied.

"Are you sure you should be running around with that would Jean?" Jack asked just as Jean fainted and fell into his arms.

He laid her gently down on the bank of the ditch. After checking that there was pressure to both of her wounds. Jack waited for her to regain consciousness before giving her back her police radio.

"Listen to me Jean. Mark has gone in the house after the Vet, the driver and Natasha. I had expected them to make a run for things out the back door. But so far nothing. Your guys are about five minutes out. I hit the Code Zero button again so they know that you are in trouble. I am going in after mark as I think he may be in trouble. If you see anyone that is not Mark or myself start shooting at them but keep your head down and hopefully they will run back inside." Jack said

"Jack its not your fight the armed response units will be here in a couple of minutes let them handle it." Jean said holding her hand to the injured part of her side.

"You know I cant do that, imagine it was me in there, you would bust a gut to get to me. Stay safe see you soon." Jack said and took off at a running crouch, holding his shotgun across his body.

Quickly Jack checked on the housemaid, no pulse. Not that he expected one. At the front door he quickly peeked inside he saw nothing. He turned the handle to the double glazed front door and it gave easily. He opened it silently and entered the large house. Snatching a look in the room on his right with the shotgun pulled firmly into his shoulder. Nothing there.

Moving swiftly and silently across the main entranceway he opened the door on his left and pushed it wide open with his muddy shoe. Then swung the double barrelled shotgun covering the centre of the room, quickly checking left and right, clear. Believing that there would be no one upstairs especially if they were trying to make a run for it, he made his way further down the corridor.

The main dining room was on his left its double doors were partially open and the was a splash of wet blood on one of the handles. From his own training years ago on the police hostage rescue course which he had attended, he knew it would be foolish to expose himself at a double doored room. The way to do it was to keep low to the ground and push both doors at the same time. Should there be anyone inside they would automatically fire at the middle of the doors. After checking that his immediate area was safe he got down on the ground and pushed the doors wide open.

The greeting he got was way more than he had expected, the wood on the doors above him, were shredded by automatic machine-gun fire. There was a slight pause in the deafening sounds and jack looked up through the smoke to see the Driver standing there with what looked like an Uzi machine pistol which had a double drum magazine. Jack fired both barrels almost mountainously and the driver flew backwards over the table before landing face down on the floor.

Jack initially thought he had killed the man, then he saw the drivers arm move. The Uzi had fallen from his grip as he had flown across the polished mahogany table. The machine pistol lay about six feet from the man, who had also been wearing a bullet proof vest, whilst some of the shot from the cartridges had hit the man in his arm he was not mortally wounded.

Jack broke the shotgun open and ejected the spent shells then struggle to reload getting just one in before the man reached his own gun Jack fired. The full load, hit the man directly in his face, shredding and demolishing tissue and bone at the same time. The driver would not get up this time.

Jack thought about picking up the UZI but as he had never fired one of these before, nor would he know how to reload it if required so he kicked it out of sight under the table.

That still left Natasha and the Vet. He knew the Vet had a rifle with a scope and that Natasha had been using a small automatic pistol. Jack could hear the emergency vehicles approaching fast. After checking the room Jack went out the door and almost lost his head as a snatched shot from the rifle, at the top of the double staircase. The shot hit the edge of the door sending large splinters into jacks face. Jack fell back inside the dining room and moved to the wall. He pulled a large shard of wood from just above his eye and the blood ran down partially blocking his vision.

The very distinct sound of Mark's Desert Eagle, was followed by the clatter of the rifle falling down the opulent stairs.

"Y'all can come out now Jackie boy. All the bad dudes are down, and the Russian bitch is tied up in the kitchen." Mark said

Jack made sure his gun was fully reloaded and carefully exited the dining room and walked into the hallway, The rifle was now on the floor. Jack looked up to where the shot had come from and the vets body was draped over the banister, minus most of his head.

Sirens were stopped at the top end of the driveway. There were shouts from outside the house.

"Armed police, come out now, keep your hands on top of your heads." Jack then broke his gun open and then dropped it to the ground. Mark removed the magazine in his hand canon before laying it on the ground. It was only then that jack realised that the vest Jean had given him to wear had a bold patch on the front saying 'POLICE'

Both Jack and Mark walked out as instructed then knelt on the ground with their fingers interlaced above their heads.

Some one must have cleared the road as there was now a police car followed by an ambulance and three more police vehicles. Two officers were helping Jean towards the waiting ambulance.

"Its OK sergeant those two are with me they are part of my team." She shouted over to where Jack and Mark were about to be tied up with zip ties.

Jack and mark now stood up and went back towards the farmhouse.

"So where did you put the Russian bitch?"

"I left her chilling her heels in the Kitchen." Mark replied as the walked down the hallway past sever ARP officers, in their black boiler suits and kevlar helmets. Jack followed Mark into the kitchen and then Mark opened the walk in freezer. He had smashed the internal release handle off presumably when he put her in there. Her hands had been tied with wire and they had been looped over a meat hook that was hanging from the ceiling. There was a trickle of blood from her nose and mouth.

"Did she try to beat you up?" Jack asked sarcastically

"No but I got tired of her whining so I had to shut her up." Mark said and directed the police to take her into custody.

Jack Picked up his shotgun from the floor emptying out the shells in front of one of the ARP police officers. Mark collected his Desert Eagle and fitted it back into his under the shoulder holster. The pair of them walked back into the afternoon sunshine. They walked over to where the medics were trying to make Jean lie down on the stretcher. The Paramedic seeing all the blood that was flowing down Jacks face wanted him to get in the ambulance. Jack refused but did allow them to place a dressing and a bandage over to stem the bleeding.

Jack took her Jean's hand and thanked her and they both said they would see her later. He would make sure that Alex, would meet her at Pilgrim hospital in Boston.

Raids just like the one that Jack had been involved in happened around the world some ended without deaths but most went the way that John and Natasha had chosen to go. They went down fighting, but the question was why die when you don't have to.

The delivery addresses of all the freezers were raided simultaneously. Apart from the Billions of dollars recovered nobody wanted to talk.

28
A Different Take-Down

After the formalities had been sorted with the police and Jean providing cover stories as well as Marie from the US Treasury Department providing more cover for Jack and Mark. They were allowed to return to Jacks home. As soon as they got there Jack arranged for his wife Janet to drive Alex over to Pilgrim Hospital.

"Did we get the print factory in the take down." Jack asked Tom.

"We did but it seems like they knew we were coming for them we got several million in fake notes and even a hundred gallons of iron infused ink. We got all the cotton and silk paper. But unfortunately we lost the plates?" Tom said

"How could we lose the plates if we had the place under surveillance?" Jack said

"We have a team in there at the moment looking to see if they have the plates hidden somewhere in the building. What is interesting is one of the people we arrested at the print factory is claiming diplomatic immunity." Marie said

"For which country?" Jack asked

"Try Russia on for size." she replied

"Are we giving it to them? And has their Embassy said anything about this yet?" Jack asked

"That would be no and no, at least for now we are getting chopper to take us over to Nottingham in about five minutes. I am guessing that you and Jack want to be in on this." Marie said to mark.

They had barely answered when the sound of a helicopter filled the air. A Bell 206 landed in the field behind Jacks house and the rotors kept turning Marie raced for the chopper with the two men in tow behind her. As soon as she was in beside the pilot she put on a headset and spoke quickly into it. Jack got in and Mark followed and pulled the door closed behind him. They had not even had a chance to put their seatbelts on before the helicopter took of and pulled a tight turn and headed back the way it had come.

Less than thirty minutes later they had landed at the print site and were directed by an armed officer to a room within the factory complex. Another two armed officers stood outside a door. The officer that had led Maries team in, knocked on the door which was then opened by a man in a business suit.

"Come on in."

There were another two armed officers in the room and a man wearing denim jeans and a hooded plain grey sweatshirt. His hands were zip-tied together.

"Who are you?" Marie asked the suited man.

"Really I should be the one asking all the questions. But it would appear that someone above my pay-grade seems to think that you are of some importance in this. Suffice to say I am with MI6. You I believe are with your Treasury Department, you are with the FBI and you are?" The man said looking at Jack

"An interested party." Jack replied.

"I would like the room please." Marie said

"I think you are forgetting who has this man under arrest." The MI6 man replied

"I am sure that you have your orders and I am also sure that you have been directed not to interfere in our investigation. I am sure you will be written in on the outcome of things. But for now I would like the room. And that includes you" she said referring to the two armed police officers.

"We should stay for your protection mam" The MI6 man replied.

"I have my protection here" She said and motioned to mark who opened hi jacket to reveal his Desert Eagle.

The MI6 man nodded to the two officers who left the room. When the door closed Marie lost no time in starting to question him.

"Name?"

"I have Diplomat Immunity." He said with a heavy Russian accent.

"Not without a name you don't?"

"I am Russian Diplomat for Trade."

"Name?"

No answer

"Name for the last time. Without a name you are a common criminal involved in terrorist activity for the last time name?" Marie asked and then she seemed to lose her temper.

She slapped him with an open hand. It hurt his pride far more than his face.

"Where are the printing plates?" and followed it with a slap. Still no answer.

"Jack can you go outside and ask the nice gentleman from MI6 if this man has been searched."

Jack did as he was bid and went looking for the MI6 guy. After being shown to the front of the building.

"The agents want to know if the suspect has been properly searched." Jack asked him

"What do you think? Of course he was, the ARP boys would have done that as soon as they busted in, Why do you ask? Ohhhhhhh shit you left them alone with him." The MI6 man said and started to run back down the corridor towards the room where the Russian was being held.

Jack followed close on his heels. The MI6 guy burst through the door, only to find the man sat in his chair, still still zip-tied and completely unharmed.

"Your man here, is Russian but does not have any form of diplomatic immunity. I am sure that someone will come and take him off your hands soon. The United States, thanks you for your co-operation." Marie said and started to walk out of the room.

"Wait please I have something to tell you." The man suddenly said.

"A little privacy please." Marie said to the MI6 man, who left while muttering something about women giving orders.

"Well spit it out or you will end up in a Ukrainian jail by tomorrow morning." Mark said

"The plates are on their way to the Russian embassy in London. One of the drivers has them." The Russian man said

"I need a name and what is he driving." Marie said as she slammed her hand back down on the table.

"Dimitri Rassamov. But I don't know what car all I know is he collected the plates about an hour before the raid." He answered

"Not good enough, get him over to the Ukraine authorities." Marie said indicating that Jack was to do as she had said.

Jack decided to play along.

"All right let's go." Jack said helping the Russian up from the chair

"No wait you promised." He screamed

"Tell me about the car or no deal." Marie said

"I don't know western car makes. But it was a red one." He pleaded.

"Fine, we will send one of our people to get you out of here," Marie said before continuing

"Jack get that Brit boy back in here."

Jack did and the suited man returned.

"Hold him here incognito. No one gets to speak to him and he speaks to no one. If you think my authority does not climb as high as yours. Then call your boss. Right we are out of here," She said and they headed back out of the building to the waiting chopper.

As soon as they were inside, she put her headset on and spoke to the pilot. Then she took out her mobile and spoke to someone else. The chopper took off and headed towards London.

They arrived at the side of a slip road there was already several cars with blue flashing lights and even an ambulance waiting. The police and some people in civilian clothing were marshalling traffic on to the M25 Outer Ring Road for London. The three left the helicopter and joined those on the road check point. They were now under the charge of Marie O'Malley

"We are looking for any red car with a Russian or Russian sounding driver. There may be just the one or possibly two in the vehicle. So make sure you check properly." Marie said to the officers who were waving the cars through.

"What we don't want if a god damn gun battle here so if you even think there is a gun then use your fucking tasers. So take them out of you pockets and hold them out of sight by your legs."

"Mam that is not UK Policy" An officer said.

"I have just come from one gun battle where a police officer was shot and seriously wounded. Do you want to be the next one. These people will not think twice about shooting you. So do you want to be safe or do you want to die?" Marie asked and all four officers took out their tasers

Over the next hour they checked cars.

"There about a dozen cars back." Mark pointed to a red SUV that was looking for a way to get around the road block.

"You two with me" Marie said and they followed her on the outside of the lane.

"Stop all the cars and don't let anyone through" Mark shouted back at the two other officers. Jack followed Mark up the inside as Mark removed his Desert Eagle and held it hidden out of sight by his leg.

The red SUV tried to reverse but there was a line of cars backed up for about a mile. The SUV tried to force its way forward again with the same problem.

Marie and the officers were now running up the outside of the line of cars, Mark and Jack were doing the same on the inside. They had to get there before the driver managed to get out of his predicament, he was trying to force his way onto the hard shoulder in order to go around the road block.

Marie got there first and was in the act of taking aim at the driver when he hit her with the front drivers side wing knocking her to the ground. Had it not been for the bus in front of him he would have run her over. One of the constables tried to rescue Marie and was pulling her back. The other officer dropped his taser and went to their aid. Mark shot through the engine block three times. The sound up close was deafening.

Jack pulled open the passenger door of the SUV and made a grab for the driver who had now tried to put it into reverse. As the car spluttered and then died. Motorists were getting out of their cars and running back the way they had come. The driver reached for some thing in the drivers door. Marie was now on her feet fired her gun once through the windscreen of the car, hitting the driver in the shoulder. Mark dived inside the car and grabbed the man by the throat and pinning the other arm to the seat. The drivers door was opened and Marie reached in and removed an Uzi machine pistol from the door pocket. She passed it to one of the police officers who were behind her.

Mark unclipped the man's seatbelt and dragged him screaming out of the passenger door. He threw the man on the ground and brought the driver's hands behind his back and Zip-Tied them. After making the man stand he walked him across to the shoulder of the road and made him sit. Jack did a quick search of the car and came out with a briefcase. He laid it on top of the damaged SUV's bonnet and clicked the latches, opening it there were around twenty engraved plates most of which still had ink on their surfaces.

"I think these are what you want Marie"

"So long as those are all there is. Then yes. I will need to check them out, though if you look on the back of the plates you will see a swastika being held by an eagle." She said

Jack took one of the plates out and turned it over in his hands, before putting it back into its slot in the case.

"Well?"

"You can stop looking." Jack said.

"We still need to interview this guy and we need to do it in private away from this place." Marks said.

"Lets go home, the Perkins place should be empty and we can use the stables." Jack said. After closing the briefcase and helping the wounded man to his feet, Mark and led him over to where the helicopter was sat. Marie spoke to the police and thanked them for their assistance and walked behind the three men. Jack got in one side and Mark shoved the man, none too gently in the other side, before following him in. Marie got in the front beside the pilot and spoke into the headset. The rotors turned and the helicopter lifted off.

"What do you think the press will make of all that?" Jacke shouted at Marie

"All what? And what press it was a drug dealer caught in a sting operation." She said. Although Jack could not see her face he knew she was smiling.

29
Ownership Of Crimes

Marie had the chopper land at the back of the Perkins farm, Alex and Tom were waiting there for them. Jean had discharged herself from hospital ad was sat in the front of Alex's car. There was blue police tape all the way around the house and also on the stable block. Jean had obviously squared the circle with the Lincolnshire police force.

The chopper landed and as soon as the rotors had spun down, they exited. The driver of the red SUV was firmly supported between Mark and Jack.

"Can you two manage him?" Jack asked.

Getting a nod from Marie and a thumbs up from Mark. Jack walked over to where Jean was sat in the front passenger seat of Alex's car.

"Hows the side?" Jack asked Knowing full well that really Jean should have stayed in hospital.

"Ohh You know." She replied off handedly.

"So how did you fix this with Lincolnshire?"

"Told them they could have the credit, for breaking an international money laundering operation. That and they can have the proceeds from the Perkins Farm Sale, after all it was bought with the proceeds of crime. So it should net them quite a few million for their next years budget. So we can have this as long as is required." Jean replied

"Nice work, giving them the credit goes a long way with inter county co-operation. We have one of the guys that were printing and I think he is pretty high up the ladder of things."

"You know we could have used John if you had managed to take him alive." Jean said

"I think had he got out from here alive, he would have died pretty quickly in Russia. They will be cleaning house by now. Are you fit to walk?"

"Just try and stop me Jack."Jean said and Alex took her arm and the three of them walked down to what was the Vets surgery. Mark had the driver attached to a hoist in the surgery and the man was almost on his toes to save his weight being carried on the wrists that were still bound together with the plastic zip-ties.

Jean sat down on a chair that Alex had pulled out for her. Tom was standing next to a steel trolley with a laptop on. Marie was now looking at the plates that they had recovered from the SUV

"Where are the $100 plates?" Marie asked their prisoner

"Russkiy"

"We already know you are Russian and I know you speak English. So we can do it simple and nice or we can do it the hard painful way. The choice is up to you. So once again where are the one hundred dollar plates?"

"Net angliyskogo tol'ko russkiy"

"Seriously you want me to beat it out of you."

"Pass me that hammer please." Marie said to no one in particular. Jack noticed the eyes on the man move towards the hammer that was on the side of the table.

Jack reached over and picked it up and made a big show of handing the chunky hammer over to the US Treasury Agent.

"You know my brother was tortured and murdered by Russian mobsters. They tortured him for days. It broke my mothers heart. She could not even recognise his face when they brought his body home. I always told her I would revenge his death one day. It would appear that fate has handed me this day on a plate." Marie said as she slammed the hammer down on to the stainless steel table so hard that it actually tore a hole in it.

"Take him down and lay him on the table with his legs apart so the first damage I can do, to this Russian is crush his manhood." Marie said as she removed her jacket and took her pistol out of its holster and passed it over to Jean.

Mark and Jack lowered the man down on to the table adding an extra zip-tie to bind his hands to the top of the table and then one for each leg to the bottom of the table. While the men were doing this Marie was testing the weight of the seven pound lump-hammer from hand to hand. This hammer had be used to break concrete and house bricks. Now she was threatening to use it on the Russians gonads.

"You two might want to step back when I do this as it is going to get real messy." She said

"C'mon Marie you really don't have to do this don't be as barbaric as them." Mark said

"Just so you know even if you cant speak English this is just business the business of revenge. For my brother and mostly for my mother." She said as she raised the hammer high over her head and poised to smash down onto his manhood.

"Stop Please please don't do it. I never harmed your brother. I will tell you what you want to know Please." The man said

"Are you Russian?"

"Yes I drive for the embassy. That is what I do." He said

"What is you name?"

"My name is Sergio Maronov" he said, and Marie looked over at Tom who was clicking away on his computer. Suddenly the drivers face came up on the screen. And Tom nodded to Marie.

"Where are the One Hundred Dollar plates?"

"They were sent to Moscow."

"How?"

"I don't understand."

"How were they sent to Moscow?"

"I took them to the Embassy and then they went in the diplomatic bag and they flew to Moscow, that was this evening."

"What airline?"

"I think the British one British Airways"

"Marie took out her telephone and called the American Embassy.

"They are on the evening flight to Moscow which will have taken off by now so you need to get it down somehow and make sure that we get the diplomatic bag. Use any means you have to, these are the Bernhard plates, we cant lose these a second time." Marie said

There was a pause as whoever was talking with Marie said something. Marie interrupted them.

"I don't give a flying fuck about laws and territories. We need them back at any cost, so if you have to shoot the Fucking plane down then do it just get those plates back and that is an Order. My orders come direct from the Whitehouse. If you have a problem with anything I tell you do do take it up with the president. Just get that plane down on the ground before it gets inside Russian airspace." Marie said and shut her mobile phone.

"I am sorry about your brother Marie." Jean said

"What? Ohh That." Marie laughed and then said

"I don't have a brother and my mother died in childbirth. I just said that to scare the crap out of him. I guess it worked especially if you all believed it. Now lets find out who is behind all this."

"Sergio I can put you on a plane to Moscow or return you to your embassy and let them know you told us where they plates are. Or you can tell me everything you know about why the fake US Bills were being made and who is behind it. If you do that I can promise you life long protection from any Russian retaliation. So which is it to be?"

"I will help you. Please do not give me back to Russia or to the embassy. For they will blame me and murder me."

"Jean can you arrange for this man to be delivered to the US Embassy, they will be expecting him. Best take him to the door under a blanket."

"I think we can accommodate that request. By they way nice acting. You had me fooled. I really believed you were gonna crush his nuts." Jean replied

"Oh that part was not acting, I need those plates." Marie said

Almost thirty minutes later Air Traffic Control for London Heathrow International Airport, relayed an urgent message having received the correct codes from MI6 that there was an explosive device on board of British Airways flight BA880. The flight had been turned around and an air corridor was opened specifically for it. There were three Typhoon jet fighters scrambled from their base at RAF Coningsby in Lincolnshire, to escort the flight back to London. Before arriving back at London Heathrow they stayed over the North Sea doing figure of eights to use up fuel. This was standard practice for any flight that may have a problem.

What it also did was to give Marie, Mark, and Jack time to fly down in the chopper. Jean stayed back at Jacks house with Alex, due to her injury. Marie and the others landed at the designated spot on the end of the emergency runway, which already had fire-tenders and other emergency vehicles lined up at the side.

Jack knew this was Just for show and that as soon as the plane touched down it would be directed to the end of the runway and then there would be a rapid decamp as per international aviation rules. No baggage would be allowed down the slides with the passengers. The Royal Air Force Bomb Disposal Squad, based in London arrived just after Marie's chopper touched down. Marie called her embassy who then called the British Embassy who then called the Bomb Squad leader who then accepted that Marie would be in charge.

One of the Typhoon fighters screamed down the entire length of the runway before pulling up and doing a barrel roll and then breaking left. It was followed a few moments later by the other two fighters. Like the first Typhoon they pulled up at the end of the runway and shot up into the night sky.

Jack looked at where they had come from and could see the Airbus A320 making its approach to the runway. A textbook landing and then taxi before stopping at the designated location. The Aircraft was immediately surrounded by emergency vehicles a series of six buses pulled in behind them.

On board the aircraft the crew had not been told that this was just a ruse to get the plane back in the UK. They genuinely believed they had a bomb on board although none of the passengers knew this. The Pilot had announced that they had an engine problem and would have to return to London immediately. He apologised for the inconvenience.

Passengers were instructed to stay seated until the plane had come to a halt. Then the passengers were told to removed their shoes and leave them at their seats the same applied to all hand luggage. It was all to be left in the overhead lockers. When the emergency was over they would all be able to get their items.

The plane turned and stopped and the engines spun down. Marie Jack and Mark waited at the end of the plane. The Officer in charge if the RAF BDU had his men bring in a long extendable aluminium ladder to the rear Port Emergency Exit.

The front starboard emergency exit and the wing exit doors were opened. The plane decamped by seat rows with those at the front of the aircraft first. These were the seats that were first class, this is where the Russian who was a chef at the embassy, had been seated. They had sent him so as not to arouse suspicion. This would prove to be their biggest mistake of all. A real diplomat would never under any circumstances ever let the bag out of his or her sight. But the chef did as he was told. He saw the bomb disposal vehicle out of the window and all the emergency vehicles. He would not die for a stupid case. So he left it in the overhead locker.

Being lead through the plane by the RAF officer. Jack and the others waited until first class was emptied. Then they went in pulling the curtain closed behind them. They started searching the overhead lockers and found the bag almost immediately. Mark lifted the bag down and laid it on the seat next to him and rapidly picked its locks. Opening the case there were several printing plates that had been wrapped in cloth. There had been no attempt to disguise them. They were all $100 plate for both the front and the back of the bills.

Jack found a British Airways carrier bag and passed it to Marie. She held it open while Mark placed the hundred dollar printing plates inside. Then closed the diplomatic back and returned it to the overhead locker, before they all went back down the plane and exited the way they had come in, then to their helicopter. The pilot asked for permission to take off and was granted as all other planes has been kept clear of the airport with a 'Bomb'

30
Market Closed

After they had all been dropped back at Jacks and before any celebratory drinks. Jack first had to go down to see his brother and sister in law. It had been fun he had to admit that to himself. But he knew that this would be the last time. Jack was over seventy and it was a young man's world. The adrenalin rush at the time had taken over all the other senses, the ones that say, are you mad, this is stupidly dangerous. Playing with guns only ever ends one way. That was. it ends with someone dying, not always the bad guys either. He nearly lost one of his oldest and dearest friends.

Jean had worked alongside Jack since she had had started out in the Swindon Police Force. as a Constable. She had worked her way up through the ranks making Detective Inspector, before Jack had retired and then getting to the dizzy heights of Detective Chief Inspector. And like Jack had done, she refused to fly a desk. Jean was a proper copper. It was what other police officers would call a Coppers Copper. She was not interested in the politics of policing she wanted to be out there fighting crime and catching the bad guys. Today she nearly died and it would have been Jacks fault for calling in a favour.

Jack pulled his BMW up outside the home of his younger brother Billy. He sat for a moment in the car, thinking about what he was going to say. He was still sat there when the kitchen door opened and Billy stood in the door way.

Jack opened the door and climbed out of the car. He walked to his brother and in a moment of genuine brotherly love he grabbed his brother and hugged him.

"Its over"

"It is?"

"Yes Billy at least as far as you and Jenny are concerned. All the bad guys are down. And their property has been seized. Everything that you and Jenny have is yours and under the proceeds of crimes act you would have to have benefited from crime. Neither you nor Jenny committed any crime and that is the way it is going to look on the books.

"So we keep the kennels, cattery and the extra land at the bottom?" Jenny asked?

"Yes its all yours. The same applies to all the vehicles that are registered in your names. Everything. That includes this as well." Jack said as he took out the ring and earring set, placing them into Jenny's hand.

"What happens to the Perkins place now?"

"Well I have been told that there are some surveyors coming down from Lincoln police to see what they can sell before the house and land are auctioned off. I have spoken to Jean and she said you should take what you want from there as a bit of a reward. There is still a lot of Vets equipment down there and a couple of tractors along with a fork lift I think they would be of use to the Marjorie Cats and Dogs Rescue Centre."

"Thanks Jack." Billy and Jenny both said almost in a synchronised unison.

"Next time you think some thing is off?" Jack said

"What?"

"Don't call me Billy, I am getting way to old for this shit. Right I better pick up the frogmen and take them back." Jack said

"They are already gone, and we don't know where too."

"Ohh OK See you soon, now I have a lot of grovelling to do with Janet." Jack replied and said his good byes and left.

Back in Jacks garage Tom was busying himself putting equipment into flight-cases.

"I think you will find some of that belongs to the CIA and I think those micro cams are the property of FBI."

"Cant blame a man for trying" Tom said.

"I have always found that those preventing crime do have a bit of a habit of being involved at the edges of of it." Mark said in his southern drawl.

"So Marie, are you going to tell us the full story behind all this fake money?"

"Only if you have some cold beer?"

"Help yourself" Jack said opening up the beer fridge that sat under his now somewhat bare workbench.

When they were all seated.

"On the face of things, it initially looked to be an effort to destabilise the US dollar by flooding the world with these almost perfect counterfeit notes. As you know more than half the dollars in the world are held in other countries outwith the USA territories. And around and estimated that somewhere between one to three percent of these, are already counterfeit. It was bad enough that the world know that about ninety percent of all US bills are contaminated with narcotics and set dogs off on false trails all over the place. Anyway I digress. We thought by these criminals, dumping all these fake bills that when the world banks tried to hand them back to the USA. The USA would have to honour their agreements with these banks and that would put a strain on the Federal reserve. Worse if it became public knowledge that more than half the dollars in the world might be fake the dollar would lose its standing on the international market, This again would adversely affect our economy as a whole, forcing the US into a recession, which would make the great depression look like a blip on Wall Street, rather than the crash of a global economy." Marie said and took a long swig of her beer.

"You said that you thought this, which makes me believe that it was inconclusive?" Jack said.

"Indeed Jack you are a smart one. Yes we thought that it was an attack on on the US Dollar. I was wrong. The attack came directly from Moscow. We only found this out yesterday in fact, not that it changes anything on the ground here. The same crime was being committed. Whilst it was sort of an attack on the USA that was just coincidental. The CIA in Moscow had a man in the Kremlin and he was able to turn a senior member of Putin's closest inner circle, in fact the closest. It was Putin's personal accountant. He became aware of a plan to obtain the Bernhard Plates, which you already know the history of. Well these plates came to surface about two years ago, then got into the hands of a small time crook in Argentina. He was murdered and the plates moved up the way from one criminal to another until they came to the attention of some of the hardline old guard of the KGB, who were now kingpins in the FSB. They have a lot of muscle, not just in Russia but would it surprise you to learn that they literally have gangs of FSB agents in most countries of the world. In the criminal underworld all you have to do is let it be known that you are willing to buy something for a ridiculously high amount and you can get it. Russia knew about these Bernhard Plates, so they offered five billion in gold and diamonds. Within weeks there were nibbles and then a single reverse plate of the one dollar bill was sent and it was easily recognisable by the Nazi stamp on its reverse. The people who had the plates wanted half up front for which they would give half of the plates, well almost they kept both sides of the one hundred dollar bill, to ensure they still had the bargaining power. A shipment of gold bars, diamonds and other precious items were taken to the meeting. And the exchange was made. A new meeting was arranged and the other half of the payment was brought to the meeting. So back to what I told you at the start of this episode. The FSB have gangs all around the world. Putin organised all the FSB agents in the whole of south America, supported by undercover soldiers from Cuba and Venezuela. They lay in wait literally surrounding the old factory where the exchange was to be made. When the deal was completed and all the plates were in the hands of the FSB. The agents left with their items and they left in its place the two and a half billion worth of gold and diamonds. This was to be split equally between the Cuban and the Venezuelan governments after they had completely wiped out the gang of criminals that originally had the plates. This they did and they took their loot. It sounds like a lot of money two point five billion. The value of the plates though would be valued in the quintillions. Or if you have heard the term a Google. That is their value on the world stage." Marie took another swig and put the almost empty bottle down.

"So we were wrong on just one thing. Most of the fake money only went as far as Europe. In this case the USA would simply say to all the EU Banks is we will not take counterfeit money. This would certainly hurt the US in world finances but the bigger hurt would hit Europe. There would be mass devaluations of every currency within Europe. Especially those that base their currency on the Euro, but not exclusively. It would damage the British Pound Sterling which as you are aware would go go from a AAA rating in the world bank to being a pariah. The Russian Rouble would then thrive. It is what would happen next that would be the worst thing for the world. Those countries and nations who had prior to the late 1980's and early 1990, had been part of the Union of Socialist Soviet Republics. Would suddenly be looking to rejoin the now wealthiest of nations. And in a week or two, we would be back to a time when there was a cold war only this time Russia would hold all of the cards. They could set the world price on something as basic as flour to a level whereby only the rouble could afford to buy it. The USA and the West would suddenly find themselves in a similar position to a soviet sub state of the 1970's. With world wide poverty. Putin was going to use the Fake Dollars to impose his version of soviet power over the world. He would be the world leader. And he almost succeeded. So just in case you were wondering why a USA Federal Reserve Agent could manage to make the gun laws of the UK disappear or call up a chopper and fly it direct into one of the busiest airports of the world and get a fake bomb alert on a commercial aircraft. This is how. You will of course never be able to tell anyone the truth behind anything that I have told you."

"Jesus it makes me glad that I retired and just grow carrots." Jack said

"I cant say I am surprised. Putin is still trying to recreate the old USSR by using force. Look at Crimea. There are other Baltic and caucuses felling very worried at the moment" Mark said

"Give me a proper criminal any day of the week." Jean said

"The just look at Putin. Murderer, Financial crook, Thief, and a lot of other things I am sure. He makes the Godfather look like a fairy Godmother." Marie said

"So about this beer fridge are you going to let the rest of us use it?" Alex asked.

They sat drinking until the sun came up on a normal sunny day. World banks opened, the stock market opened, no rumour of the fake money had got out. Putin was seriously pissed off. He asked the FSB to bring him his accountant. Putin threw a screaming tantrum and threw a chair across his office. The FSB who had supposed to be watching those that came to the USA embassy, were sent for. Putin had them shot in his office. Then he had their families come in and clean the office after which they were disappeared. The accountant and his family flown out on an Aeroflot flight to London the night before landing after a slight delay due to a bomb scare at London Heathrow.

Printed in Great Britain
by Amazon

19023339R00173